MRS. RAHLO'S
CLOSET

and
Other Mad Tales

MRS. RAHLO'S CLOSET

and
Other Mad Tales

R. E. KLEIN

For information address iPublish.com, 135 West 50th Street, New York, NY 10020

ⓦ A Time Warner Company

ISBN 0-7595-5016-6

First edition: July 2001

Visit our Web site at www.iPublish.com

To my parents, Harold and Rosalie Klein
and to my Grandma Goldie

CONTENTS

CONTENTS

MRS. RAHLO'S CLOSET

I was poor and about to begin graduate school in an unfamiliar city. Having completed four years of college in my hometown in the West, I won a fellowship to the Hartley Medical School in New England—enough for tuition and textbooks, with very little left over. I indulged in the luxury of plane fare across the continent; henceforth, to complete my medical studies, I would have to live as economically as possible.

It was an early afternoon in late September when I arrived. I headed immediately for the college and over to the information center to ask about on-campus lodgings; nothing was available. Next I consulted a list of students seeking roommates. I called a few numbers, but the small amount I could afford for my monthly share of the rent was insufficient.

Armed with the classified section of a local newspaper, I

tried various neighborhoods and examined many lodgings, but I could afford none of them. I wasted half a day in pointless searching, till one of the landlords suggested I visit the older district. I would find cheap rooms there, he told me, though the renters didn't advertise in the papers. So I took the streetcar and went to Old Town.

Old Town may once have been a prosperous seaport, but now all was changed. As the streetcar turned eastward, I could glimpse the brown flats of a silted harbor, hideous in its desolation. The ships had long ago departed, the water turned to reeking mud; the stench assailed me even from a distance. Only the lonely, shrieking gulls inhabited the putrescent wastes.

The streetcar took a sharp turn inland. The squalid shops and dismal warehouses of the commercial district gave way to rolling hills and broad, empty fields. Then we entered the residential section. I left the streetcar and walked many blocks.

Here I found an abundance of richness and decay. Many of the houses I saw were mansions, multistoried structures elaborately gabled and cupolaed: opulent symbols of baroque fancy or neoclassical elegance once, but neglected now, cracked and stained by time. The colossal wooden piles looked empty and sepulchral, rotting in places, with broken windows; a few collapsed roofs completed the picture of abandonment. Enormous shade trees masked the houses, along with giant mounds of dusty, unpruned bushes.

I walked down many narrow streets winding among a profusion of foliage. Deliverance Lane, Evangelical Way, Comber's Alley. Queer names. Still, by streetcar I was only twenty minutes or so from campus, and judging from the appearance and age of these buildings, a room might just be affordable.

Eventually I came to Grantham Path, a narrow, twisty street full of tottering old ruins whose paint might have begun peeling at the time of the witch trials. I stopped before a house half-hidden in foliage. Dry, cordlike vines twisted over all its walls and through the chinks in its rotten timbers. The September sun flashed red diamonds off the house's latticed panes. It was now early evening.

As a boy I often explored the stretches of shabby tenements in downtown Los Angeles. One late afternoon as I wandered down Temple Street, the setting sun at my back threw a great plate of light at the dingy buildings in front of me. Suddenly brilliant, the hovels glowed with glory, transfigured to palaces till the splendor grew too dazzling for the eyes. Then the sun sank, and the vision ended.

Some such remembrance I had on Grantham Path in Old Town, some such correlation of disease and glory. I continued on, and saw the sign.

It was a small placard placed in an upper window of the most dilapidated mansion I had seen so far—four stories of weathered boards and grimy windows buried in clusters of foliage. Unlike the surrounding houses, which fronted the sidewalk, this building stood in isolation behind a garden of dead weeds, guarded by a tottering fence of wood and wire. Beyond the fence a footpath ran to a veranda.

The sign said ROOM FOR RENT. I opened the splintered gate and navigated the weedy path to the house.

Stepping onto the veranda, I found it solid enough but empty: no worn wicker lounge chairs, no split-bottomed settees. Just dust and odor.

Odor. Whiffs of it haunted the veranda. I knocked on the ornately carved door, waited a minute, and knocked again, harder. I fancied I heard sounds inside and knocked a third time. The door glided silently open.

I was shocked at first by the person who appeared. She was a very tall, very massive, and ancient woman, her skin pale and wrinkled, her white hair wild and profuse. Most striking were the eyes: huge, black, protuberant, they seemed to burst from the surrounding pallor.

"Hello," I stammered. "I'm William Ashley, a student at Hartley. I saw your sign." As I spoke, she seemed to awaken from a long dream.

"My sign," she said in a rasping voice. "You saw my sign. Come in."

She made way for me, and I stepped into musty darkness. There was that old-house smell, compounded of mold and mildew and rotting timber and improper ventilation, a kind of dry rot of the air.

"I'm Mrs. Rahlo," she began hoarsely. "The room is upstairs."

My first impression of repulsion was mitigated by her civility. I felt ashamed of my initial reaction to her.

As my eyes grew used to the dark, I could see well enough to follow her up a broad, thinly carpeted stairway. We came to a landing.

"It is the first door on the left," she rasped. We entered.

She opened the curtains and windows, admitting a flood of late-afternoon sunlight into two small adjoining rooms: one a sitting room, the other a bedroom. The sitting room contained an armchair, a table, and a desk; the bedroom, an iron bed, a chair, a chest of drawers, and a large antique clothespress. The windows faced the back of the house and looked out upon a seemingly limitless expanse of overgrown fields, beyond which were hills.

"I'll show you the bath." Her voice had lost its harshness; she

4

spoke softly and gently. "It is just down the hall." This was, of course, a later addition of perhaps the last century, some spare room having been fitted up with bathroom fixtures. But the plumbing worked.

"How much," I asked, when we were back in the sitting room, "is the rent?"

She considered a moment, then named a ridiculously low sum.

"I'll take it," I said. "I can move in right away. I have a few suitcases waiting down at the college. I can pay you now."

She smiled. "Your rent includes meals."

I stammered a bit, wanting to be off and get my things before she changed her mind. She smiled again.

"There is one thing," she said, pointing to a door I hadn't noticed. "That closet in your bedroom, you are not to use it; it is not part of your apartment. I use it to store things. It is locked. Please do not try to open it."

Assuring her I would do no such thing, I left to get my luggage.

• • •

It took her a long time to answer my knock, but she came eventually, opened the door, and presented me with my key. I started again at the wrinkled white face and bulging eyes—I couldn't help myself—but she affected not to notice and even offered to help me carry my suitcases upstairs. Despite a repellent appearance, she seemed a pleasant old lady.

She was a thoughtful hostess. When I entered my rooms to dispose of my luggage, I found by my bedside an antique bowl of dark crimson flowers.

She gave me dinner, too, though I had to suppress a childish revulsion to her touching my food. We sat in a huge dining room, scantily furnished, meagerly lit by an unshaded bulb screwed into a makeshift fixture.

A kind of fish comprised the major course, bland and unfamiliar to me, and we drank a sweet red wine. She was cordial, even friendly, but I did not like the way she smacked her gums and seemed to play with her food. The wine, too, she purled in her mouth, swishing it around, almost gargling.

While we ate, I had the opportunity to observe her more closely: the goggle eyes, the chalky skin, the frayed black dressing gown. Whenever our eyes met, I instinctively looked away.

"Does anyone else live here?" I asked after dinner.

"No one," she said. She took my hand. "That is why I am so happy to have such a nice young man here." I was surprised at her strength; her hand had caught mine unawares, and her grip hurt.

We drank a great deal more of that red wine. I could not tell whether it had any effect on her, but I was beginning to feel disoriented. I remember she asked questions about my family and background. I tried to answer coherently. Eventually she surprised me by asking if I wouldn't care to move into the parlor to watch television.

The parlor was a vast, dark, dusty room immediately off the entrance hall. It was empty save for two straight-backed chairs flanking a squat wooden table supporting a black-metal device with an oval screen. This was a "homemade" television, she told me, built by a friend of hers who made them as a hobby. She gave me more wine and switched the machine on. The screen flashed to a white blur.

The reception was poor, or else I had drunk so much that

my senses were awry, as I could not easily distinguish picture or
sound. But I could not leave off drinking. While in the throat
the wine satisfied intensely; but immediately after, it left a
thirst that burned for more.

We watched some sort of program, I think; but I really
could not be sure what it was. Only gradually did I become
aware that my hostess was speaking, that she had been speaking
for some time. "Will you take him?" she asked. "Will you take
him?" She seemed to speak not to me but to the eerie phos-
phorescence of the screen.

● ● ●

I fell asleep almost as soon as my head hit the pillow. But I
awoke in the night. Great whiffs of that dry-rot odor assailed
my nostrils. Was it this that awakened me? No. It was the
scraping sound at the foot of my bed. I sat up. Could it be a rat?
Pressure on my feet. Something had jumped onto the bed.
Kicking out, I grabbed for the bedside lamp and switched it on.

Something red—the size of a cat—sprang with a flurry of
legs to the floor.

I leaped off the bed and whipped around to the foot.
Nothing. But there was that scraping sound again, coming from
under the bed. I crouched down to peer beneath the bed.
Nothing there. Then I stood up. In the corner of the room, near
the locked closet, a red oval shape nearly two feet wide was dis-
appearing through the solid door.

The whole thing was too uncanny. I started to throw on
some clothes to leave the house—until I remembered the
wine. I caught hold of myself and lay back down. Surely no rat,
or anything else, could pass through a locked door. I laughed as
I pulled up the covers.

I had a poisonous nightmare, a revolting masque of frenzied men and desperate women hurling themselves into frantic debauchery. A child was in it, too, whimpering. Then something appalling happened which I could not remember. The dream ended in the cold luminous glow of the television in the parlor.

• • •

I awoke to sunshine streaming into my room. All the wine I'd drunk had left no aftermath. My head was clear as I surveyed the flowing fields outside my windows.

It was Saturday, the end of summer; no school till a week from Monday. I had a week and over to settle in my new house. After I'd bathed and shaved, I went downstairs to find Mrs. Rahlo awaiting me with a plentiful, steaming breakfast.

In the cheerful sunlight I laughed at the repulsion I had felt for her. Not only was Mrs. Rahlo not repellent, she seemed rather pleasant-looking.

"Did you sleep well, dear?" she asked gently.

"Well enough," I said. I had all but forgotten the frightful dream I had had.

"Sometimes it is difficult to sleep in an unfamiliar house." She smiled and passed me my plate.

The food—some kind of vegetable concoction—was abundant and hot, but, like the previous night's meal, bland and tasteless.

While I ate, she praised me for being such a well-mannered tenant.

"Have you had many tenants?" I asked.

"No, dear. The last was a middle-aged gentleman who came to study the old buildings. We were very happy until a telegram

8

came and he had to go back to Boston. He left in such a hurry he didn't have time to pack his things. He said he would send for them later. He never did."

Her face brightened. "I'll bet his clothes would fit you. Why not try them on? They are just where he left them, in your room, in the big drawer at the bottom of the clothespress." I had paid little attention to the clothespress; my meager clothing all fitted into the chest of drawers. I thanked her and promised to examine the clothes.

Breakfast over, Mrs. Rahlo inquired how I should spend the day. I told her by exploring the neighborhood.

"Oh dear," she said with concern. "The streets around here are not—exciting, though there are some fine old trees." Then she whispered, "I wouldn't go close to any of the houses; many are empty and falling to pieces. You may injure yourself. Someone else might . . ." here she broke off. "You are my— tenant; I feel responsible for you, dear."

I promised to be careful.

I threaded my way through the bright, crazy streets, past the drowsy houses, slumbering in morning sunlight. I met no one, though here and there I fancied I saw faded curtains move in upper-storied windows. Through the spaces between the crumbling houses I could see hills in the distance, one mound in particular. But every time I found a path I thought would lead me there, I was confronted by more tottering, ruinous houses, many of them with ROOM FOR RENT signs. Eventually I headed back.

Mrs. Rahlo was gone but had left me a vast vegetarian lunch. I wondered what all those vegetables were. There was something like lettuce and something similar to squash. But the rest were pale leguminous things, totally new to me.

After lunch I decided to explore the fields behind the house. Starting with the front yard, a series of mounds and craters covered by knee-high weeds, I gradually worked my way around to the side, skirting the line of tall, dead gladioli spiked along the narrow bed next to the house. Passing by a ventilation grate, I caught an updraft of the house odor.

Suddenly I had the sensation of being watched. Were Mrs. Rahlo's bulging eyes staring from some uncurtained window? The house smell seemed to pour out of the ventilation grate at my feet. Something scraped against the wire screen. I bent down and peered through the grate.

Behind the rusty screen squatted something oval-shaped, with hinged appendages protruding from its body. I shouted, and it scurried off with a scraping sound into the black caverns beneath the ancient mansion.

It was as weird as it was incongruous; though, after all, we weren't far from the sea. Perhaps an inland channel flowed nearby. This is what I told myself as I stood sweating in the sunlight. For what I saw behind the ventilation screen was a monstrous crab.

Old buildings are often infested with vermin, I assured myself as I continued alongside the house. Maybe the large crustacean helps to keep down rats and roaches. I had a mental picture of a crab devouring a roach and turned my thoughts to other matters.

It was not until I walked the entire length of the house and entered the back grounds, that I realized the *immense size* of the building. The rear part had deteriorated much more than the front. Here and there great gaps rent the outer wall, and I peered into gutted, rubbish-filled rooms disfigured by cracked partitions and raw, splintered crossbeams. Glancing up, I could see that certain upper rooms had collapsed entirely—tons of rotted wood and shingle, supported by the lower, still-intact portions of the house.

The back grounds stretched moundy and vast, mostly, I thought, like a succession of old empty lots running to weed. In places I could make out bits and byways of a onetime sanded path. But mostly there were white weeds, as tall or taller than I, great clusters of them. A huge, empty jungle lot, like the house and neighborhood, full of the mystery that breeds from sunlit squalor. I could find no trace of Mrs. Rahlo's kitchen garden, if she had one.

It was pleasant breaking my way through those weeds. At times I scaled some bare, hard-packed hummock that commanded a fair prospect. Other times I descended into tiny valleys from where I could no longer see the house. But the weeds in these places rustled, though there was no wind, and I thought of the monstrous crustacean beneath the house; perhaps others inhabited the weeds. I returned to the house, bathed, looked into a novel, and napped until dinnertime.

For dinner we had more of the same vegetables I had for lunch. When I asked the names of these, Mrs. Rahlo smiled and shook her head, telling me she ate nothing but these vegetables, which she grew in a back garden, insisting that they were rare, choice, and exceedingly healthful. I nodded agreement; for, despite her sickly pallor, she did look remarkably healthy.

I told Mrs. Rahlo about my morning's walk through the neighborhood, mentioning I thought it strange I hadn't met with anyone.

She smiled. "We keep to ourselves. Most of us are very old."

"Do you go much into town?" I asked.

"I never go out, dear. I used to, a long time ago. But people were unkind."

"You were out this morning."

"No, dear. I was in the house somewhere."

"If you don't go out, how do you shop?"

"I have a friend—the one who made my television set. He brings me all I need."

"I'd like to meet him," I said.

Her eyes glowed. "I'm sure you will, my dear."

After dinner we moved to the parlor and drank more of her red wine. The television was gone; she said she sent it away to have it repaired.

She told me many more things, about the old days and the way the old-fashioned people would dance in the streets. My throat was dry, so I helped myself to more of the delicious wine, as she talked on and on.

I interrupted once to tell about the creature I saw beneath the house. She said all sorts of things crawled up the sewer channels, which ran down to the sea. She promised to call in an exterminator.

"I hope it didn't frighten you, dear," she added.

"No, it surprised me. That's all."

She told me she was frightened once, by stern and cruel old men.

"How is that?" I asked.

"When I was a girl. They tried to stop everyone from having pleasure. Ah, but where are they now?"

"Things are different now," I said. "These days nobody cares what anyone else does." She grinned and nodded and told more stories.

• • •

The old woman's stories blended with my dreams that night, along with the memories of my morning walk. Once more I threaded the overgrown pathways. Only now it was night, and the streets no longer empty. Dark things, masquerading as people, dragged themselves beneath the shrubbery. The scene changed. They were dancing now, pirouetting in a graveyard by a black church in a vast and empty field, a frenzied string, delirious, weaving in and out, laughing insanely, till the church exploded, except for one stone wall. Still they laughed; the night quivered with their laughter.

I awoke. It was night. The house odor was very strong. The laughter continued. But no. It wasn't laughter. It was a click— click—click from the locked closet—almost as though the door was opening and closing.

The bedside lamp revealed all as it should be. Nonetheless, I made sure the closet door was locked. Yet I was uneasy for thinking the sound I heard was that infernal crab, dragging its claws behind the walls of my room. My thoughts reverted to the thing I imagined had jumped up on my bed. No, that was a dream. Crabs or anything else can't disappear through locked doors. Still, I was glad that Mrs. Rahlo planned to call the pest exterminator.

• • •

I awoke refreshed but dimly troubled. I found a note in quaintly archaic handwriting tacked to my door.

> *You see, I went out after all,* it read. *You'll find your meals laid out in the dining room. I moved the sofa onto the veranda in case you feel like sitting outside.—Mrs. R.*

The morning was brilliant. After breakfast I went outdoors to lie upon the overstuffed sofa Mrs. Rahlo had provided and read up on my medical statistics. I wondered vaguely how she could have single-handedly moved such a massive piece of furniture. Then I remembered her friend. I read a chapter or so till I suddenly thought of the clothing the former tenant had left behind. I went upstairs.

The clothespress occupied nearly half of one wall. The bottom drawer was crammed with personal belongings. What first engaged my attention was a fine blue woolen overcoat, seemingly new. It fit me perfectly. I could never have afforded a coat like that.

I removed the coat, as the room was warm, and examined the rest of the drawer's contents: trousers, socks, underclothing, shoes, suspenders, handkerchiefs, shaving equipment, and two parcels—one bulky, one small—both wrapped in brown paper and done up with string.

The first and larger package proved to be books of folklore. The titles were curious: *Witchcraft in Old and New England*, by G. L. Kittredge; *The Wonders of the Invisible World*, by Cotton Mather; *The Malleus Maleficarum of Kramer and Sprenger*; *Translunary Cults*, by Larsen and Myers; *Demonolatry* by Remy.

The second parcel contained a single calfskin volume considerably older than the other books. It was in manuscript and looked like a diary. I put the clothes and other objects back in the drawer and took the ancient volume downstairs to read on the veranda.

I had no difficulty deciphering the spidery handwriting. On the flyleaf was written in faded brown ink: JOURNAL OF NATHANIEL BRADLEY/SOMETIME CUSTODIAN OF THE KING'S GAOL/1712. Beneath this, in modern hand, someone had added in pencil: STEPHEN WYCLIFF, BOSTON, MASSACHUSETTS.

Wycliff, the former tenant, was evidently a serious student, for entire pages as well as single passages were underscored and interlineated with marginal comments. I read these marked portions while seated on the veranda that sunny afternoon. When I'd read enough, I tucked the volume into my side pocket. I have it still. Here is what I read.

Some twentie years since were these Colonies vex'd and annoyed by many damnable Witchcrafts. The Witches, it is sayd, worship'd a Black Man, whom they called the Divell. Whether this accurs'd Monster was Satan himself or merely one of his minions it is useless to speculate. Some would have it he was a mortall albeit very wicked man. Most curious of all, I have heard it whisper'd by the very Witches themselves, cag'd and awaiting the scaffold, that this Monster was neither Satan, imp, nor wicked man, but a ferocious Goblin from the Starrs.

The next marked passage began three pages later:

In exchange for the Divell's promise of eternal life, each Witch doth pledge herself to him: eats his "flesh," quaffs his "wine"—blasphemous mockery— and proffereth living human sacrifice—that the Dark Daemon may sate his hunger upon their Souls.

So doth this evil, obscene Horror oblige his disciples with gifts, termed *Familiars*—Monstrousities in the shapes of common beasts—Toads, Hares, Crabbs, Catts, and the like—none seeing them clearly, they seeming to dissolve into air. The Divell teacheth the Witch to talk with the Familiar, who is the messenger betwixt them. When the Witch is away or at sleep, she sometimes putteth herself inside the Familiar, so shee can be ever watchful. I have heard that the Divell can spy when he is far away in Hell or in the Starrs, by means of an infernal Engine he giveth his witches, though none I spake with know much of this.

I skipped over a few more pages to the next underlining.

Some specially favour'd ones the Divell did fore-warn of the trials to come. These witches he immured in coffins, standing up, and did conceal in secret places. But first did he pour *lightning* into the coffin, to serve the Witch as meat and drink for all the years that shee must sleep to await the Divell's return. For with the Godly action of our Pious Magistrates the Divell was weak and did fly far away from New-England, promising he would return in times when men were less vigilant, though, such a time I pray may never be.

All these things I learn'd while I was Custodian of the Gaol at Salem, Massachusetts, during the years 1690–1697.

Thus ended the quotation. Curious reading indeed. I rose and paced the veranda for some minutes before returning to the overstuffed sofa. Throughout the following pages the mark-ings extended only to a sentence or two, and I did not bother with them. But about two-thirds through the book I came upon another sizable section underscored with dark pencil.

> Some do connect the explosion of the Congregational Church with these same Witches, though many do judge the building unstable for having been erected upon an existing foundation of ancient heathen stonework. One Hallowmass Evening a curs'd chant bellowed from the empty Church. So fierce and loud was the noise that people all over Town heard and wonder'd, I being with a small party that ventur'd to investigate. We were some goodly distance away when the entire building filled with fire and exploded with a roar that did send us sprawling to the Earth.

> The explosion was like no blast ever seen. Had the Church been charg'd with gun-powder, the wreakage surely had been strewn about. But the church exploded inwardly. All burst to rubble, save a wall of black stone, the ancient foundation, some said, upon which the builders did raise the Church.

> Ever after men avoided the site as accurs'd; though rumour had it that shortly after the destruction, in the depths of the Night there came to the Church-Yard a deputy of Parsons, Magistrates, and other godly men, who digg'd up the coffins of the dead corpses to lay them anew in consecrated ground, and then with mighty Hammers did break the head-stones and other monuments so that none could know the land once was hallowed. I have visited this site but newly and find all covered by long grasses.

The narrative sent me back to my terrible dream. I had dreamed of an exploding church and a black wall. For a moment I lived the horrid sensation of being caught up in some ancient evil. But in warm sunlight how easy it is to dismiss such freakish correlations.

I caught myself yawning. Being out so long in the sun had made me drowsy. Nevertheless, I roused myself to read one more short passage.

"That the Divell's especial favour should be known, he has shapen their faces to swell with long Eies." Written in the margin, strongly embossed with pencil, were two words: "Mrs. Rahlo."

Despite the warm day a shiver crawled up my back. Mrs. Rahlo? Yes, I could see it—in the seventeenth century, an era intensely aware of evil. A physical peculiarity, a cleft palate or an oversize wart—or a pair of bulging eyes—doomed an old woman to red torture. Puritan minds moved close to hell. The magistrates—those iron-willed, self-righteous old men—they were the real purveyors of evil; it couldn't be otherwise. To take their words seriously made life a mindless horror, defenseless before inconceivable malignancy. Modern people must not believe in witches. No wonder Wycliff never sent for his belongings. He was probably dead or in an insane asylum.

I pocketed the journal and stretched out on the sofa. The afternoon sun felt pleasantly warm. My mind drifted to my father's house in California, where I was surrounded by kind, familiar faces.

• • •

I awoke shrieking in the sunlight. I had had a hideous dream about witches embalmed with electricity, standing white-faced, with open goggle eyes, in long rows of vertical coffins.

It took me some moments to recover. The dream fading, I looked about me. It was late afternoon. Had Mrs. Rahlo returned and failed to wake me? Surely she must have returned by now. It must be near dinnertime, for I was hungry. I went into the house to look for her.

The dark house seemed cold as I stepped inside; a momentary flash of those hellish white dream faces made me shudder. Then I reminded myself of the pathetic delusion of the last tenant. I wondered where Mrs. Rahlo was.

This was my third day in the crumbling old mansion, and I was familiar only with my rooms on the second story and with the front room, parlor, and dining room on the first. A quick inspection showed me that my hostess was in none of these. If she had returned, where was she?

"Mrs. Rahlo," I called. "Mrs. Rahlo?"

I was oddly timid of shouting, uncomfortably aware of my voice dimly vibrating in dark rooms. Nevertheless, I had a notion that I would find Mrs. Rahlo in her chambers, wherever they might be. So I determined to explore the house. There would be basements and cellars, not to mention nests of attics, but Mrs. Rahlo's rooms would undoubtedly be in the main part.

I proceeded to examine the ground floor. Empty rooms, dozens of them, ruined and filthy. Empty closets. Not a scrap of furniture, save the two seats in the parlor and the table and chairs in the dining room. The kitchen, too, was empty. No refrigerator, not even an icebox. No oven or stove, merely a wrecked counter and a massive fireplace choked with weeds and rubbish. I saw that she had used a spirit lamp to prepare my food. But there was no evidence of food at all, just mounds of dried weeds piled high in the corners.

Only the entrance hall, parlor, and dining room had been swept clean and scantily furnished. The rest was bare, carpeted with dust, reeking with mildew. Many of the rooms to the rear were wholly ruinous, the walls caved in, floors taken up or rotted away. One I could not enter for a fallen ceiling.

I ascended the stairs to the second floor. Knocking on doors, I called my hostess's name. No answer. Only my own voice echoing down disused corridors—all the rooms bare, all open and empty, some deformed by frayed shrouds of wallpaper—others gutted, exposing an eerie skeleton of raw, splintered framework. Over all there was dust.

I found the dry rot even more pronounced on the third floor. I could not easily advance to the fourth, for the staircase at a certain point became blocked by a mound of rubble and collapsed timbers. I thought for a moment of trying to climb over the obstruction but stopped when I saw the two hellishly glowing pinpricks of jeweled light. That hideous crab squatted atop the mound on the rotting stairway, its fierce pincers opening and closing. I gave a cry and raced back to the landing.

I decided then that either Mrs. Rahlo called in the exterminator immediately, or I would leave the house, regardless of the cheap rent. I retreated to my bedroom and stood staring out the window in the late-afternoon sunlight, waiting for Mrs. Rahlo.

I heard a doorknob twist and then rattle. I swept round. It was the closet door. Was someone locked inside? I grasped the knob and tried to wrench the door open. It was still locked. I knew then that I badly wanted to open that door, had wanted to do so for some time. Beyond that door lay some mystery, and I must have a look. I reached for my keys and tried first one then another. The keys proved useless. Almost feverishly, I tried to slip the bolt with the blade of my pocketknife. Inserting the blade between door and jamb, I began to maneuver the knife.

"You promised you wouldn't do that, dear." Mrs. Rahlo stood directly behind me.

• • •

We ate a cold vegetable supper and drank of the red wine. Far from being upset with me for having tried the closet door, Mrs. Rahlo fluttered with solicitude. I had never seen her so animated.

"I was thinking," she said, her voice suffused with excitement, "we'll have a full moon tonight. Maybe you'll want a turn in the garden. It is neglected now, but there are still some nice walks and a very pretty fountain."

"A fountain? I didn't notice it on my walk yesterday."

"You didn't go far enough," she replied.

We drank more wine. I told her of searching the house as far as the third floor. Her rooms lay on the fourth floor, she said, accessible by a back staircase. She started when I mentioned the crab and vowed to call in an exterminator the next morning. She laughed then, as though she had made a good joke.

The summer day continued far into the night, for the retreating sun left behind a resplendently bright moon. After dinner, still sipping the sweet wine, we moved to the veranda. I talked more about my previous day's adventures among the streets and about the hill I never could get to.

She brightened. "We call it Bigmound. You can get there if you climb the wall at the end of my garden." She poured more wine.

"I'd like that," I exclaimed, "—to see the hill by moonlight." I knew I should drink no more wine, but I could not help myself.

"But, my dear, you shall. Perhaps you will meet my friend, who comes there sometimes. It is only a few feet from the wall you are going to climb. Go into the back garden and find the main path; it starts at the fountain that used to splash blood."

"Blood?"

"Oh dear, it must be the wine; it looks like blood, doesn't it? No, I meant *water*; the fountain used to splash water until they took it up and cracked the pipe."

"Somebody 'took up' the fountain?"

"Oh, no. No. My garden I mean. Somebody tore up my garden, dear. Here," she said, filling my glass, "take some wine with you. If you should meet my friend, greet him for me. Find the fountain and take the path; climb the wall and see the mound!"

Yes, precisely the thing to do. I must see the mound; I had to. The moon was shatteringly bright. Clutching the glass, I made my way to the rear of the house and entered the weeds. As I staggered on, I thought I heard a cry from the veranda. Was Mrs. Rahlo weeping? Could she be laughing?

My body throbbed with motion as I thrashed through those eye-high weeds, wading farther into those fields than I had the day before. I had not realized the vastness. Where was the fountain path? Once I came to a bare brown hill. All about me shone a crazy patchwork of moonlit blotches interspersed with black ruts. It is bad art, I thought——the hills too silver bright, the hollows too black. Then, for a moment, I wondered what I was doing, running and sweating in the moon-haunted fields, a wineglass in my hand.

The path, a voice told me, your path lies just ahead. Find the fountain. Odd bits of masonry littered the ground, but I could not stop to investigate. I had to find the fountain. Just ahead.

I lost my footing and came crashing down among the weeds and broken masonry. I gained my feet, took a turn, and found the fountain.

How like a tomb it was in the blinding moonlight. Tall and white it stood, surmounted by a stone cherub; but time had cracked the cherub's face. Cracked, too, was the fountain's wide rim. Empty, dry and cracked. The blazing whiteness burned my eyes. I licked the dregs out of the wineglass, which I found I was still clutching, and set the glass delicately on the rim of the fountain. The cherub smirked now like a devil. I turned to the path that lay just past the fountain.

The mound. To the mound! I raced down that bright moon-silvered path, dense weed walls on both sides. Abruptly the path gave way to an open place; there before me was the wall. The wall I must climb to see the mound. That worn black wall, it was only a few feet high. I could scale it easily—then on to the mound, where something colossal waited for me.

I made a quick turn—and tripped again. I lay on the ground and saw I'd fallen over a half-buried chunk of masonry. I'd hurt myself. My hand was bleeding. I still clutched whatever it was that had cut my hand. I felt a small sharp stone. I opened my palm and held the stone in the moonlight. It was a tiny stone cross, intact save for a jagged edge where it had broken off from something.

Still on my knees, I cleared the weeds from the half-buried stone that caused my fall. It had words carved upon it. It was a tombstone. I thought of those other white slabs of shattered stone that lay around me. And I knew I was in a graveyard. The whole field was once a graveyard—ancient, desiccated, demented. A dead graveyard. A graveyard's ghost.

All was wrong; I mustn't climb the wall; I wouldn't. I stood up and began to make my way back to the house. Mrs. Rahlo screamed.

"Climb the wall. He is waiting for you."

The wall. Of course, I had to climb the wall. The wall was only a few feet away. It would take but a moment to climb over. I reached up with my wounded hand. Pain coursed through my arm. In the moonlight I saw I had left a small bloodstain on the wall's surface.

"Climb the wall!" shrieked the piercing voice. But my hand hurt too much. I started back to the house.

"I am coming to make you climb the wall."

Suddenly I had a vision of Mrs. Rahlo pursuing me with outstretched arms, hands curled to claws, and I realized she was not human.

Avoiding the tinseled path, I crashed through the wall of white weeds, running, tripping, stumbling in my haste. I lost all sense of direction, but still I ran. As often as I fell, I picked myself up and ran on.

I paused momentarily on a slight ridge to gather breath and look around me. The weeds waved like an ocean. Far beyond lay the dark shadow of the house. Then I saw something moving at a tremendous rate, some low crawling thing parting the weeds as it swept on. I knew it was Mrs. Rahlo looking for me.

I was exposed to sight. I leaped off the ridge and plowed through the weeds. Sweat-blind, I raced and swam and crashed—and suddenly left the weeds.

And found the fountain. Tall and white it stood, but not empty, no. It was full of blood. Gushing blood, pumping blood, spewing blood out of the cracked cherub's leering mouth. Blood filled the wineglass I had left on the rim. Blood poured from the wide, split basin, dyeing the ground crimson.

My one chance was to make my way to the front of the house and escape through the crazy, winding streets. Gradually, I stole through the weeds, burrowing through the thicket, inching my way, sometimes crawling, till at last I crouched hidden beneath the house's massive shadow, then I crept stealthily along the side of the house till I was clear.

The street lay only a few paces ahead. I paused to gather breath, then sprang onto the sidewalk. And stopped. Black, misshapen figures shambled from the ancient houses, pouring into the streets as if in some weird procession. One slouched toward me.

I bolted back the way I'd come and again entered the weeds. The night was nearly spent. I had a notion that if I held on till daylight, they would all be powerless to hurt me. I buried myself beneath a mass of weeds, insulated from the feverish light of the sinking moon.

I knew then the probable fate of the former tenant, Mr. Wycliff. *She* had fed him to the horror from beyond the stars. Did it see him as it saw me—through the "television" in the parlor? Had it found him, too, an acceptable offer? Did he climb the wall? For generations now, Mrs. Rahlo, charged with satanic lightning—like a stored battery—had lain mindlessly in her death sleep—periodically roused to life by callers at her door. I awoke her, just as Wycliff had a few years earlier. What would have happened had I not hurt my hand? What was behind that wall?

Something tickled the side of my face. Casually I turned to brush aside a wisp of weed—and peered into red-jeweled eye-stalks. The crab squatted two feet from my face. Its antenna had touched me.

It lunged suddenly. I kicked out. It was thrown back. I

leaped to my feet and raced through those hideous dead fields, the monster just behind. It moved with incredible speed, like a bloodhound. I hurled myself through the white walls of weed, not daring to draw breath. I came to the fountain of blood. I had to know. The crab. Where was the crab? I glanced back.

Something leaped upon me.

"I have got you," Mrs. Rahlo shrieked, and bore me to the ground. Above me the fountain gushed.

Blackness. Dank, damp-house smell. A crawling sensation all over my skin. I was standing. I put out my arms. A narrow space, rough, splintered wood on either side.

"I'm in the closet," I said. "I'm in the locked closet of my room."

"You're in a coffin!" said a voice behind me. "And I am with you, my dear."

"No," I shouted. "I'm in the closet. I can get out."

"Yes, go back and climb the wall. Someone's waiting for you."

It was hard to breathe. The overpowering smell of decay. That narrow closet. And the bulging-eyed horror was in there with me.

"You really must see him, my dear; he is tall and black and full of power."

"No."

"He will give you secrets and wine."

"No."

"You have drunk of his wine, eaten his flesh; now you must yield him your pledge."

"His flesh? I've eaten his *flesh*?"

"Our vegetables, my dear; they are part of him."

"I can get out of this closet," I screamed. "I must find the

26

door." Here I feverishly clawed at the boards around me.

"It isn't a closet, dear; it only looks like one."

"There must be a door——"

Then my hand, already wounded, must have struck a splinter, for my head grew bright with pain. And in the brightness directly ahead, I saw the outline of a door.

"The handle should be about here," I said. "I must make a handle."

"No," said the voice. "You must go the *other way* and see him."

I felt the handle in my aching hand; I twisted the handle and pushed the door out from me.

And I came into the room. Early-morning sunlight flooded it. The room shook to an agonized shriek of despair, a wailing ululation that died abruptly.

I turned toward the closet. Only there was no closet. I saw only a coffin, upright against the wall. The sun's full rays impaled the tattered thing that squirmed inside: a goggle-eyed heap of shriveled skin, its appalling head framed in a profusion of wiry hair, its howling mouth gaping in a silent scream. Electric sparks crawled over the body.

Then the coffin shrank back to a closet, then became a coffin again, crackling with sparks as the mummy writhed. The coffin brightened to a blinding brilliance and went out. Only the locked closet remained.

I left that house then, slowly, quietly. In the morning sunlight I left Grantham Path, too, with its silent tottering houses. How many other Mrs. Rahlos, I wondered, infested those rotting piles? I walked, the morning sun on my face, through those sinuous streets drowned in vegetation, past those leering houses with ROOM FOR RENT signs in upper windows. I walked west, away from the heart of Old Town, until I found people and noise. It was only after I found a seat aboard the streetcar bound for the college that I fainted.

I am well now. I am living on campus and pursuing my studies. Sometimes I think of Mrs. Rahlo in her closet, waiting for other callers, and I am troubled. I think she knows where I am. I wonder how far she can roam from her house.

Sometimes I think I'll return to that mansion on Grantham Path and wrench open the door of that locked closet. I'm sure I'll find her remains; if I burn them, I'll probably make an end of her. That was our mistake. In Europe they burned them; in this country the creatures were pressed to death or hanged.

SCOURGE OF FIRE

In the words of those interviewed, everything seemed to "go wrong" about eleven o'clock. The early-summer heat shimmering off the baked pavement on that brilliant, dusty June morning suddenly vanished; the sunlight dimmed, the air grew opaque. There were strange sounds and stranger odors. One woman, washing her clothes, witnessed the soap bubbles crash to the floor and shatter. Two men, smoking their pipes while discussing the affairs of the day, found their rising smoke to be solid like a screen. Another man put his arm through the wall of his house. A young girl, listening to her radio, related how the music changed into a "funny smell." Some workmen tearing up the street had the opportunity to survey the scene around them. The buildings, they said, behaved like collapsing shadows. One old gentleman was observed to run through an alley, his shadow audibly flapping behind him like an old coat.

Another man, dashing into the living room to join his family, suddenly disappeared. For the next few hours they heard his voice moaning from somewhere in the room. But perhaps the strangest occurrence was that cited by a motorist who covered his eyes as he braked to avoid collision with a giant lizard rising from the unbroken asphalt of the highway.

• • •

"Queer things," the doctor was saying, "are the life's blood of sanity. Tales of strange disappearances, of monsters rising from the sea, of men transformed into wolves keep the mind from stagnating in its own complacency. They force us to accept the world as a perpetual enactment of mystery and wonder. They remind us that beneath the paved highways lies dark, cold earth."

"Yes," agreed his friend. The two corpulent, middle-aged men sat in Dr. Rosen's study, a book-lined, comfortable room downstairs in a mellow old house in the city. "It is life's strangeness that makes life worth living. It is the butter of our daily bread."

"Our daily drudge," said the doctor, absently tugging an immense black beard. "Take you, for example, a marketing executive. You rise each day at six, breakfast at six-thirty, arrive at your office at eight. Then you're busy for the day—no, don't say it; I know you enjoy your work. You're home at four-thirty, you relax, you listen to a bit of music, eat a good dinner, read a good book, and so to bed. Life blankets you cozily with sameness. But is this the path for which we are intended? I have the impression that most of the world lives life as though it were something to be 'got through' as painlessly as possible."

"Yet one must work."

"Of course, unless one is endowed with independent means."

Here the doctor coughed modestly. "A person must go through the motions of life—paying taxes, for example—but not lose sight that these motions are not life itself. Life is something deeper."

The late afternoon had darkened with the declining sun, and twilight entered the room. Dr. Rosen adjusted his gold spectacles, stood up, pulled the drapes closed, and turned on the light. Returning to his seat, he filled and lit his briar pipe.

"I'll give you an example," he continued, puffing. "You, William, are on your way to work. It is late spring. The morning is especially bright. Seized by a whim, you decide to walk. Every object you pass seems fresh, as though viewed for the first time. Without your being aware of it, a great sense of well-being has stolen over you. On your way you pass a garden with a few rose-bushes. Impulsively, you stoop to smell a rose. The fragrance remains with you. As you step through the office door, you greet your secretary with a smile born of the rose fragrance. Thus you transmit your rapture to her, and she too becomes radiant. Now perhaps she regrets being too hard on a certain young man who tried to impress her. All this because of a rose, a walk, the season—and each of those things derives from causes still more remote, mysterious. Consequences, you see, cause and effect. Causes result from mystery; effects scatter to infinity."

"Well," said William Shanks, rubbing his bald head, "this is all very fine. But I don't see the connection between werewolves and finding a husband for my secretary."

The doctor smiled.

• • •

About the time this conversation took place, a truck rumbled along a dark and particularly desolate stretch of road. The driver stretched and yawned. On either side of the highway great tracts of wasteland reached as far as the eye could see. Suddenly the headlights picked out a figure in the road. It was a woman dressed in white and waving her arms wildly. She was burning. Even as he braked, he saw her plunge into the field. By the time he reached her, she was only ashes.

This was the first of the fires.

Many fires followed. So many that the city began to suffer an "epidemic of fire," as one newspaper put it.

It was the hottest summer in years; and, of course, there was a drought. People were careless; too many air conditioners overloaded circuits. Too many hot plates were put too near inflammable curtains. Perhaps too many children played with too many matches.

It was a summer of cremation.

An elderly woman—nearly three hundred pounds of wrinkled fat—presumably fell asleep on a sofa by a cold, empty fireplace. A heap of greasy ashes and an unburned arm remained. Most of the sofa was intact. The coroner ruled death by misadventure.

A wife returned from the grocery to find her husband seated in a chair, unaware that he was burning. He was consumed in seconds.

Because of his hectic schedule, Shanks had not seen Rosen in some weeks. Now, as the fury of July rose to the furnace of August, the marketing executive ascended the worn steps leading to the doctor's study.

"Ah," said Rosen, "how good of you to come. Sit down, and I'll find you something cool to drink." The visitor sat close to the air conditioner and luxuriated in the wet, refrigerated breeze. Through the windows he could see the heat shadows reflecting off the pavement.

The two men refreshed themselves with lemonade and sank back into overstuffed armchairs. Rosen was the first to break the silence.

"There are fires," he said.

"Yes," his friend agreed. "It has certainly been a summer of fires."

"Do you recall the conversation we had the last time you were here?"

"Something about my secretary's happiness depending on my smelling a rose."

"Causes and effects, yes. Your secretary's nuptials the effect—at least one effect—of your smelling the rose. And the rose was, of course, the effect of very different causes. The union of your secretary with her young man must surely produce still other effects."

"Children, probably." His friend laughed.

"Now there are fires," Rosen said seriously.

"It's been a brutal summer."

"I wonder." Rosen leaned forward. "If the fires are our effect, what do you suppose is the cause?"

"Why, different things, just what one reads in the newspapers—smoking in bed, overloaded circuits, the drought. Why, the very lawn has become kindling."

"But cannot you see, William, that these fires are different? They are cases, pure and simple, of spontaneous combustion. A woman lying on her sofa is burned to ashes. Nothing else is destroyed, except that the sofa is a little scorched."

"Well, yes, that *is* queer. But spontaneous combustion—Dickens wrote of that in *Bleak House* and Charles Brockden Brown in *Wieland*. It has something to do with electricity in the air, doesn't it?"

"Something in the air. Yes, perhaps." The doctor removed his gold spectacles, wiped them with his handkerchief, and replaced them carefully on the bridge of his nose. "William," he said slowly, "I've a big favor to ask. Might I get one of your bright research assistants to find some information on his computer?"

"What do you need?"

"I would like a geographical chart plotting all the known locations of our mysterious fires. Also, a list of the victims, showing the common elements among them."

Shanks grinned. "You'll have your data by tomorrow night."

• • •

The night was uncomfortably warm when the two friends met in Rosen's study. The doctor poured out two glasses of chilled wine.

"Tell me what you have learned," he said.

"The combustions are restricted to certain areas of the city, the heaviest concentrations being here, here, and here." Shanks pointed to portions of an elaborately annotated city map.

"Ah," said Rosen. "Yes, I see. Around the stockyards, the dump, and—here, what is over here?"

"Why, the paper mill—also the tool and die works, and the foundry."

"Now the victims."

Shanks handed over a folded printout. "Here is a breakdown into age, sex, physical condition, occupation, and everything else we could think of."

"Excellent." Rosen ran his eyes over the papers. "Ha! Age and weight . . . age and weight. Well, well, well . . ."

"Well?"

"Most of the victims are old and fat. William, that would describe us."

He spent some time poring over the document, tugging now and then at his great black beard or pausing to polish his spectacles.

"This is not random," he said at last. "If we set aside the accidental fires that occur in all seasons, these fires, *our* fires, are deliberate."

Shanks was on his feet. "Deliberate? Are you sure?"

"Yes. Someone is burning people to death." Rosen folded his hands over his belly. "Perhaps not an agency that exists in the natural order of things."

"Are you suggesting the supernatural? My dear Emile!"

Rosen looked grave. "Once there were sirens," he said. "Desirable and deadly, they sang men to death—remember your Homer. Medieval France witnessed a plague of lycanthropy; people attacked and devoured one another. Or take all those queer pestilences that seem to have arisen from nowhere, scorched civilization, and quietly sunk out of sight."

"I'm afraid I don't see your point."

"My point is this. As old mysteries die out, cannot new ones be born?"

"For some *agency*, some incendiary force, to come suddenly from nowhere to destroy human life—why, our world would be a horror!"

"What is as horrible as a shark?" Rosen asked.

"Very little."

"What if there were no sharks, and suddenly one day a shark appeared? Would you call the world a horror?"

"I see your point. Familiarity lessens our terror of things. But things don't just appear."

"Things do appear, William. What of those accounts of stones falling from the sky, or of inundations of frogs and fishes?"

"Curiosities."

"Yes, they are merely curious, because they are harmless. It might be different now."

"What you are saying is——"

"Something sharklike may have come among us."

• • •

When the two met again, it was late the next day.

"I hope you have dined," said Rosen.

"Quite well," Shanks said. "And you?"

"I have not had the time. Forgive me, would you much mind if I feed myself while we talk? I've had some wine and cheese brought in. Pray help yourself to either." Despite signs of weariness, the doctor seemed well pleased with himself. His cold blue eyes glistened behind the gold spectacles. "I spent the day at the university library," he said between mouthfuls, "taking endless notes from forgotten texts. I've found things." The doctor finished the last of his meal and wiped his lips. "Do you remember our conversation of a few weeks back? About causes and effects?"

"Go on."

"Think of the queer events in June. That was the beginning. That is when the thing broke through. A motorist claimed to see a giant lizard emerging from the highway.

"Now, recall your medieval science. Remember the humors, and the elements behind them?"

"Yes, earth, air, fire, and water. The four primal elements."

"Precisely. And each element has its corresponding spirit, or elemental. In air there is the sylph; in earth, the gnome; in water, the undine; in fire, the salamander. All four tribes accommodate a hierarchy of elementals. The greatest is slightly lower than the lowest angel; the least has the character of a demon. Each tribe inhabits its own sphere and is hostile to the other tribes. Yet all four maintain a precarious alliance. They keep one another in balance."

"But this is mythology," Shanks insisted. "Such things never existed."

"Clear your mind," Rosen said. "Wipe away the textbook fallacies and newspaper learning." He produced the printout. "Here are incontestable facts of fires." He looked earnestly at his friend. "Are you aware of the abundance of fire gods in ancient civilizations? You know Haephestus. What about Agni in India? Loki in Scandinavia? Or Xiuhtecutli in Mexico? Have you heard of the vestal fires in ancient Greece? And there are not only fire gods but earth gods, air gods, water gods—it is all there in the true history, the essential, kernel history that passes by the name of folklore.

"These elementals, mistakenly called gods, what are they like? We have answers for this, too. Neither good nor evil, they sometimes traffic with mankind. The gnome will reveal secret treasure; the undine, the lore of the sea. But the salamander, he serves the philosophers. Have you read much alchemy? Do you know of the secret fire of the philosophers? Of the elixir that transforms base metals into solid gold? Think of your historic pacts with the devil. The salamander will make the alchemist's gold, but in exchange for what?"

"Preposterous," protested Shanks.

"Remember Prometheus. Recall Nero's burning of Rome. There are hints throughout history. There are hints!" Of usually a sanguine complexion, the doctor flushed nearly crimson with excitement.

"What you are saying," said Shanks, "is that the fires—*our* fires—in the city—"

"Yes," Rosen almost shouted. "We are dealing with a fire elemental!"

• • •

Shanks slept ill that night, his dreams tormented by cowled shapes, burning gold in half-timbered garrets—but gold in exchange for what?

For his part, Dr. Rosen worked almost till daylight, indexing and arranging his mass of notes, correlating them with Shanks's data. Even as he worked, near the stockyards a laborer coughed into flame.

At first Shanks thought he had a fever. No, it was the room, stifling with heat. In the night he had thrown off the covers, but the sheet clung to him, cemented with his perspiration. A cold shower provided some relief; still, he'd have to step outside into the blast furnace of the summer morning. Silly of him never to have installed air-conditioning, yet he never really needed it. Till now.

His car was unbearable; even with the windows and the vents open, the upholstery scorched his back as with electric coils. The steering wheel seared his hands. The engine drove sluggishly, the pistons beating more heat into the cylinders; there was a tire smell of burning rubber. By the time he reached Rosen's house, he needed another shower.

The study felt delightfully cool; icy wind from the air conditioner stung his dry nostrils.

His friend's eyes glistened behind the gold spectacles. His black curly beard in the morning light shone almost copper. The two sat in the book-lined study, sipping tall glasses of lemonade. The doctor reclined in his chair and stared out at the heat waves rising off the pavement and parked automobiles.

"Halfway around the world," he said, "fire elementals have been seen in the great Gobi Desert, where they're known as Djinns. Lonely travelers tell of immense fiery columns burning at night in far-desert wastes, where the only fuel is desolate rock. Who knows? Perhaps it is these elementals that made the land into a desert."

"Do they never leave the desert?"

"No. According to old authorities, there is a perimeter around the point where they enter our world, and beyond that line they cannot travel. But it is complicated. Within each circle, each elemental inhabits a distinct area: the undine, west; the sylph, east; the gnome, north; and the salamander, south."

"Then, our city—"

"Yes, the man's disappearance, the monster in the highway, all the strange events of last June—everything took place just a few miles north of where we are. Have you any other questions?" The study remained an island of coolness and repose within a fiery, shimmering sea. To Shanks the heat and all it symbolized began to seem faraway and unreal.

"Where do these elementals come from?" he asked.

"From somewhere else," the doctor said. "Someplace beyond, whence they work their influence. From time to time one falls into our plane of reality, perhaps, as one philosopher suggests, as a substitute for something removed from us. Remember, a man vanished in front of his family—in his own living room."

"Well," said the marketing executive, "this is all most learned and logical, but, Emile, what are we going to do about it?"

"My friend, we must know our enemy. I mentioned that within each category of elemental there are hierarchical divisions; we must determine just where on the scale our creature belongs. If it is of a high order, we may be able to communicate with it, maybe even persuade it to return to its proper sphere."

"Communicate with it? How?"

Dr. Rosen smiled. "We will hold a séance."

• • •

A week went by. The heat continued—searing, scorching, steaming the body in its own sweat.

Seated in his office one blazing afternoon, Shanks received a phone call.

"It is tonight," Rosen's voice told him. "Can you pick me up at seven? Good. Perhaps we shall speak with our elemental."

"Queer things indeed," Shanks mumbled, and continued with the day's work.

Sunset brought no abatement of the heat, as the dying sun sent a great scarlet flare bursting across the horizon, to turn the air itself into fire. Shanks arrived at Rosen's. A few minutes later, the two men drove down the baking highway.

Rosen sat strangely silent, speaking only to give directions. But Shanks could sense the suppressed excitement in his friend.

The car swept through the East Side, the old district, region of industry. Here were factories, machine works, tool and die firms, loading docks, chemical smells, and the muffled clang of metal against metal. Concrete warehouses stood with faded cream exteriors rust-stained beneath tiny barred windows. They passed an auto wrecking yard: piles of corroding metal on hard-packed, oil-stained earth. They went by parking lots abandoned for the evening fortified by chain-link fences topped with barbed wire. All around were clumps of withered crab-grass breaking through cracks on discolored asphalt; papers; tin cans. Rubbish-filled plots.

They turned down an alley and into a street of shabby houses whose peeling stucco revealed the chicken wire and tar paper beneath. Dead weeds served as front lawns.

"Here is the address," Rosen said abruptly. They parked in front of a stucco box.

A stout redheaded old woman in a florid silk gown answered their knock. Rosen introduced her as Madame Medina. The three stood in a musty room lit only by an old brass lamp burning perfumed oil. There was little furniture.

"Ah, Doctor," she said in a heavy accent, "I have accomplish what you tell me. You will see. Please come into the séance room."

As they followed, Shanks gave his friend a quizzical look.

"She has an impressive record," the doctor whispered in his ear.

The séance room contained nothing but a deal table and three metal chairs set in the middle of a crude five-sided figure painted on the bare floorboards. An assortment of glass uten-sils littered the table.

"Doctor, and you, sir," the medium said, "your equipment all here. Do we try now to reach the other side?"

"Yes, but a moment of explanation first," said Rosen. "William, no elemental is ever without the other three. In order to invoke our fire spirit, we must invoke all four. Madame Medina here has undertaken the preliminaries for this by conse-crating the four elements—that is, the physical realities that are the earthly emblems of the spirits we propose to conjure.

"You will notice on the table a large glass globe. Inside, as you can see, is an arrangement of concave mirrors. I had it constructed according to a design of Paracelsus. If we are successful, within the globe will appear a manifestation of the salamander."

"All well and fine," said Shanks. "But how do we protect ourselves? Remember, this thing has burned people to death."

"No," interrupted Madame Medina. "No danger. Look. Here I have salt, camphor, resin, sulfur—all mixed together. If demon try to hurt us, I throw into fire. He go away fast."

She extinguished the oil lamp. A metal brazier standing on a tripod in the corner of the room provided a weak red glow. All three silently took their places at the table.

Whispering at first, the medium passed imperceptibly into a dreary, sustained monotone. Rosen sat stiffly erect, concentrating.

To Shanks it was a wearisome affair. Madame Medina droned away in Spanish, a language he had never learned. The room felt uncomfortably warm. He shifted in his chair. The droning began to get inside his head. He shifted again. It was all theatrical in the worst sense, this ridiculous old woman muttering to herself in this dark, stuffy room. The whole thing was ludicrous, vulgar.

Somewhere the Spanish had given way to another tongue. Shanks could not say which. The closeness of the room was making him sleepy. He shook himself awake and realized the medium was chanting.

"Gob, Peralda, Djinn, y Necksa—" Her body swayed spasmodically. "Djinn. Djinn. Djinn. Djinn. Djinn. Djinn." "Gob, Peralda, Djinn y Necksa—." On and on and on.

The air had grown thick and stale. He should probably get up and walk around a bit. Or go outside. But that would hurt poor old Emile's feelings. The glass ball, he noticed, shone with light. Emile had said something about that.

He closed his eyes and sank deeper into his chair. He really should get up, but in a minute. His head felt stuffed with cotton. It was better to rest first. The medium—the whole thing was absurd. He opened his eyes.

The room was uncomfortably bright. What caused that unpleasant smell? The medium stood now.

She was burning.

She was still chanting. "Djinn! Djinn! Djinn!"

She doesn't know she's on fire, mused Shanks. *Emile and I ought to tell her.*

White flames crawled up her arms, her neck, her face.

She's stopped chanting now, thought Shanks. *Maybe she will start again.*

"William," a voice called from far away. "William."

It sounded like good old Emile. Only it couldn't be Emile, because he and Emile were at a séance, where—

"William, wake up! We've been hypnotized!"

What? Oh, it *was* Emile, and—Shanks stood up.

"Water!" Rosen shouted. "Or our coats! Something!"

She was like glowing iron. Cowled in a robe of fire, she collapsed to the floor. The flames vanished. Nothing remained but ashes.

"Behind you!" Rosen yelled.

Shanks turned to the wall behind him—then threw his arms before his face as he staggered back.

The entire wall was a saurian head, bulging into the room, a rapid tongue—a grinning, wedge-shaped mouth, and an eye staring, staring,—boring straight to the backbone, paralyzing, hollowing out, emptying.

A ferocious sound like a blast of steam sent them reeling into the hall. They returned moments later to find the wall empty and unbroken.

• • •

They drove home in silence. Once back in Rosen's study, Shanks found comfort in scanning the familiar titles of the leather-bound books on the walls. Rosen sat absorbed in thought. Neither seemed willing to disturb the silence. It was only after a long while that Rosen spoke.

"We now know that our elemental is not of the type that spoke to the alchemists, or it would have spoken to us. It is of a considerably lower order—more a force than an intelligence. Yet, like the higher powers, it wants one thing."

Suddenly Shanks felt anger. "Yes, it wants to kill. We've established that. That poor woman."

"Kill? It wanted to marry her!"

"What?"

"Think back to all the tales you know of elemental spirits." The doctor was his old animated self. "Recall the love stories of the undine, or mermaid, luring a man to love and doom. Why, these spirits, these elementals, live a very long time, yes; but they are mortal—their souls are mortal. Their highest desire is to put on human immortality—achievable only by putting on human flesh—hence the 'marriage' or possession. Our fire elemental covets a human body and a human soul."

"But it kills people."

"Yes, because the victims are unwilling—or the vessels are too frail. It is the classic satanic pact. The devil delivers gold, but in exchange for what? For the body and for the soul. In the end they are the same. To gain the devil's gold you must yield him your body and your soul. Mark what I say: sooner or later the creature will find a willing subject able to contain all that incandescent energy; then the spontaneous combustions will cease, at least for such time as the body holds together."

"And then?"

"Why, then it shall seek another body."

"Emile, we have to notify someone about all this. Someone in authority, maybe the FBI."

"I'm afraid they would only hinder our work."

"Our work? What work? The séance was a failure. What can we do besides wait for the monster to possess somebody?"

"We dare not wait!" the doctor thundered. "When it fell from its sphere of fire, it upset the balance of things. It now feeds off the other elements; witness the abnormal heat. That is one reason we must not wait. Another is this: you see what it does now in its unembodied form; once it gains a human body, its appetites may be even more shocking. But there is a third reason not to wait. And that reason is our own safety. When that salamander's head came out of the wall—"

"Yes?"

"It saw us."

• • •

The newspapers at this time joyfully shouted the misdeeds of a popular film couple, and lambasted as well a whole raft of political figures for crimes unspeakable but not, apparently, unprintable. Occasionally, on some inner page, one could find an inch-long column devoted to a death by fire, but the public had long since tired of this. After a while, fire ceased to make the news at all.

As for Shanks and Rosen, they met to weave elaborate plans

based on the doctor's almost constant research into folklore and demonology. In September came the rains.

Without transition the air smelled fresh one evening. The citizens raised their heads to a cold sky pouring rain. In an instant the heat spell was forgotten, as woolen garments were hastily pulled on and long-disused raincoats sought for in spare closets. The rains lasted nearly a week and continued intermittently for a few days more.

In the study, Shanks released billows of sweet-smelling pipe smoke as he sat in his armchair contemplating the droplets of water coursing down the slick windowpane. Rosen, too, stared out, but he peered into the night.

"No more heat," said Shanks. "No more heat, no more fires, no more elemental. It must have burned itself out or returned to its otherwhither."

"You forget the third alternative," added Rosen. "It may have found a body."

The rain hit harder, propelled by a sudden wind. Rosen drew the curtains.

"If it has found a body," the doctor resumed, "we must be ready for it. I read recently an ancient account of an elemental spirit exorcised by means of a stone tablet bearing a potent inscription."

Shanks sighed. "Lacking any better suggestion," he said, "I suppose we ought to put in an order for one."

"You are too flippant," Rosen sniffed. "I am having one made."

• • •

Two weeks passed. September became October. The news was all of the virulent new "wasting sickness," which exhausted and emaciated and was nearly always fatal. October passed into November.

Toward the end of November the friends spent two weeks fishing mountain streams for trout.

When Shanks returned to the office, his secretary greeted him with a multitude of new work, then left the room but was back immediately.

"I nearly forgot," she said. "A man came here every day while you were on vacation. Some sort of foreigner. I kept telling him you were away. But he didn't seem to understand. He just stood there, whispering your name—till I had to ask him to leave. Every day. I think he was an albino. I suppose he'll be back. What should I do about him, sir?"

Shanks told her to use her own discretion and began to assemble the threads of business. By the time he finished, it was evening, and the office was empty. A glance at the clock told him he was nearly late for an appointment. To save time, he left the building by the rear exit instead of his usual way through the front, since his car was parked on a side street. He started the engine and turned the corner, past his office entrance. It was only when he was some blocks away that he realized he had seen a figure standing in the shadows by the office door.

For some reason he could not sleep that night. He tried reading, then counting backward, and finally formed wordless pictures. Still he could not sleep. What was bothering him? Was he hungry?

Shanks pulled the bedcovers away, got into his slippers, and made his way to the kitchen. When he opened the refrigerator, he decided he wasn't hungry after all and settled for a glass of milk.

He carried the glass into the dark living room and sat on the sofa. When he finished his milk, he remembered reading some-where that people often suffered insomnia during a full moon.

Was it full tonight? He went to the window and parted the curtains.

Someone was standing in front of his house.

Half-hidden by the big cotoneaster arch that fronted the sidewalk, a figure stood facing him, stood with its arms at its sides, stood and did not move. Just then a passing automobile lit the front yard for an instant. Shanks gave a start: the figure seemed to be wearing a white mask.

What was it his secretary had told him? Something about an albino. His impulse was to call the police to report a prowler. But, even as he watched, the figure moved away and disappeared down the street.

● ● ●

The first thing he did on arising the next morning was peer out the window. In the street he saw only neighbors. He had slept late. When he called to inform Rosen of what had happened in the night, there was no answer. The doctor had probably gone to the library.

Business was heavy that day. It was nearly closing time when Shanks remembered he had meant to call Rosen. He reached for the phone.

This time the doctor was home. Briefly Shanks told him what had occurred.

"It is probably nothing, Emile, but my secretary told me that a similar character has been calling at my office."

"I have a suspicion," Rosen said in a strange voice. "William, you may be in terrible danger."

"What?"

"I thought it instinctive, like a shark. I was wrong. It is acutely intelligent. Listen, my friend. The man with the white

48

face. It is our creature. It has found a body. And it is coming after you."

The intercom buzzed.

"Sir," came the secretary's voice, "that man is here again, the foreign gentleman I told you about. Shall I send him in?"

"Not just yet," said Shanks. "Emile? He's here. He's here, now, in the outer office."

"William, get out. Go! Run!"

"You don't think——?"

"The wasting sickness we hear so much of——it is that creature keeping itself alive. It has become a vampire. Leave immediately. Use the back door. Drive home. I'll meet you. Hurry!"

As Shanks stepped through the private exit and into the alley, he heard the inner door opening. Then he was off, sprinting like a boy.

• • •

The evening came moonless and cold, with a slight wind spilling through the streets, rustling the shrubbery that grew alongside the house. Rosen had arrived a few minutes after Shanks. Together they hefted a heavy stone tablet from the trunk of Rosen's car onto the front porch.

They sat in the unlit living room, peering from the window. The wind increased. Shanks's gaze kept returning to the swaying branches of the cotoneaster arch. By now they shook so fiercely, he expected to see a white face each time they clashed. Rosen put a hand on his friend's arm. "What is the time?"

"Ten to twelve," came the whispered reply. "Listen——"

A pause. "It is only the sylphs working their wind," Rosen said softly.

Outside, something metallic scraped discordantly every time a tide of wind flooded the passageway between Shanks's house and the house next door. The tossing shrubbery sounded like the sea, the grinding metal like the hoot of a foghorn heard in delirium. The wind sang louder.

"On such a night, the salamander is doubly strong," whispered Rosen. "The sylph goads it into a fury of combustion."

"Why does it want me, Emile? It saw us both—why me?"

Rosen shrugged. "Maybe you were easier to find. Maybe it can concentrate on only one at a time. Who knows? Perhaps it is drawn to you."

"Why do you think it will come here—tonight?"

"I suspect it comes here every night, just as it haunts your office by day. I think it will continue to do this until it finds you."

"Do you really believe the tombstone will work? That that thing will take the time to read all that foreign writing?"

"It is Chaldean," the doctor said. "And our creature doesn't have to read anything. The writing is a spell to attract it to the stone, which, by the way, is chalcedony. Buried inside are seven semiprecious amulets. According to my old Babylonian author, if the creature but touches the stone, the lapidary charms inside will catapult it back to where it belongs."

Rosen's hand gripped Shanks's shoulder. There, by the shrubbery—a flash of white.

A figure stepped out of the shadow.

"It's coming for the tablet," Shanks whispered. "It's making for the porch."

Something split the air with a cacophonous crack.

"It worked!" cried Shanks. "He's gone."

"Wait!" His friend restrained him from tearing open the door.

"Wait? Why?"

The doorbell rang.

"The tablet?" Shanks whispered. Rosen shook his head.

All was quiet except for the wind.

Then, from beyond the door, a hollow voice uttered a monosyllable.

"Shanks," it repeated, over and over. "Shanks."

The knob of the locked door rattled. The wind was howling now, the scraping metal shrieking.

But then the rattling ceased. The wind stopped. The house lay calm.

"The window," Rosen whispered.

They looked out in time to see a figure retreating down the street.

Rosen opened the door. Fragments of the tablet littered the walkway. Rosen stooped to retrieve the amulets and some of the fragments, then closed the door and turned on all the lights.

"What stopped it from breaking in?" asked Shanks.

Rosen tugged at his beard. "I don't know," he said. "Maybe it was the amulets." He held them tightly in his fist. "I need more time to study." The wind started up again.

"I own a pistol," Shanks said. "We can always shoot it, you know."

"What use would that be? To have the creature once more indulge itself in an orgy of burnings until it finds another body? I begin to despair."

"Despair?" Shanks said angrily. "I despair that there are such things as elementals. I despair that my well-ordered universe has been kicked upside down. I despair that every elemental that ever existed was not stood up before a celestial firing squad and blasted into hell!"

Rosen's eyebrows lifted. "No elementals? Why, then, no life! Without the salamander, no fire,—no sun, no warmth. Our planet a mere spongy rag dripping with cold, wet earth. Without the undine, no water—the world a shriveled, bone-hard ball. Would you banish the gnome? No solid substance—no earth at all—a whirling mass of gas, fire, and water. And the sylph—do you not like to breathe? No, my friend, elementals in their proper spheres spell life and substance. It is only when such a spirit falls out of its sphere that there is death and chaos. We must restore it!"

"How?"

"Produce an undine. Fire and water are inimical; water must prevail. Do you know where we can find an undine?"

"No."

"Nor do I. Yet there is a way. There must be!" he shouted. Excitement lit his face. "Where does the creature go, William, when it is not attacking others or spying on you? It has a body, and a body requires rest. Where does it go to rest? It must have a lair. We have to find that lair, surprise the creature while it is resting, and capture it. Then we must immerse it in a large body of water. That will send it back to where it came from. The amulets are our key."

"Brave words," said Shanks.

Rosen produced a handful of fragments from the shattered tablet. "Brave words are not enough," he remarked dryly.

• • •

Daylight found Shanks at Rosen's house, groggy and dispirited from lack of sleep. He looked about him irritably as he sipped his coffee.

His secretary had orders to phone him as soon as she completed her project—also orders not to admit the foreign man for any reason. He yawned again. Rosen had gone to the library. Shanks lit his pipe. It tasted ashy.

Without enthusiasm he took up their old memorandum of fire data and with a compass began drawing circles on a city map. According to Rosen, somewhere within one of those circles was the creature's lair. A half hour passed.

The phone rang. It was the secretary. No, the foreign man had not come by, but the figures were ready.

Shanks scrambled to copy the information. He hung up. Now he had another sheet to work from, a list correlating the outbreaks of the wasting sickness. Excitement rose in him as he added circle after circle to the city map. When the last circle was drawn, he hurriedly phoned Rosen at the library.

• • •

The next few days were busy ones. Rare gems had to be bought and carved to specification. An important meeting had to be arranged for two in the morning. Then, too, there was the matter of the large asbestos box.

It is not uncommon for the head of a marketing research firm to superintend the testing of a new product. A certain amount of secrecy is also expected, to protect a manufacturer against his competitors. A 2 A.M. appointment, then, did not seem suspicious. After all, tremendous profits might be made from a totally heat-resistant container.

A strip of moon glowed dimly behind the clouds as Shanks and Rosen once more passed through the industrial district. As always, it was Shanks who drove. But this time he drove a rented van that carried an asbestos box.

As the van navigated the narrow back streets, Shanks

thought of the eerie cremation of the Spanish medium. What would this night bring? The sight of the foundry cut short his dark thoughts. He pulled the van up before a sprawling colossus of winking fires blazing in the night. Shanks parked at the receiving dock in the rear, ascended the loading platform, and pushed an electric bell. Almost immediately a foreman came out, accompanied by two workers, who lifted the asbestos crate onto a metal dolly and wheeled it inside.

"You gentlemen won't need your coats," the foreman said. "It's always summer here."

The inside proved cyclopean. Enormous blast furnaces lined the walls, their iron doors constantly opening or shutting with loud clangs, throwing a lurid red light on the sweating workmen.

"Welcome to the caverns of hell," the foreman said with a grin. "This heat"—he stretched out his arms—"you never get used to it. And you're always cold when you're someplace else." The two workmen donned protective masks. The foreman handed similar ones to Rosen and Shanks.

"This place never stops," he said. "The fires never go out. If anything goes wrong, the mechanics come and fix it. Here's the one you insisted on, Dr. Rosen, the one that burns hotter than the others."

The workmen lifted the crate off the dolly and onto a roller slide. The foreman pushed a button to open the furnace door. Though the oven was only in the pilot position, a terrific blast of heat hit them, and an appalling glare.

"Say the word," said the foreman, "and I'll take this gaff and slide your box right in. You can see everything through the glass panel in the door. Say, why is the top still up? And what you got in there? They look like jewels."

"To test the heat," Rosen said darkly. "When I am satisfied

with the experiment, I'll operate the mechanical rod to give the lid a nudge. A spring trap will lock the case."

At Rosen's signal the box went into the furnace. The fires were turned up. Shanks stared into the white heat. Despite his protective mask his eyes could peer only for a few seconds at a time. The heat was unspeakable.

The workmen left for another project, but the foreman lingered by the furnace. Rosen had told Shanks to divert any onlookers. The foreman was easily diverted.

"Do I like working here?" he asked in response to Shanks's question. "Look around you. Do you know what this place is, Mr. Shanks? This is Gehenna. Have you heard of Gehenna? It's in the Bible, sir, the place where they made sacrifice to Moloch. He was a devil, you know, and we've got devils—lately. We've got that wasting sickness bad here. It's all that heat and light—they never hurt anybody much before. They shrivel a man now. They start by affecting the eyes." He lowered his voice yet still had to shout to make himself heard above the din of the foundry. "Last week I thought I saw a lizard in this furnace." He pointed. "A little lizard, climbing over white-hot steel!" He laughed, and Shanks laughed with him.

Rosen did not laugh. For he, too, saw shapes in the fire. It was not a lizard he saw, but a full-sized human body squirming from the back of the furnace. In the fierce white light he watched its mottled face and dead eyes, dormant but moving instinctively, the tongue darting in and out of its mouth to lick the flames. The body made a half turn and shrank to a tiny salamander with jeweled eyes. Lured by the amulets, it crawled dreamily up the side of the case and dropped through the opening. Rosen worked a lever; an iron rod came down and closed the lid.

"Enough!" he cried to the foreman. "Remove the case, please."

The workmen returned to gaff the box back up the metal rollers. Despite the intense heat, Rosen had the case immediately loaded on an iron gurney and wheeled to the van.

"Help me attach these metal bands," he cried, when the workers had left. "It may wake any second." They labored feverishly until they had the case banded in four places with strips of metal.

"Now—to the reservoir. Drive! Go!"

The reservoir was all the way across town. Out of the factory district onto the highway, they sped past closed buildings and empty lots. A whirl of city blocks shot by. The highway opened up to broad fields.

The air inside the van grew uncomfortably warm.

"It is awake," said Rosen, "and exerting tremendous pressure. Please drive faster."

"Can it break out?" called Shanks, increasing the speed so that the van shook as it roared along the highway.

"It doesn't matter. If the lid cracks open just a hair— Never mind. Drive faster."

Shanks leaned forward, his head nearly touching the windshield, his hands shaking on the wheel, his eyes fixed hypnotically on the unstable highway. The speedometer registered its full 120 mph. The van rattled dangerously.

"There!" cried Rosen. "Up that steep hill—it is the reservoir!"

The air stifled, smothered, singed the eyes, cracked the skin.

"Slow down. Don't miss the turnoff. There, just ahead."

Overlooking the city, the reservoir was accessible only by a steep and winding road. Shanks hit the brake; the van nearly capsized as they veered into the narrow curve. Now the van did not shake; it crawled up and around each painful turn. The air was scarcely breathable.

Rosen leaned over to glance at the dashboard. "We're overheating," he said. "The temperature gauge is all the way to the red. The reservoir cannot be much farther."

But it was. The road went up and up—till suddenly they reached the top. Sparkling in the faint starlight a large body of water gently rippled a hundred yards below. A three-foot wall of concrete blocks separated the water from the embankment.

The van stopped.

"The engine has quit," Rosen whispered. The intense heat made it difficult to speak. "Get out. We'll let the van coast down to the water." Rosen heaved his bulk out of the passenger side. But Shanks remained.

"William, release the brake and get out!"

As though awakening from a daze, Shanks stepped out of the van as it began to roll down the inclined road. Gradually it picked up speed, hurling itself faster and faster at the wall. It hit the concrete with a resounding thud, taking pieces with it as it partially burst through and came to rest with its front wheels overhanging the water by a few feet.

"Down!" roared Rosen. "We must push it all the way into the water!" They raced to the van.

"Push," Rosen panted. Their feet braced, their backs straining, they strove with every sinew to dislodge the van. It was wedged fast.

"Inside," Rosen gasped as he fought for breath. "Grappling hooks. Attach them to the metal bands. We'll heave the case into the water."

The impact of the crash had sprung the rear doors. The box was in full view, surrounded by an almost palpable wall of heat. Nearby a pile of blankets was beginning to smolder.

"Gloves," Rosen whispered. "And wet the blankets."

They drew on heavy gloves and immersed the blankets in the reservoir. Shielding themselves with the dripping blankets, they attached short grappling hooks to the blistering metal bands.

"Hoist!" Rosen yelled through the fiery heat. "Hoist, hoist—there! Now into the water. What is wrong? Why don't you help?"

Shanks's gaze was not on the case but up into the sky, where a giant glowing salamander was forming above them, its claws twitching, ready to pounce, its razor teeth grinning down.

"It is an image," shouted Rosen. "It's only an image. Help me with the case!"

"It's going to spring!"

"Get the box into the water. The bands are melting! Heave it over the wall! There!"

It hit with a splash and a hiss as of a thousand snakes. The vision overhead disappeared.

The case glowed as it sank, lighting its descent with a gleaming green. Then abruptly it began to rise. The men leaped back to run high up the road as hissing hills of steam boiled from the water.

"We have outraged the balance of elements!" Rosen shouted in triumph. "Fire cannot burn water. Watch!"

Steam billowed up in ever-changing shapes, eerie and ectoplasmic, to meet overhead in a canopy of cloud. Music, clangorous and plangent, welled up in wordless, nonhuman song that sent the senses throbbing to an ancient, longing sadness.

For a moment, within the cloud canopy a face peered down, weirdly beautiful, its eyes eloquent of all the waters that ever were.

"The undine!" whispered Rosen with awe.

A fountain of fire spouted suddenly from the waters below like an ignited oil well, burning exultantly, forming ghostly hills of vapor. The water hissed away in a volley of steam.

The dolorous song rose an octave. The seething waters piled into a single liquid column, steadily rising till it seemed that gravity alone would send it crashing to drown everything below. Still it rose, and more, overtopping the fountain of fire, then moved quickly to engulf it.

For a moment all was quiet. The fire blazed through the green water like the sun inside an emerald. Then, with a thunderous crack, the shaft of flame erupted skyward, as the wave cascaded down to shatter in a burst of flying spray.

"It has gone back," Shanks heard someone say while the stream of fire shrank to a spark above and vanished in the upper atmosphere. Rain poured down. The sky held only clouds.

At the top of the reservoir a dazed Rosen tugged at his friend's passive arm. "Come," he said. "It is a long walk home."

THE TOWER IN
THE JUNGLE

Even as a child did I first go alone to the mummies. The Old One sent me to retrieve his golden scroll, left below in the catacombs. Never had I been without his strong presence to guide me. They frightened me, crouching in their cold tunnels. Dust lay everywhere, pieces of them. I remember a whim I had to extinguish the torches rather than look upon those grinning human fragments. Instead, I thought to sing an ancient song the Old One had taught me about a foolish barber and his drunken slave. This made me laugh so that I tarried long, dallying to hear my voice echo along the corridors. I emerged only reluctantly to the light, scroll in hand. Thus perished my dread of mummies.

From my earliest awakening the mummies shadowed all. Every freshly opened catacomb yielded mummies. Mummies by the thousand infested the ancient, oppressive ruins, which haunted the rotting jungle like an insidious spell. Great heaps of megalithic blocks those ruins were, dazzlingly white, carven with savage design. Their unstained whiteness extruded from the persistent foliage like newly stripped bones.

The Old One and I lived in a solitary tower, the only ancient edifice left standing. About us swept the ocean of jungle, vast beyond my computation, constantly growing, shifting, burying what remained of the ruined city. Stifling and copious, the jungle cast its waves, save in the clearings, where the mammoth ruins glowed by moonlight. By moonlight, too, the jungle exuded a pungent perfume, disturbingly like the spices the ancients used to preserve their dead.

And there were the apes who inhabited the ruins and nearby caves. Sometimes by brightest moonlight, when the night fragrance grew strongest, would I ascend to the stone casement midway up the tower and peer down upon the apes swarming over the blinding stones like maggots on bad meat.

And there was the Old One, forever adrift among his alembics, retorts, and crucibles, or conning the script on a worm-eaten parchment while he took meticulous notes on his golden scroll. Ever in pursuit of the Grand Experiment, ever seeking the rectified red powder to force the dead to whisper their secrets.

The Old One was the only living human my boyhood knew. From earliest infancy had I looked upon his distended orbicular eyes and leathern skin with an awe born of the awful spaces his wizard's mind had penetrated. He had come to the jungle ages ago from the iron-walled city that stood somewhere near Ur. He it was who taught me to chant and to read the ancient tongues, though rarely did he speak to me in those latter days, withdrawing himself instead to the very top of the tower to ponder, alone, in the alchemical chamber.

Now this room was wonderful to behold, hung on three sides with a vast tapestry in gold and vermilion depicting a league of hunters pursuing some nameless monstrosity across a background of hurling planets. Lacquered tables bearing wonderful instruments straddled the stone flooring. One device stood there of polished wood, a nest of concentric hemispheres couched one inside another, the whole beautifully emblazoned with zodiacal signs of amethyst and ruby.

Most beautiful of all was the multiplicity of glass bowls, domes, balls, tubes, and cylinders forming a network that thrummed with bubbling liquids of the most exquisite reds, greens, and ambers. Thus was the alchemical chamber perpetually awash with color.

Weary of his experiments, the Old One sometimes retired to a stone throne set within a shallow recess at one end of this room. Across the entrance hung tawny curtains of tiger's skin; these he drew together, then sat and pondered ways to glean the Secret.

For a certain Secret was known to the ancient race whose mummies glutted the tombs below the jungle. But this secret the ancients had neither incised in stone nor limned on parchment, for it was a terrible secret, a secret of infinite power, learned just before the race perished and known only to the highest sorcerers among them—the wizard priests who whispered it in an oblate room beneath the most ancient of their temples. I spent my days opening tombs, seeking their black-robed, turbaned mummies, while aloft amidst alchemical apparatuses or on his stone throne behind tiger-skin curtains, the Old One brooded on a formula to make them speak.

Always he pursued the Grand Experiment, the recipe for the rectified red powder that would unlock the dusty tongues of the mummy wizards, so that whichever knew the great secret could whisper to him the terrible words. So time passed as the Old One came ever closer to perfecting his powder.

I have told you of the apes. One I feared above the others, a large old bull more erect than its fellows and clearly the leader of the other apes. It stood always in the forefront, its red eyes and murderous fangs perpetually twisted into a mask of malignant ferocity. On moon-haunted nights it gave the impression of a hideously deformed maniac. Yet it was the mane—that odious shock that crowned its misshapen cranium—that made the creature abhorrent to me, a profusion of shaggy wires distending—almost twitching with its own life. This being I called Nazzla, after the Atlantean word for maniacal horror.

Many times did I brave the wet, weary heat of the jungle, ever seeking new catacombs among the fallen stones, in quest of the mummies of ancient sorcerers, distinct, as I have said, in black robes and turbans. So far I had gathered only thirteen, and the Old One would have me harvest all I could, against the time that he should perfect the rectified red powder to make them speak. For he reasoned that among the turbaned dead, surely one must know the secret of infinite power.

These sorcerers' mummies we laid on trestles in a long room on the ground floor—a sumptuous room, full of lacquered cabinets loaded with canopic jars overflowing with fragrant spices. Amid these aromatic surroundings the sorcerers' mummies lay in mute and awful dignity, carefully preserved against the day that the Great Work should be perfected. Then, one by one, would each black-robed, turbaned mummy be summoned forth to yield the secret, if it knew. The lesser mummies, abundant in every catacomb and cellar, we used for experiments at the top of the tower, though I was seldom privy to these experiments.

So I spent my boyhood harvesting mummies in the catacombs beneath the jungle. The apes never offended me unless I happened to be carrying a mummy. Then they screamed. They followed the mummy and me, always at a distance, shrieking until I had borne the mummy inside the tower.

And this was the labor of my childhood and early youth.

But there came a time of great change. It happened in this wise. Obeying instructions, I ascended late one afternoon into the tower room. The crystal tubes and cylinders bubbled their red-, green-, and amber-colored liquids as I tiptoed to the curtained alcove.

"Master," I called. "It is sunset."

There was no answer.

"Master."

Then I heard a sharp intake of breath as the Old One's face appeared between the tiger-skin curtains.

"Moisture from the thag beetle," he said.

I raced down the stairs and out into the jungle. Not much sand had sifted to the bottom of the Old One's great hourglass when I returned with a pouchful of clicking, scraping insects.

Selecting three of the largest, the Old One, with thumb and forefinger, deftly squeezed out their moisture over a bowl of beaten copper, nearly brimming with seething white ichor. He stirred the mixture till it turned pink, then dipped a cloth into the bowl and began to anoint a mummy on a nearby slab. No sooner had the mixture met the mummy's skin, than the mummy began to change color. The deep brown faded to a light tan, then bleached to a deathly white. Tiny ripples played about its wizened carcass. It raised its head to peer at us with the ghost of eyes.

"Rise up," the Old One commanded in a tongue of magical lore.

It left its slab and went the way pointed by the Old One's finger.

"Yon stone door," the Old One thundered, "the trap to the lower chamber—lift it."

The mummy knelt for the iron ring set in the stone floor. It wrenched the stone free, then broke apart. For some minutes after, the pieces continued to writhe.

"Master!" I cried. "You made it move; soon you will make them speak; you will learn the great secret!"

"Pah," he said. "It was too fragile." He withdrew behind the tiger-skin curtains.

Something screamed in the jungle, a long, loud ape scream. Instantly echoed an uproar. I held my ears as I peered through the casement. The jungle below seethed with apes, their heads tilted to rage at us in the tower as they howled and screamed and pounded their chests. Behind me I could hear the soft whisper of the mummy's fragments twitching on the stone floor. Below, like a captain disposing his troops, one ape roared the loudest of all. I did not have to see the long cranial hairs to know that it was Nazzla.

• • •

Now that the Old One had learned to make the mummies walk, it amused him to animate many. About the tower they wandered or out into the jungle. Occasionally a mummy broke and left its fragments twitching.

Seldom quiet now, the apes prowled ever nearer to our tower, yet gave way whenever I escorted a mummy through the jungle. Always the apes kept their distance—just out of sight— but the violent screams died not until the mummy and I were far away.

The second momentous event happened in this wise. The Old One sent me down one morning to gather some of the giant scorpions infesting a certain stagnant pool. This I did and brought back many plump ones with scarlet stingers.

Hours later he sent a mummy down the tower steps. As I sat conning a curiously runed parchment, the mummy laid its thin hand on my shoulder and beckoned me to follow to the tower room, where the master awaited.

Before I could speak, the master pointed to a brown and twisted mummy propped against a wall.

"Behold yon mummy," he whispered.

"Yes, Master."

"I can make it scream."

In a moment he produced a carven box of cinnabar and prised off its lid. Out sprang one of the larger scorpions. Catching it in a pair of tongs, the Old One briefly immersed it in the pink mixture within the bowl of beaten copper. Instantly the liquid turned a bright red. Then he released the insect. It leaped across the floor, crawled up the mummy's body, and perched upon the face. The master spoke a word of power. The mummy gaped open its jaws. With a flurry of multijointed legs, the insect crawled inside the mummy's mouth. There was a sharp crunch as the mummy's teeth broke the hard shell; a scarlet ichor shot from the desiccated jaws.

At that moment the mummy opened its ghost eyes and screamed. Again and again, shrilly, as though the very night were affrighted with horror. The jaws closed. But the screams persisted, echoed from a hundred throats in the jungle. The apes. Their screams rent the air till the glass balls shook on the tables. Then the night went quiet.

Its jaws shut tight upon the dying insect, the mummy stood

motionless against the wall. The mummy's skin was no longer brown; the mummy glared a deadly white.

"Master," I cried. "You made the mummy scream. You made the mummy scream. Soon they will all speak and whisper secrets!"

"Pah," he spat. "Not with such a bug. It was only a game." Folding his silken robe about him, he retired behind the tiger-skin curtains.

Another effect of the Old One's experiments was the way the mummies attached themselves to me. Thus I found myself, on an oppressively hot and overcast day, entering the jungle to collect a certain variety of bloodworm. Vapor rose in thick, wet clouds from every tree, fern, and creeper. As I penetrated deeper, the way grew darker till I felt my way through an opaque wall of hot gloom. The steam cushioned every sound. The silence overwhelmed. Suddenly a titanic network of light tore the sky apart, followed by an earsplitting explosion of thunder. Then the steam closed in once more, and the world contracted to opaque silence.

I had made my way so far when something crossed my path. I started, then realized it was only a mummy. Glad of the company, I smiled a greeting, and with the mummy tramped farther into the jungle. I could feel the electricity gathering in the air; sparks fell from the mummy's face and fingers. Another shock of thunder shook the world to its foundations. I covered my eyes against the burning flash of lightning. When I looked up again, I found I had picked up another mummy.

By and by it began to rain, slowly at first, then a persistent patter that gradually increased to a flood. A dreadful gash of lightning exploded overhead, and I saw that I had picked up more mummies.

The rain became a deadly downpour of stinging, wounding arrows, vicious and overwhelming. The hissing was deafening, surpassed in volume only by those terrific thunderclaps that seemed to flatten the jungle. There was neither safety nor shelter—only rain and affliction and the sense of drowning.

Then abruptly the rain ceased. One moment the world drowned; the next moment the sky was dry. The steam floated away. All about me I heard the pat-pat-pat as the jungle dripped from every leaf. It was good to be free from the deadly drops that struck the head like a hammer. I stood up to find myself surrounded by mummies. I laughed happily. Now that the storm had ceased, I could resume my task of gathering worms for my master.

Thunder stamped the earth once more with a concussion that left my ears ringing. The storm had not passed. This was merely a lull. The steam rose, twisting to impenetrable wraiths. The mummies dripped electric sparks.

Directly ahead a figure loomed. Another mummy, I thought. But it was not a mummy. Massively it moved through the mist, fire sparking from every point. Its head—misshapen in some way—blazed, too, as the creature loped toward me through the oppressive gloom. A big bolt of lightning crackled. The figure raised its face to scream at the booming sky. It was Nazzla.

The apes attacked from every bush and tree, ripping the mummies' parchment skin with fierce, murderous fangs. Thunder boomed as a mountain of water burst like a tidal wave. I raced through the flood even as the hate screams shrilled with the roaring rain.

I ran as I had never run before. Eventually I reached the tower. Pausing only to fill my lungs, I fled up the stone steps into the great room bubbling with colored lights. Not finding the master, I turned to the recess covered by the tiger-skin curtains.

"Master," I cried. "The apes have broken my mummies."

The master's head appeared between the parted curtains.

"I had not thought of the apes," he said, and closed the curtains.

When the dawn's feeblest rays barely pierced the gloom of my chamber, I looked up from my bed to see a mummy standing over me. There was movement about its mouth, and I saw it was chewing a scorpion. With a sharp snap it crushed the shell, then opened its mouth, and said, "Come" in a sepulchral voice. So I sleepily followed the mummy aloft to the room of alchemy.

Wearing a plain brown robe, the Old One sat writing figures on his golden scroll. I waited respectfully. When he was finished he looked up.

"I dreamed of a tomb beneath a great boulder shaped like an ape's head. Enter the tomb and bring me what grows on its walls."

"Yes, Master."

"To reach the tomb begin now and walk with the wind until sundown. The failing rays will light the ape's head."

"Yes, Master."

"Tarry not; and take no mummies, lest the apes molest thee."

Then did I notice a coil of rope and some copper tackle upon a stone bench.

"Master," I said. "You have a rope and implements."

The Old One wrapped his brown cloak tightly around himself.

"I, too, go into the jungle," he said. "But a different way."

There was no path leading to the tomb of the master's dream. I wielded a great knife to slash through coils of spiny creepers barring my way. Twice did venomous serpents pass close to my sandals. Vermin drove sharp needles into my legs as I plodded through sucking mud. Still I followed the wind, never doubting the wisdom of my master's dream.

Throughout the daylight hours I burrowed through dripping foliage. I stood up at last in a clearing just as the dying sun painted the jungle blood-red. My heart nearly leaped from my rib cage. Waiting for me was Nazzla.

But, no, it was the boulder, the white ape-headed boulder the master sent me to find. A mass of vegetation topped its summit and, in that awful and uncertain light, resembled nothing so much as a mane of wiry hair. As the dying sun withdrew its fires, the head dimmed cold and white. The foliage at its summit fluttered with an invisible wind against the darkening sky. I found the entrance to the tomb, the gaping hole I had mistaken for the mouth of the colossal head, an upright tunnel ending abruptly in a great iron door encrusted with verdigris.

Not since infant years had I felt aught of dislike or of dread for mummy places. Yet this tomb I much misliked because it was carven in an ape's head. I hung back some moments, hesitating whether to sing my ancient song of the barber and the drunken slave. Instead, I unsheathed my great knife to prise open the massive door.

It opened easily, though none there could have been to oil its hinges. Beyond the door was darkness. I tarried some instants, then, with shaking hands, drew forth my tinderbox, struck steel to stone, lit my tiny lamp, and stepped inside.

I stood in a long chamber, excessively damp, filled with slabs bearing the largest mummies I had ever seen. Something about their posture I did not like, though as yet I dared not shine my lamplight fully upon them. One mummy caught my eye even in the indirect lamplight, for it seemed to wear a fanciful head-dress of black iron. I raised my lamp high to peer along the chamber to the farthest end. It was riven with tunnels. I stepped back to lean against the wall.

A soft wet thing touched my bare arm. Hastily I jumped away and flashed my lamp around. Soft mold furred the walls, wet mold, quivering slightly, like a thing alive. I shed the lamplight fully on the mummies. They were frozen to a rigid posture, reaching for the growing mold, their mouths gaped greedily open.

Hastily I gathered some of the mold inside my leathern bag, my hand shaking so the lamp sent eerie shadows against the walls. In my eagerness to withdraw, I must have bumped the mummy with the crown of iron. For the crown rolled off the stone slab and clashed to the pavement, awaking echoes in the corridors that reached far down inside the rock. I raised the lamp.

I beheld an apelike head with a mane of white hair. I lifted the lamp higher. This mummy lay next to the wall; the mold nearly touched its dried lips. I fled the tomb.

What—my mind raced as I ran through the jungle—what would happen—my heart surged in rhythm to the words—what would happen when it tasted the mold?

Hours later I tramped familiar paths and was much elated when I reached the tower.

Though greatly wearied, I lost no time in climbing to the tower room, for I knew the Old One waxed impatient for my return.

Instead of being greeted by the bubbling of red and amber liquids in crystal cylinders, I found the alchemical room cold and lifeless, save for a lonely copper lamp emitting a sickly fume.

"Master," I called. "I am returned." I stepped to the tiger-skin curtains.

"Master?"

I heard a sharp intake of breath. The curtains parted. There on the throne sat—Nazzla. Now it was neither ape nor man. Now it was white. The fierce fangs, the mask of murderous hatred—white, all white. Slowly shaking its grinning ape-head, it peered at me through ghost eyes. Now I know why the master had gone into the jungle. He had embalmed Nazzla.

Back and forth the great ape rocked on the throne, its ghost white head lolling from side to side, its distended mane swaying like a pendulum.

I fled shrieking down the stairs, through the lower chambers, and into the room where lay the turbaned mummies of the priests.

There stood the Old One, flagrantly attired in a robe of scarlet and gold. The beaten copper bowl simmered on a tripodal brazier.

"The mold," he said.

"Master, upstairs—Nazzla!"

"It took a piece of mummified ape to perfect the solution. The mold."

I handed him my leathern bag. He spooned a quantity of mold into the bowl, and blew upon the coals. The liquid within bubbled, rose high, then dried and collapsed to a red powder.

"Master," I said. "Nazzla sits on your throne."

But he was unmindful of all I said. His eyes seemed to light the room.

Now he passed to the thirteen black-robed, turbaned mummies on their wooden trestles, and deposited a spoonful of the rectified red powder between every pair of withered lips.

One by one, the mummies turned white. Each opened its eyes.

The master stood away and said a single word of power.

One by one the turbaned mummies rose to whisper in his ear; as each did so, it passed out of the chamber.

Twelve times did this occur. Twelve times did the Old One scowl and say in deepest scorn, "Pah, it knows it not."

At last uprose the thirteenth, the tallest and most withered. It walked stiffly to the master and bent down to his ear. Then it passed out of the chamber.

A beatific look illumined the Old One's face, and he smiled a terrible smile and spoke the words: "Now I wield the power of the ancient dead." Then his smile fell as his face began to whiten. He laid himself upon a wooden trestle, turned stone white, and passed into mummification.

A shadow fell upon the wall. I looked behind. Nazzla's mummy opened wide its jaws and screamed.

Vibrant with power, screaming their death screams, the apes surged into the chamber, shattering the instruments, hurling the trestles against stone walls. Foaming madness raged in their maniacal effort to demolish all they could seize.

Down came the shelves of priceless ointments, the lacquered cabinets. Pungent fumes arose as canopic jars cracked, spilling attars, oils, and unguents over the littered floor. Inlaid chests burst to splinters beneath thunderous feet.

A flash of gold and vermilion. The vast tapestry had become a cloak across the slouching shoulders of a great ape descending from the tower room.

The Old One's scroll was tossed aside to lie among the mounting heap of wreckage.

Then, lo! Amid the cacophony, the black-robed, turbaned mummies filed in from the adjoining chamber. As the apes turned to meet them, the mummies raised shriveled arms, made claws of shrunken fingers, and sank black splintered teeth into the apes' throats. Three apes died on the floor, strangling in their own blood, while others fell upon the mummies, snapping the dried, thin bones, gnawing black integument off yellowed skulls—till the mummies burst to dust.

Now the apes slouched toward my master's body, lying supine upon its trestle. But I was quicker than they. Brandishing my great knife, I planted myself before the Old One.

As the first ape lunged for me, I stabbed the knife point into its throat, withdrawing the blade as the mighty ape, gurgling with blood, went crashing to the floor. Then I wielded the knife like a sword—slicing, biting deeply the apish necks, severing tendons, chopping away at hair, muscle, and flesh.

Suddenly the very air exploded with screams. The apes gave way as out of the jungle countless mummies poured into the chamber. Apes died, but mummy after mummy cracked to powder. The room became clouded with mummy dust.

Something dealt me a blow that sent me reeling to the floor. My knife was gone. I had one last glimpse of that hellish scene, then fled the din and devastation, that accursed jungle, and eventually fell in with Sumerian traders.

Though much I wander down the years, that last sight remains as a scar sealed with corrosive acid. Upon its trestle lay my master's ghost white mummy. And its lips—its moving lips spoke to one bending low to catch the words. I screamed when that one stood up. Towering beside my master's trestle, a look of terrible intelligence on its mummy face, was Nazzla.

EDNA

Beware my anfractuosities, Edna. They can be mordacious."

"Were you speaking to me, sir? My name is not Edna."

The large man paused to wipe his sweat-spotted face with a red bandanna.

"It does no good to inspissate, Edna."

They stood at a deserted bus stop. No bus in sight.

"You mistake me for somebody else." She edged around to the other side of the bench to stare in the direction where the bus would come. She looked fortyish, blond, petite. He was perhaps fifty-five.

He removed his straw sportsman's hat and wiped his mostly bald head with the red bandanna. He stared at her, stared through her in the direction from which the bus still had not come.

In a moment he was beside her. "I can growl, Edna. Want to hear me growl?"

She walked, fast, but he remained beside her.

"Why do you keep up this futile pretense, Edna?"

She stopped long enough to look him squarely in the face.

"I will call a policeman if you do not go away."

"Police, police." Only it was he who called. "Police!"

The street remained empty of all but a few parked cars.

"I can call the firemen next, Edna. Shall I call the firemen? Firemen. Hey, firemen."

Then a squad car did arrive, passed them, turned around, and stopped. Two uniformed officers got out.

"My wife," the big man explained. "She pretends not to know me."

"Is that right?" the first policeman asked her.

"No, I don't know him. He came up to me."

"Her name is Edna," the big man said.

"No, no it isn't. It's Lucy, Lucy Mulcahey." She popped open her purse, fumbled for identification.

The second policeman took her wallet, scanned the cards inside. "Just a moment," he said. The two policemen retired a few feet away to confer. The big man produced the bandanna and began to swab his face. The woman's fingers made little twitching movements, like a bird's legs etching along a perch.

The policemen came back.

"You'd better go along with him, Edna," the first policeman said.

"I tell you my name is Lucy Mulcahey. My identification."

"Yeah." The second policeman winked. "We crossed that out. It says Edna now, just plain Edna." He turned to the big man. "Last name?"

"Monkhouse."

"Monkhouse." The policeman wrote it down. "Well, you

go with hubby, Mrs. Monkhouse. You go home and make it up."

She ran now, crazily, her legs flailing against the hard pavement. After three-quarters of a block she stumbled but caught a lamppost and hugged it. She turned to look back. The three of them stared at her.

Suddenly the bus arrived. She waved, and it stopped, and she was aboard and found change in her purse; then she collapsed onto an empty seat.

The bus halted at the bus stop where she ran away. The big man got aboard.

She did not faint or even scream.

He paid his fare and walked right by her, sitting in the seat just behind. She sat rigidly, eyes forward.

"Hello, Doll," a male voice said behind her.

"Charlie. Where you been?" A female voice.

"Been arguing with Edna. She's mad at me."

Someone whispered in her ear.

"You shouldn't tease Charlie so much."

She turned around. It was a large brunette. She turned back again and began to sob wildly—to leave this bus, quickly—to get home—somehow—

The bus stopped again. She looked up to see a belt buckle.

"You mustn't make trouble, Miss."

It was the bus driver.

"This man—" She was crying uncontrollably.

"My wife," Charlie explained tactfully.

"She ain't well." This from the large brunette.

"He's not my husband."

"Edna"—this from Charlie—"the children. Please come home now. It's at the next stop, driver."

Before she knew it she was off the bus and herded between them, Charlie and the large woman—each supporting her by an arm. They walked her down a tree-hung residential street.

A police car passed, executed a U-turn, and stopped. The officer at the wheel rolled down his window. "Everything all right, Edna?" He tipped her a wink and drove off.

They took her to a white wooden house and pushed her inside. They led her upstairs to the back part of the house, into a room, and onto a bed.

Charlie smiled benignly. "We're locking you in while Doll and I fetch our surgical tools from the basement. Be right back." The door slammed, and she heard the lock click. The window stood open. There was a narrow ledge and a drainpipe, and she got partway down, then fell and hurt herself, but she did not hurt herself so badly that she could not run away.

She wandered for blocks till she found herself crossing a main intersection. A taxi turned the corner. Somehow she gathered courage to hail it and give her address.

• • •

The spare figure of her husband waited in the open doorway. She handed the cab man a bill, then ran to her husband, pulled him inside, and slammed and locked the door.

"Jack, I've been through horror. Jack? Jack!"

"Why are you so late? What's happened? Your dress."

"There was a man at the bus stop—and the police——"

The doorbell rang.

"Our dinner guests. Just when you're upset—I'll tell them you're ill and send them away."

"Our guests——?"

"The man from Phoenix—he's bringing his wife. I told you."

"I—I can't think. Wait, yes, he wants to invest in your business. It's terribly important—Oh, they keep ringing! I don't know—I must be in shock—"

"I'll send them away. I'll get Dr. Jim."

"No. Later. This means too much to you. Later, after they leave, we'll get Dr. Jim. I'll tell you everything, and we'll discuss what to do. I'll be all right till then."

She washed and brushed and changed her clothes and was able after a while to control her trembling. Twenty minutes later she returned to the living room.

"My wife Lucy," Jack said to his guests. "Lucy, this is Charlie and Doll. Lucy?"

She found herself on the sofa when she came to. The big man stood over her.

"I let you escape, Edna. I thought we would have more fun here. Jack's gone over to fetch your neighbor Dr. Jim. Doll is upstairs going through your things."

"Who are you?" she managed to whisper, her eyes wide but unseeing.

"Don't go telling on me, Edna. People who tell on me lose pieces. Now let's have some sex before your husband gets back." The door banged open as Jack returned with the doctor.

She tried to speak, but her feelings were too wide for her throat. She could only cry, wildly, brokenly. The big man made drinks for Jack and himself and Doll. The doctor led Lucy into the bedroom and closed the door.

"That man—that man in there—" Suddenly she could speak. The doctor looked grave.

"Your pulse is dangerously fast." As always, his booming voice attested authority. "Try to stay calm. I'm going to nip home for a sedative to give you, Lucy. I'll be right back to talk to your friend. Don't worry. I'll leave the door open. If you get nervous, call Jack."

Before she could say "Don't go" he was gone.

She counted silence for six beats of her heart.

"She have these spells before?" Charlie's voice.

"No. She was upset." Jack spoke now. "Something about what the police did at a bus stop. I didn't hear the whole story."

"Your poor wife." It was Doll. "You look sick, too. You should get some fresh air. You got a garden? You stay here, Charlie, in case the doctor needs something." Their voices moved off.

Alone in the house with Charlie.

She could scream. She could surely scream. Jack was only as far away as the garden. Dr. Jim would return any second. No one could hurt her with Jack and Dr. Jim so near.

What if she couldn't scream?

"Lucy." Dr. Jim was back.

"Take this now. Swallow it. It will calm you down."

"Oh, Dr. Jim. That man."

"Swallow the pill, Lucy."

She swallowed the pill.

"That's better. It will relax you. You don't have to do anything but lie there. Jack and I will do the rest. Now excuse me one more time." He was out the door. She heard him as he passed from the hallway into the living room.

"I say, Mr——?" his voice boomed.

"Charlie."

"Yes, well, Charlie. Lucy has mentioned some things. Come with me a moment. The kitchen will do. I want to ask you a few questions." She heard the kitchen door slam.

It will be all right now. Dr. Jim is in charge. He will make everything all right. She lay for several minutes thinking of how right everything would be.

The kitchen door banged open.

"Hey," Charlie's voice said. "Something's wrong with that doctor. I think he's dead."

Everything collapsed inside her until the voices came.

"Look at his face," yelled Jack's voice. "What happened?"

"He fell over," Charlie's voice said.

"I'll call an ambulance. Doll, will you look after Lucy?"

"I'll do it, Jack," said Charlie.

Now was the time to get out of bed. Now was the time to kick her legs onto the floor and stand up. Now was the time.

"It's me, Edna." A figure filled the entrance. "Upstairs in the master bedroom is better. We'll have more fun there." He took her arm, oh, so gently, led her upstairs, and put her on the big bed, then stood between her and the doorway.

Oh, Jack would fix him. Jack was small, but he was wiry. Jack would throw this man out of the house forever. Why was Jack taking so long? Her shoulders heaved. What was he doing down there? Her breaths came fast. Her eyes leaked scalding tears. Why didn't Jack come up?

Charlie sat on the bed.

"Want to know who I am, Edna? I'm the guy who just killed your husband."

Now she could not even cry.

"Jack's a corpse on the floor. I put poison in his drink. He's dead like that doctor. How about a kiss now, Edna?"

Doll came into the room.

"Charlie, her husband called the ambulance. You gotta finish her off quick."

Charlie's hands began to stroke her hair.

"Did you hear that, Edna? Before I killed him your husband called the ambulance. He called it for your friend the doctor, whom I also killed."

"Charlie," from Doll. "I hear the siren. Do it quick and let's go." Charlie's hands moved to her face.

"Now tell me that you love me and that you love Doll," he whispered.

The siren got loud, and then stopped. She heard a banging of doors.

Doll had her head out the window.

"Charlie, they're coming in with a stretcher."

Charlie's hand came down hard on Lucy's mouth. He held her firmly with his big hand. Doll remained at the window.

"They're bringing the doc out, Charlie. They're loading him aboard the ambulance. Jack is helping."

Jack.

"I lied about the poison, Edna. Jack is still alive. I'm going to tell him you begged me for sex. Then I'll cut his throat." There was a slamming of doors. The siren sounded, diminished in volume, and faded out.

"They're gone, Charlie."

The hand came off the mouth and onto her body. His big lips moved close to her face.

"Charlie," said Doll. "The police are outside."

Charlie stood up.

"Don't say anything to embarrass me, Edna," he whispered.

She took a breath. She would tell them everything. She would not be afraid. Any moment now. She breathed out slowly and took another breath.

Heavy footsteps pounded up the staircase. Two policemen burst into the room—and Jack—Jack was with them.

But they were the same policemen who were at the bus stop.

"Is this the man?" the first policeman asked.

"Yes," Jack shouted. "Arrest him. Get him out of here."

They were the same policemen.

Charlie pulled out his red bandanna.

"Officers"—he smiled—"Jack here tried to rape Edna."

"Well, ain't he naughty," exclaimed the first policeman.

"Oh, bad Jackie," said the second.

"You may want to take him downstairs and hurt him," said Charlie.

Jack fought hard as they dragged him outside. He shouted and screamed all the way downstairs. She could still hear his voice dimly from a far part of the house. Then she couldn't hear it anymore.

"It's good to see old friends." Charlie winked at Lucy.

A shrill cry of pain momentarily welled up from the floor below.

Doll began to whistle.

Then the house grew silent again.

"I'm going to cut you now, Edna. You watching, Doll? Here follows dolorous pain, Edna, attended by a sordid and meaningless extinction—you'll like that, won't you? It is a digladiation that to oppugn were feckless, to resist were vain. First abrogation of conspectuity, next consopiation, followed by cessation of viability and adscititious conspurcation. Fetch me a large kitchen knife, Doll."

Doll stopped whistling. "You ain't going to pull out her intestines, or something like that, are you, Charlie?" She looked worried as she left the room.

Charlie sat down once more on the bed.

"There are two things you should know, Edna. One is that I met your husband at an entrepreneur's convention in Phoenix. I made friends with him, told him I would invest in his business. I followed him home, and I followed you." He smiled down at her.

Doll returned, handing a butcher knife to Charlie.

"Oh," he beamed, "this is the knife I've seen advertised; the blade is almost supernaturally sharp."

He licked his lips.

"The other thing you should know is that our two official friends downstairs are members of the coven."

"Maybe she don't know what that is, Charlie."

"I'll put it simply. Pain and fear. As much as possible." He smiled. "It's for Satan, Edna. It's all for Satan."

Charlie bound his red bandanna around Lucy's eyes.

"I might cut the eye or perforate the belly. Maybe right away, maybe not. That's the fun of it, Edna, not knowing where or when it's coming. Be alert now and see what happens."

She screamed, but the scream stayed inside her, echoing through all the dark passages of her body.

Her body lurched spasmodically.

"Wrong, Edna. That was only the tip of my ballpoint pen. Stimulating, huh? The next time it might be the knife."

She screamed silently till her consciousness became one torment of sound.

Again her body wrenched.

"Nope," said Charlie's voice. "Only the earpiece of my glasses. Gave you a turn, didn't it? Maybe it'll be the knife next time."

The screams stopped. She did not have even them anymore.

She had only Jack's face to think about. And Dr. Jim. No, they did something to him. She couldn't remember what. But he was gone. Jack, too.

"Blindfold off. What? Don't you like my handsome face? Look at me, Edna."

There was nothing left now.

"Look at my face, Edna."

Not even fear.

"She's gone, Charlie. Her mind's gone."

"Oh, bad Edna. No use then for the bad old knife." He laid it on her bosom.

No, there was something. On her chest.

Something screeched outside.

"Charlie, there's another squad car pulled up," Doll said at the window.

"Pain and fear." Charlie smiled.

"Charlie, I don't know these cops. Look, the doctor's with them."

"We had fun, didn't we, Edna?" Charlie said.

"Charlie, we got to get out."

Charlie shook his head. "Good-bye, Edna." She was left alone. Except for the knife on her chest. He would be back for that. He would miss his knife.

A lot of noise. Even now he was coming back for his knife. Someone bent over her.

"Lucy. Jack, up here! She's all right. They got them, Lucy. They got the bad cops. They got them all."

"Lucy?" another man burst into the room.

"All right," said Dr. Jim.

"Thank God." Jack hugged her. "Thank God, Lucy."

She blinked as the room filled with uniformed men.

"My name is Edna," she said.

THE APPRENTICESHIP OF
ALAN PATCH

I

It was cold inside. And dark. The boy shivered, but not because of the cold, damp stone surrounding him. There was a faint odor of ash and rancid fat.

"Mr. Corson," the boy pleaded.

No answer.

"Mr. Corson!"

The boy was alone. Mr. Corson had retired into the house, or hitched up the team and driven to town.

"It's cold in here." He giggled nervously. His palms groped along the cold stone, coated with frozen grease. "And it hadn't oughta be."

He bent to feel the perforations in the stone floor, beneath which ran the icy furnace pipes. The disturbed air wafted an acrid taste of ashes though no fires had burned for weeks.

"There's no way out," he whispered. "I have to wait for Mr.

Corson to unlock the door; maybe he won't come till morning.

"Mr. Corson," he screamed. "I'm so *afraid!*"

Silence.

"Please, please let me out. I won't run away anymore." He leaped to bang his fists against the iron door, then collapsed to the floor, huddling himself against the greasy wall.

It had all happened so suddenly. He never had time to consider it. Till now. Till on a bitterly chill November night he crouched, terrified and whimpering, locked inside the black vault of the crematorium.

• • •

"Alan, ya got ta do it."

"Please, Pa."

"The money's been paid."

"Pa, no. Let me be a farmer like you."

"They ain't much use fer farmers no more. Ya got ta think o' yer future."

"Then make me a blacksmith, Pa. I'll work hard, I promise."

"Ya ain't got the strength, son. Yer too little."

"Then anything, anything but *that*."

"Mr. Corson's a successful man—not like yer pa. 'Sides"— he scratched the stubble on his lean cheek—"he's taken on yer 'prenticeship fer next t' nothin'."

"Pa, I don't want to be an undertaker. I'm scared of dead folk."

"I paid the money, son." He stared at the boy. "Yer fourteen now. In seven years y'll be out o' yer indenture. Someday y'll have yer own business."

"Pa, don't send me to Mr. Corson."

The old farmer laid a skinny arm across the boy's shoulders. "It's only forty mile away, son. Maybe, now 'n' then, if Mr. Corson says it's all right, one of us c'n visit t'other."

"Sure, Pa." The boy wept. The lean farmer turned to repair a broken washtub. Tears rimmed his tired gray eyes.

• • •

It took two days to walk the forty miles to Mr. Corson's undertaking establishment. A mile past town it was, a freshly whitewashed pine house adjacent to the graveyard; behind it clustered half a dozen shacks. The stone one farthest away looked vaguely like a smokehouse. No neighboring houses stood nearby. Only this house, the outbuildings, and a nearly empty graveyard full of weeds. He arrived in late afternoon.

A shiny new sign hung over the door:

J. W. CORSON

UNDERTAKER

COFFINMAKER

A violent urge seized him to turn back. It was futile. He knocked on the door.

No answer.

He waited, then knocked again.

Nothing.

I can still go back, he told himself. But he knocked a third time, and it was too late. The door opened.

A burly, hearty-grinning man in rolled-up shirtsleeves opened the door. His brawny hands were wet, and he was rubbing them together to dry them.

"Mr. Corson, sir, I'm Alan Patch."

The undertaker continued to rub his hands. "Come in, boy," he boomed. "Let's have a clear look at you." He ushered the boy into a chintz-covered parlor.

"This here's the waitin' room"—he beamed proudly—"where the grief-stricken call on their dead. Sit down." Alan sat. The undertaker took both of Alan's small hands in his own powerful ones.

"You're a little thing, ain't you?" He laughed. "Oh well, it don't take much strength to pump chemicals into a corpse." He was thoughtful for a moment. "Of course, you'll be digging graves; that takes a heap of strength. You ever dig a grave, boy?"

"No, sir, but I've done lots of digging—helping Pa on the farm."

"I see. Good, good." His large, handsome face shone with pleasure.

"Say, you hungry?"

The undertaker took him to a kitchen and sat nodding and smiling as the boy bolted pork and beans.

"I live upstairs," Mr. Corson said. "You'll sleep in a little shed I've fixed up for you outside." He pulled out a massive pocket watch. "It's late now. I'll show you where your shed is." He smiled happily. "I'm goin' to town. Tomorrow I'll start schoolin' you in the business."

Alan nodded sleepily.

The shed was old and musty-timbered—and too near the graveyard. But the bed was soft. Before he knew it he slept.

The sunlight woke him.

"Morning," he mumbled. "Time to help Pa." Then he remembered. He washed up from the pitcher and tin basin on the table next his bed, then climbed into his pants. Leaving the shed, he timidly knocked on the back door of the pine house.

"You don't need to knock," said Mr. Corson, opening the door. "Just come in, make up the fire, and feed us our breakfast."

"Yes, sir."

Mr. Corson seemed pleased with himself.

"I just come back from town." He winked slyly. "I ain't been to bed yet." They ate in silence. Maybe things wouldn't be so bad, Alan thought. The bright sun glowed behind the chintz curtains. Mr. Corson sat and beamed as Alan finished the dishes.

"Come into the workroom," Mr. Corson said. "I want to show you something."

Alan followed him into a big, semidarkened room, shielded with thick linen curtains. Metal tables occupied the workspace, all empty except for the ones bearing objects draped in black blankets. Mr. Corson walked over to one of the laden tables.

"Come here, boy."

Alan hung back.

"Come here, I say. You paralyzed?"

Alan found himself standing next to the table.

"Now what do you suppose is under this blanket? A couple of suitcases? Maybe some cabbages. Or a lot of old meat!" He tore off the blanket.

The boy froze at the sight of the old lady. She was so white and wrinkled. She was so still.

"Used to be a woman, Alan, jus' like your ma—my ma; she was someone's ma—someone's grandma. Ain't much of her, is there? She's wrinkled all down to nothin'. Our job is to make her look pretty—where you goin'?"

"Her eyes are open. They're supposed to be closed."

"*We* close 'em; and we'll paint her, too. Come over here."

Alan backed away. Mr. Corson grabbed him.

Mr. Corson shoved Alan's face against the wrinkled dead one.

"That's a corpse, boy. You're going to live with them things." He released his hold. Alan retreated to the wall. "There ain't nothing to be a-scared of." He laughed. "Sometimes they're real funny. See that door? Open it. It's *only* a closet. Open the door. Nothin's goin' to rush out and grab you."

"Please, Mr. Corson, I've—I've seen enough for one day." The undertaker laughed loud and clapped him on the back.

"Boy, you can't be a mortician if you're scared o' cadavers. That's a joke. Come on, you got to get used to the carcasses. You'll be handlin' 'em every day. Open that closet door. No, here, I'll do it. See? There ain't nothin' inside but a big old iron coffin, and it's *sealed*."

Alan had closed his eyes with the opening of the closet door. Now he saw that what Mr. Corson said was true, only a big black iron coffin.

"Even I wouldn't want to open this one." The undertaker winked.

"Last spring we had an awful flood. Lots of folks was drowned. A couple of men discovered a horse and rig hard by a big pool of water; they didn't find the driver, so they brought the horse and rig back to town.

"It took weeks for that pool to drain back into the river. Some boys was playin' in a field one day, and they saw something left behind by the water. *Him*," he said, pointing to the iron coffin.

"The sheriff had a fella haul the remains over to me. I locked 'em in this thing. I'm keepin' it here in case any heirs show up." He contemplated the black iron.

"Wow! All that time in the water. Wonder what he looks like. Want to open it and see?"

Alan shook his head repeatedly.

"I was only teasin'. But, say, if you lean way over, you can get a whiff of him. Wowee! Ugh! What do you say?"

"No, sir, no. Please let me go outside for a while; I don't feel well."

"Sure, boy, sure. You run around for a while. But you got to get over bein' scared. I'm the one to help you do it."

• • •

He knew Mr. Corson would be displeased with him for staying out so long. But he didn't care—anything, if only temporarily, to leave the sick fear of that dreadful house. He roamed for hours, haunted by the white wrinkles on the dead lady's face, conjuring unspeakable sights to picture the remains inside that iron coffin. He came to the graveyard; a slight breeze stirred the dead weeds. *Even this place is better*, he thought; *here they're all underground, and I can't see 'em.*

Unlike the things beneath the blankets in Mr. Corson's workroom. Who knows what grisly plan the undertaker might adopt to rid him of his fears. Then he remembered Pa—skinny old farmer, all alone—scratching a living in the eroded, worthless soil. He wept.

• • •

"You been away the whole day."

"I'm sorry, Mr. Corson. I . . . I just have to get used to things, that's all."

"Of course"—the undertaker grinned—"that's all. Them dead—they just take gettin' used to. Now how's about makin' us some supper? I'm so hungry I could eat a corpse!" He seemed to find this a good joke and collapsed laughing while the boy carried a lamp into the darkened kitchen.

The dead woman stood by the fire.

Silence, a long silence. Then the boy screamed. When he came back to the sitting room, his face was white.

"I couldn't move," he gasped. "Mr. Corson, I was that scared I couldn't move. Why'd you do that, Mr. Corson? Why'd you dress her up in a hat and veil?"

"You got to get used to them, boy; you got to." He brought the corpse back to the sitting room. Alan shut his eyes.

"If you close your eyes, I swear I'll touch you with these here human remains." Alan opened his eyes. "I'm a patient man, son, but this foolery has got to end. If folks knew my 'prentice was a coward, I'd be the laugh of the whole town. Now I'm a-carryin' this back to the workroom, but you've got to do all like that from now on. What do you think I need a 'prentice *for*? Now go and make supper; no tricks this time, I promise you."

Alan was too ill to eat, but he made a pretense of doing so. After supper the two sat by the fireside in the parlor. Mr. Corson had a bottle of store-bought whiskey, from which he took occasional gulps.

He was talking. Alan hoped he'd continue—despite the subject matter. He did not relish going out into the dark night to his shack that lay too near the graveyard.

"That stone buildin' yonder is the crematorium. I built it myself—though most folks prefer buryin'. There's a little observation panel that lets you look inside. I tell you, sometimes them corpses is better than a circus. Once I had a deader whose whole body was frozen into a scream. I guess that's the last thing he did in life—tried to scream, only he never finished 'cause he died. Well, when I turn the furnace up and he gets good and hot, he sits up sudden-like, spreads his eyes, and lets go with a horrible shriek."

"Please, Mr. Corson, please don't tell me any more; I have to go outside and sleep in the shed."

"Boy, you gotta leave off bein' scared, don't you see? You gotta. Listen, here's one about a skeleton with hair——."

Somehow he made it to the shed. He flashed his lantern inside. Empty. But there was no bolt on the door. What if Mr. Corson came in the night, bearing something horrible? The words echoed in this mind: "You got to get over bein' scared, boy. I'm the one to help you do it." What if—but, no, he mustn't think of such things. Where was Pa? He wanted Pa. He cried himself to sleep.

He woke. Were those footsteps outside the shed? Was there labored breathing, as of someone bearing a heavy burden?

The door was opening.

"Is that you, Mr. Corson?"

The door closed. The footsteps retreated. He lay awake till morning.

• • •

"Sometimes you got to uncover the head," Mr. Corson was saying. It was morning again, and they labored in the work-room. A new one came in during the night, his forehead mashed by a lead pipe.

"It takes strength," the undertaker continued. "First you make the incision—so. You see?"

"Yes, Mr. Corson."

"Next you plant your foot firmly on his chest, and *pull!*" The scalp ripped away like torn canvas.

"There. Now you take a little plaster of Paris—not too wet—and rebuild the front part of the skull. When that's done, you merely paste the scalp back. Nothing easier."

The boy miserably looked on and nodded.

"Would you like me to sweep up outside, Mr. Corson? Maybe I could go into town for supplies?"

"We're just beginnin'. Heck, I just patched that skull to show you how it's done. We got to do that old lady now; her funeral's tomorrow. Fetch her, will you, while I wash this blood and plaster off my hands."

"You want me to . . . *pick her up?*"

"That's the gen'ral idea. Say, didn't you tell me you was losin' your childish fears?"

The boy nodded. He had lied to Mr. Corson. In order to escape the undertaker's grim fooleries, he pretended to be growing used to the dead. "Just give me a little more time, sir," he told Mr. Corson at breakfast. Mr. Corson was pleased.

Now his eyes were narrowing.

"Boy, I did a mean thing last night, puttin' that corpse in the kitchen. And I almost done a meaner one when I thought you's asleep. I drug the iron coffin to the shed.

"Now look y'here. If what you told me is true about your growin' used to the work, we ain't got no quarrel. But if you try to bamboozle me because of babyish fears, I'll tie you mouth to mouth to a corpse that's comin' apart. You want that? Now haul up that carcass!"

It was astonishingly light. He looked away from it as, with arms outstretched, he carried it to the worktable and set it down.

"You're actin' like a man now," said Mr. Corson. "Just take a wet sponge and wash her down." He sniffed closely. "Gee whillikers, we'd better hurry; she's beginnin' to smell."

He dipped the sponge. After all, she wasn't a monster or a Halloween skeleton. She looked more like that 'Gyptian mummy he saw at the circus. He began to wash the body. Maybe he had not lied; maybe he *was* getting used to the dead.

Somebody pulled the front doorbell.

"You go see who that is. I've got to put on my coat and tie. And mind you look solemn."

"Yes, sir."

Alan returned. "It's a Mr. Jones; says he's the foreman over at the mill. I showed him in."

"Good boy. Now you watch what I do." They stepped to the waiting room.

"Ah, Mr. Jones," said Mr. Corson dolefully. "And how may I be of assistance?" Mr. Jones—a short man with a close-cropped head of bristly red hair—was pale.

"It's one of the hands—got trapped in the big grinder. Just happened. Got him outside in a sack."

"Ah, I see." Mr. Corson put his hands together. "Does the . . . unfortunate have any survivin' kin?"

"I hear he's got a sister somewheres, but never you mind; I reckon the mill will pay for the buryin'."

Mr. Corson expanded. "Indeed, I'm sure you'll want the very best fixin's—him, no doubt, bein' a loyal employee. Alan, show the gentleman a casket, the deluxe mahogany and silver one."

"What'll I do with *him?*" The foreman pointed toward the wagon standing in front.

"Never mind about that, Mr. Jones. My assistant will see to it, won't you, Alan? Mr. Jones, how's about havin' a drink to the dear departed?"

• • •

99

"It's the best business in the world, m'lad," said Mr. Corson. "People got to die." They sat after dinner in the parlor. Mr. Corson took a generous drink. "Once I sold washtubs. I was good, too. But sometimes folks bought, and sometimes they didn't. Now this business—here—" He laughed. "It's like I said: People got to die."

• • •

Another day. Somehow he'd got through. He actually helped Mr. Corson prepare the old lady's body. Now they were at supper.

"You done good today. I'm real proud."

"Thank you, Mr. Corson."

"You're growin' up, ain't you?"

"Yes, sir."

Mr. Corson took a big bite of lamb and spoke while chewing.

"Why, that old lady—you rouged her up terrific. Say, you've got a real talent for them corpses.

"Hah! When I first started, I made some dumb mistakes— like the time I squirted too much embalmin' fluid into a gent." He gorged another mouthful.

"It didn't do no harm, not until the funeral. Ha, ha, ha. They was all there—the family, guests, and, of course, preacher. Well, suddenly—in the midst of things, like—that ol' corpse, he starts a-sittin' up, with a oozin', suckin' kind of squishy sound. He sits up and—whoosh! he vomits gobs of that black embalmin' fluid all over everything.

"Preacher—he was the first to light out. The rest? They was a-runnin' and a-screamin'. I lay low to watch the fun. They all run off, 'cept one small boy about your age.

"'Hey, you,' I says to him; 'why didn't you run off like the rest?' He looks at that corpse, and y'know what he says? Says he, 'I thought he was goin' to speak to me'—meanin' the corpse. 'I thought he was goin' to speak to me.' Ain't that funny?"

Mr. Corson helped himself to whiskey.

"Say, you put that sack in the closet, like I told you?" The boy nodded. "You look inside?"

"No."

Mr. Corson took another drink.

"You're my apprentice, right?"

"Yes, sir."

"Which means you got to do what I tell you, right?"

"Yes, sir."

"What if I was to ask you to get that sack and spread the remains all over the workroom table—you'd got to do it, wouldn't you, 'cause you're my apprentice."

"Please, Mr. Corson."

"You'd do it; you know you would. You'd got to." He drank more whiskey.

"Now I ain't sayin' I'm *goin'* to ask you to do that." He smiled slyly. "And then again, I ain't sayin' that I'm *not* goin' to, neither. (Here, pass me that whiskey, boy.) I'm sayin' that I *might* ask you to spread out those human parts just as a kinda test like—to see if you's all growed up."

The boy writhed in his chair. The man's eyes grew small and mean.

"Let's adjourn into the workroom."

Alan never entered that room at night. The oil-burning lamps cast weird shadows.

"Go and get the sack, boy. Let's see who's in it." Alan

brought it. "Now undo the string. Undo it! Why's your fingers shakin'? Here, I'll undo her.

"Now, as I was a-sayin', if I ask you to pull out these here pieces, you got to do it, right?"

"Mr. Corson, sir. Please."

"Right?"

"Yes."

"In fact, I might ask you to stick your head inside the bag, right? Boy, why don't you answer? Sure, you're some scared, just like I figured. Ha, ha. I was jokin' with you. You clean up them dishes and go to bed. I'll do a little work in here."

At least he was in the kitchen—no horrors there—no crushed workmen inside misshapen sacks. He washed, dried, and carefully placed each dish in its appointed cupboard. Then he went out into the night.

Compared to the terrors of the workroom, the shack seemed snug and secure. He searched it with his lantern. Nothing. Empty. He removed his shoes and trousers and tried to tuck himself under the covers.

My feet, he thought, *I can't get them all the way down.*

He pushed. Some obstruction prevented him from stretching out at full length. His bare feet touched it. It felt like burlap. He sprang off the cot. He wouldn't look. He wouldn't let himself look. Gingerly he peeled back the old quilt.

He screamed loud and long. From the house came Mr. Corson's raucous laughter. Laughter was the last sound he heard as he grabbed for his trousers and ran shrieking into the night.

He dressed quickly as he stumbled along. To run. Anywhere. To get away. His bare feet carried him over the dusty hills. In his panic he ran into the burial yard. Thoughts screamed in his head. *They're reaching for me through the soil. But the ground's too hard. They'll never break through in time.*

He was out of the graveyard. *Take a breath. Better. Where now? To town?* Mr. Corson might see him there and take him back.

"I'll never go back!" he raved. Where then? To Pa. Back to Pa.

• • •

Customarily the old farmer spent his mornings scratching in the fields. Alan could not find him.

"Pa?"

No answer.

Alan went into the house. "Pa? It's me."

"Alan?" from the bedroom.

His father lay in bed, his face yellow and drawn. "I'm sick, son," the old man said weakly. The boy hugged him.

His father smiled. "So Mr. Corson let you come home."

"No, Pa. Mr. Corson's a real mean man. I run off."

The old man raised up in bed, his face white with rage.

"Ya run off? Ya run off from Mr. Corson?" He struck the boy across the face. "Son, they ain't no name for the badness you done. I give that man all I had. Ya hear me?" He stared for some moments; then he softened. "You have t' go back, son."

"Pa, no!"

"Tell Mr. Corson yer sorry ya run off."

"Let me stay here and take care of you."

"I ain't goin' t' get no better knowin' a son of mine was low enough to run off from his indentures. You promise me, son. Promise y'll go back to Mr. Corson. Promise y'll become a undertaker."

"I promise, Pa."

• • •

Two nights later when Alan returned to the mortuary, Mr. Corson dragged him, shrieking, to the crematorium and locked him in and went away.

"Come back, Mr. Corson. Please come back."

But Mr. Corson went away.

"Mr. Corson."

Silence.

Except for the wind.

The eerie wind whistled through the ventilation holes. He was alone in this ash-smelling, dark furnace of human inciner-ation. The wind began to scream like the corpse who screamed at its own cremation—here in this very room, where fires burn the grinning dead to white ash. He could see their skin peel into flame, hear their white bones crack to talcum powder.

"Help me," Alan cried.

The shrill wind piped uncannily, like a demented organ at a lunatic's funeral.

He was locked in with the dead.

"Pa, save me. Get me out of this."

But there was no Pa, no Mr. Corson, no escape.

Only the dead.

"Let me *out!*" He pounded cold walls with his fists, his arms, his head.

The dead groped for him from unseen corners.

"No," he shrieked. "Oh, no-o-"

White-shrouded shapes crouched just out of sight.

"Someone help me."

They sprang with outstretched claws.

"Please."

Skeleton hands wrapped him in winding gauze. The ashy wind played organ music. Corpse lights burst in his head.

He began to laugh then. He rolled over the stone floor, laughing uncontrollably. He laughed himself to sleep. He laughed all through his dreams. He awoke laughing.

Iron grated. He stood up.

The door opened. Mr. Corson's burly figure stood in the doorway, etched by morning sunlight.

"Sleep well, boy?" He laughed.

"I guess I'll go make breakfast," Alan said.

"I didn't want to lock you in there. I had to." He looked at Alan. "It ain't right to run away."

The boy nodded. "I won't run away anymore."

II

"Now let's give him some eyes—real glass ones, boy—rejects from the veteran's hospital. We'll make some eyelids—out of his thigh there—to cover 'em up. That way there'll be little bulges under the eyelids instead of holes. I get more for real glass eyes."

He was sixteen now and mastering his trade. Nearly two years had passed since the night Mr. Corson locked him in the crematorium. In two years he had learned to embalm, to restore, to enliven the lifeless with plaster and paint.

"That's real good, Alan. I always knowed you was cut out to be a first-class mortician."

"I'd like to embalm the whole world," said Alan. Mr. Corson clapped him on the back.

Pa had provided the finishing touch. He came in one day just two weeks short of Alan's sixteenth birthday. "He's your pap, boy," said Mr. Corson, "and I guess you'd better do him." Poor skinny, overworked farmer. How frail he looked stretched out on the workroom table. His pale chest and legs contrasted harshly with his copper face and arms.

"I'll do you good, Pa," the boy whispered. He caressed the tired, worn face.

•   •   •

The next two years proved even busier for Alan. He studied the dead—their hard white bones, their network of sinew, the marvelous muscles which when properly tamed could frame a face into trancelike slumber, or contort it to a yawning horror. The dead became his teachers, his companions, his only friends. Once there was a timid boy named Alan Patch, but he was burned to ashes in the crematorium one windy November night.

Mr. Corson grew brasher, more dissipated, increased his paunch with fatty tissue. And how he made Alan work. There was more business as the town spread. Alan sweated over bodies far into the night, while, a diamond stickpin in his tie, Mr. Corson sampled the perfumed palaces in town.

On a grim December morning, back from his nightly debauch, Mr. Corson caught Alan striking a dead man and shrieking "Corson, Corson." He slapped Alan alongside the head, mouthed an obscene word, and drifted to his room upstairs. Alan ground his teeth and said nothing.

Two months after Alan's eighteenth birthday Mr. Corson suffered his stroke. Too much beef and red-faced whiskey drinking. Too much frenzied dissipation. It happened in town. One moment the undertaker bragged to the barkeep; the next, he collapsed, meaty paw to head, hollered, and went down.

Alan tended him for the six weeks he lay in bed. Alan fed him, bathed him, doctored him with medicine. When Mr. Corson left his bed, he left behind fifty pounds of flesh. Gone were the handsome face, the braggart laugh, the paunch of the successful. The stroke had broken Mr. Corson. He was thin now and prematurely old. And he was weak.

In town, Alan, a slim youth of eighteen sporting a neatly brushed suit, smiled at the apothecary.

"He'll be his old self in no time," said Alan. "You just wait and see."

"Thanks to you," said the apothecary. "Folks are sayin' Corson would be dead but for you."

"He has much to live for," Alan said, "much to experience before he dies."

"I guess so. I'm just sayin' what's common talk—that you couldn't do no more if Corson was your own father."

"He's like a father to me." Alan climbed into the rig and jog-trotted back to the undertaking establishment.

"Mr. Corson?"

"Hello, Alan. Been to town?"

"To the 'pothecary's. I brought you some more medicine."

"Ooh, thank you. I been sick all day." Mr. Corson limped along painfully. "I feel old, boy. Someday the business'll be all yours."

Alan beamed. "Mr. Corson, someday I'll embalm *you*."

"That ain't funny, Alan."

• • •

He spent his nights in the bowels of corpses—the knives, the scissors, the embalming fluid, the needles and thread, the paint and putty. Mr. Corson lost more weight but could move freely now, and could work after a fashion. But Alan handled most of the business, Mr. Corson weakly assisting when he was able. Now was Alan grown to a pale, thin, precocious youth. Responsibility—and something else—had matured him. Working silently in dark hours taught him style; reflecting on his employer gave him innovation.

•   •   •

"A new one for us," Alan said one morning. "A ten-year-old boy with a hole in his chest you could put your fist through. Gored by a bull." They stood in the workroom, Mr. Corson assisting as Alan cheerfully poured molten wax. Suddenly he stopped.

"Let's have a party," he said. Hastily he lifted four bodies from their respective tables and propped them against the wall.

"Here's Lantern Jaw and Quasimodo and Elephant Eye and Scary Tommy."

"Alan," said Mr. Corson angrily, "you stop that. I was glad years ago when you quit bein' a-scared of them things, but this sort of conduct just ain't right. It's . . . it's morbid." Alan whistled as he returned the bodies to their slabs.

•   •   •

"Happy twenty-first birthday to me!" Alan sang happily. He contemplated the sign.

CORSON AND PATCH
UNDERTAKERS
COFFINMAKERS

Then he strolled inside to join his senior partner in the workroom.

"I never did like doin' infants," said Mr. Corson. "Poor little mites." Alan snatched it from the table and dandled its tiny carcass on his lap.

"Alan!"

"Whoop! Jounce the baby on your knee," he chanted, bouncing it up and down; then he replaced it on the table.

"Mr. Corson, did you see the tall man we got this morning? Boy, do I have plans for him."

"You ain't goin' to do nothin' bad to him, are you—like you done with that fat woman—graftin' on them extra arms?"

"Wait and see." Alan smiled.

Later that night Alan entered Mr. Corson's bedroom.

"It's under your bed, Mr. Corson."

"Oh, Alan, Why? Is it to pay me back for all them pranks years ago? You know why I done that."

"You made me what I am," cooed Alan.

Mr. Corson bent his frail body down to peer beneath the bed.

"Gah! That's horrible; he looks like a devil."

"Good, Mr. Corson; that's exactly it."

"How'd you get them steer horns to stick onto his head?"

"Just bored little holes."

"What'll you do for the funeral?"

"Why, take the horns out and fill the holes with plaster, just like you taught me."

• • •

"Oh, Alan, leave me alone. I'm too sick for such pranks. Look at me, I'm a skeleton." Mr. Corson spent nearly all his time in bed now.

"Come on, open it. It's a present to you on my twenty-second birthday. Open the nice powder blue coffin. It's Parson's grandson," he whispered.

With tremulous hands Mr. Corson unclosed the lid.

"Alan, you've given him three eyes."

• • •

"I'm a better embalmer than you are, Mr. Corson."

"Alan, stop all that nonsense."

"No, sir. I'm an artist; compared to me you're an amateur. You embalmed Miz Willey seven years ago, and I embalmed George Bradley at the same time. Now I've dug them both up. Come see whose work held up better." He dragged the old man into the workroom.

"Miz Willey surely is no beauty, Mr. Corson. That face wasn't ash black when you embalmed it. Now look at it. Here's Mr. Bradley—just as handsome as a department-store dummy, isn't he? I did that, Mr. Bradley," he said to the corpse.

"Alan, put 'em back in the graveyard."

"No, sir, not yet. Let's give them a bed for the night—your bed, Mr. Corson—with you in the middle to keep 'em virtuous."

"Alan, you're crazy. No!"

"I'm afraid we must."

• • •

Completely bedridden now, Mr. Corson saw Alan only when the younger man brought his meals. Sometimes he wondered at the contents of those meals.

"Mr. Coor-son!"

"Eh? Oh, Alan. I been sleepin'."

"I've good news, Mr. Corson. I'm moving you down to the

shed where I used to sleep, remember? Remember when you shoved that sack of remains underneath my covers?"

"Alan, please. I can't sleep in that shed. It's too cold and drafty."

"But, Mr. Corson, it's near the graveyard, where you'll soon be going. I'm going to embalm and bury you, Mr. Corson."

Alan carried the senior undertaker to the shed and laid him on the long-disused cot.

"Pleasant dreams, Mr. Corson. I may come to lock you in the crematory later on tonight."

"Oh, Alan—"

"Ta-ta!"

• • •

"Good morning, Mr. Corson. Look what I've baked you."

"Alan?"

"We had a fine cremation last night; too bad you missed it. I saved you some leftovers. Look."

"Alan," the old man gasped weakly, "you put that stuff away. It goes in an urn."

"Later perhaps. Mr. Corson, this is Mr. Conroy, the freethinker. I thought you might like to kiss his ashes. Come, Mr. Corson, kiss his ashes. You hear me, boy? Kiss the pretty ashes, or I'll lock you in the crem-a-tor-i-um," he sang. Mr. Corson kissed the ashes.

• • •

Another day.

"Where are you carryin' me, Alan?"

"To the graveyard. I'm going to bury you today."

"What?"

"You're weak and sick, but you might live on for years. Nope. Got to bury you, Mr. Corson. I'll dig you up in a few days and give you a proper embalming."

"Alan, please! Please, Alan!"

"I'm going to bury you alive, Mr. Corson," Alan sang happily.

•   •   •

"Can you hear me down there?"

"Alan," said the faint voice. "I can't breathe in this here coffin. Please, oh, please let me out!"

"Here comes the earth, Mr. Corson. Splat!" He sent a shovelful down into the grave. "And another. And one more. Now I'll cover up all of you." He whistled as he filled the grave.

•   •   •

"Happy birthday, thirty-five!" screamed Alan. "Mr. Corson, I'm thirty-five, Mr. Corson."

Mr. Corson sat still in a chair and said nothing.

"I'm thirty-five, and I'm the senior partner." A happy thought took him. "Mr. Corson, you're the *silent* partner." The embalmed waxwork said nothing.

How happy he was. The town had grown considerably in the last years. "Pa was right," Alan mused. "I'm a successful man."

Periodically he exhumed Mr. Corson's perfectly embalmed body, just to see how he was getting on. It was good to see old Corson again. Sometimes, in a fit of pique, Alan locked the silent figure in the crematorium for the night, only later to explain apologetically why he had to do it.

It was on a late September afternoon, as he was spooning soft cheese into Mr. Corson's propped, gaping mouth, that he heard a timid knock on the door. Opening it, he was surprised to see a helpless-looking, frightened child.

"Mr. Patch, sir," the child whispered, "I'm your new 'prentice."

"Come in, boy," said Alan heartily. "Mr. Corson and I were just having dinner. Won't you join us?"

HARLA

I never thought it wrong to murder—bad people, I mean. Killing good people is imprudent and wasteful; goodness knows there are few enough good people. Bad people one can pluck like leaves from an artichoke and never get to the heart. Take my boss, for example, Leonard Rose. He was rude, brash, boorish, foul-mouthed, and insolent. He is the first of the bad people I killed. It happened this way.

I stuffed a sea urchin down his throat.

Oh, it was a crowded Chinese restaurant. I had brought the sea urchin in a minithermos strapped inside my coat. As we sat drinking in a private booth curtained off from the rest of the eaters, I roused Leonard with tall tales about one of the waitresses till his evil face shone red and perspiring.

"She will kiss," I cautioned, "but only anonymously. Now close your eyes, Boss. Loosen your jaw; any moment her winsome face will part the curtains with kisses unimaginable."

The second he complied I extracted the sea urchin and ram-rodded it down his throat with the tongs.

The next person I killed was Marian, the evil old lady next door. You will enjoy this. We had a community apiary in our apartment complex. One day I got my gloves on and filled a paper bag full of bees, then thrust the whole thing over Marian's face while the bees stung every bit of face they could. To top the comedy off, I made her swallow battery acid till everything smoked inside her.

Then there was Steve. There was nothing particularly wrong with Steve except that he invariably sat in front of me each week at church. And Steve was tall.

I did not kill Steve; at least I did not kill him all the way. After all, he was a nice enough fellow; his only crime was blocking my view of Parson. I only partially killed Steve.

I tripped him one night as he was jogging home and dragged him into his own garage. There I cut his legs off with a chain saw.

You might think by all this that I am some sort of demented maniac; if so, you have misread me. I have never, knowingly, harmed anybody who did not irritate me in some way.

Except for Joe Saunders, the newsboy—but that was merely an experiment to test the toxic quality of fly spray. Anyhow, all the stuff did was make him blind. The good side is that from then on the flies left him alone.

But all this is background, so you will empathize with me in the light of what is to follow.

I was lonely. I had few friends, and even these seemed not to like me.

I wanted a wife.

The least of men is a paragon if he has a woman to believe

in him. The most repulsive offal—a human running sore—is made glorious by a good woman's love. And I was none of these. I am, in all candor—rather kingly. But still I lacked a woman's heart. (I didn't say—but I once had a woman's heart, a bad woman's. I buried it in the sandbox of the school yard. Some other incidentals I tucked into the Goodwill bin.)

The woman I hoped for finally came into my life.

And her veins ran sweet with plasma. Every tissue had a smile in it, every organ a grin.

She was younger than I, about thirty-five. And she was tall and big, with green eyes and hair the color of marmalade. She wore a short green dress and cowgirl boots the night I met her at the bowling alley.

"You bowl good," I said, adapting my grammar to the surroundings.

Her green eyes took me in. Then she smiled.

"You was watchin' close. It made me bowl extra."

I felt the love mechanism tightening. I could have proposed to her then, before I even knew her name.

It was Harla.

"Call me Mr. Tim," I said. "Let us bowl together."

We did. She let me win. I am sure of it. That is the sort of person she is. We bowled and ate tongue sandwiches, and I was a ball of love and thought only of her, Harla.

Now Harla lived in a little apartment on top of a garage. We spent our evenings cuddling there while we listened to her Leonard Spevack records.

It was summertime, two weeks after we met. Through the screen door tiptoed all the summer smells of night-howling plants. Harla wore her shorts, I my swim trunks. Outside, the plants butted heads, the he-plants courting the she-plants.

The landlord stepped up then, a brash man, mostly bald head and belly. He climbed the stairs, thrust his head against the screen door, and peered in at us.

"That's too loud. Turn that imbecile stuff off, now!"

I knew he had to die, and at once, but I did not know how my darling might react. It might mean losing her. Even murder was scarcely worth that. I tried to choke it off, to focus on the beautiful music of Leonard Spevack.

"Turn off that hog vomit!"

I decided to hazard all.

"Uh, Landlord," I said. "Bide. Harla, darling—Landlord, I say, remain on the stairs. Harla, dearest, kindly hand me a weapon of some sort."

Reaching into a kitchen drawer, she handed me a barbecue skewer.

"Here," she winked. "Stick him good."

I paused to kiss her. Next I twirled my wrist and shot the skewer right through the screen door and into Mr. Landlord.

"How loud is that music?" I asked impishly. Harla laughed. The landlord gurgled as he thumped his way down the stairs.

"Come again for another song," Harla called after him.

Landlord staggered into his own kitchen and died by the sink.

But I had no thoughts for Landlord, only for Harla, for she had done more than participate in the murder.

She reveled in it.

Do you know that rapport when people pelt each other with revelations? This was the euphoria Harla and I swam in. It must have been hours we sat smelling the plants while we exchanged tenderness to the music of Leonard Spevack. Abruptly Harla sat up.

"Mr. Tim, all my life I put up with sass and meanness. But

you have shown me a better way. Now you start kissin' on me while I think back on all the enemies I ever had."

There must have been many; I could tell by the kisses. Mostly I just kissed and let her think.

We began in earnest the next day with a chronological list, beginning with those who wronged her in childhood—three or four names—and continuing with the abusers of her teens—say, seven or eight. The last part cataloged the predators of her adult years—perhaps two dozen. By an amazing coincidence one such name was that of my old boss, Leonard Rose. (See *supra*, pages 115–16.); we laughed uproariously over this, as we looked up names and addresses.

• • •

We married two days later, honeymooning in pursuit of her enemies. Some we could not find at all, so we pretended they had met gruesome deaths by spontaneous combustion. Others had already died; we dumped garbage on their graves. But close to a dozen remained alive and reachable, although many affected not to remember her. We spent two agreeable months in this fashion. When the last of them had perished from unremitting pain, she came to me with a coy little smile.

"Mr. Tim, darlin', you cleaned my life good. Now it's time you make your list and watch me clean yours."

Her eyes filled when I told her I had done so myself shortly before we met.

"Well, darlin', you'll think I don't love ya if I don't kill some o' your enemies. Can't you make new ones?" Her eyes radiated hope.

I put my arms around her.

"They will come," I said. "They always do. We will not force it."

"Well, couldn't we kill some o' your friends?"

But I had none to spare.

"I surely would like to murder all kinds o' your enemies," she sobbed.

So for love of Harla, I set out to make an enemy.

First I insulted the druggist, but he was a forgiving soul and apologized to me. Next I made derisive gestures at a traffic cop; he laughed uproariously and told me to go along. Finally, I threw a pail of cold water on the postman. He remarked that the weather was warm and thanked me for the refreshing bath.

I sought consolation in Harla's arms after each successive failure. She was, of course, supportive though her eyes betrayed a sense of secret injury. I tried twice more to make an enemy, both attempts ineffectual. Still, Harla's arms remained soft, her manner gracious and forgiving. Yet the unspoken reproach persisted to torment, until, in desperation, I closeted myself one entire evening to ponder the problem. Resolutely did I pace the room, conjuring all the successful enmities of my career, only to contrast them with my current social bankruptcy. Why, I asked over and over—how was then different from today? Is it Harla? Surely, it could not be Harla. Twice I nearly gave over to despair. Then, shatteringly, after steadily resisting through hours of vain cerebration, the solution suddenly exploded all over the room.

"I have figured it out," I said, dashing into the parlor, where Harla sat at her needlework. "I know why I am such a washout at making enemies."

"Yes?"

"Do you know that all my life I have gathered enemies like burrs on a woolen stocking?"

"I do."

"And that I am no longer able to do so?"

"So you tell me, darlin'."

"Why, it was killing all your enemies on top of my own that did the trick."

"I don't understand."

"Don't you see? Killing sweetens one's temper. You know I am right if you will think about it. Are we not much kinder, more tolerant of others after each homicide? Well, I have been killing for years. It did not occur to me before, but subtly, imperceptibly, I must have been sweetening with each murder. Then, in the last few months you and I enjoyed such a banquet of murders as to produce in me an overdose of sweetness from which I may never recover. The inevitable result is that I am too sweet-tempered to make enemies."

"Oh, darlin'"—she sobbed convulsively—"is it bad as all that?"

"Tell you what," I said, kissing her, "why don't we search out some nice young fellow, find out who his enemies are, and kill them for him?"

She brightened at this.

"Well, sweetheart," she said, "it's not the same, but we can try it."

We went out every day during the next two weeks, seeking an agreeable person with a superfluity of enemies. We met many potentials, some of whom we seriously considered during our discussion each evening after dinner. But for one reason or another, none was satisfactory.

Then one day we stopped to buy a pipe wrench.

His name was Rick Puter, and he was short and skinny and sold aluminum siding at a third-rate hardware store. Right away we knew he was our man when a customer tried to get him to lower a price.

"Ehhh . . ." he said timidly, "I can't do that, sir."

"Then damn you," the customer retorted. "Damn you to hell!" and walked out. Harla nodded at me and followed, while I engaged the young man in conversation. In about thirty seconds a piercing little scream arose from the parking lot. Then another. Then another. Harla returned with the pipe wrench.

In the next week Harla and I extinguished two more of Rick's customers. One by glass splinters, the other by forcible ingestion of a liquid intended for other purposes. Rick's immediate boss had an unfortunate experience with some rats.

We became friends, the three of us. We had Rick over to dinner a few times, while sometimes he invited us out to a barbecue place.

"Ehhh . . ." he would say. "Mr. Tim and Harla . . . ehhh? I surely wish I could invite you folks over to where I live, but Mother don't like me to have friends. She don't even like me coming over here. In fact, she don't like me to do much at all."

Not too long after, Harla paid a visit to Mother.

"You shoulda seen her, darlin'," she whispered as we cuddled for the night. "She was all over fat and—well, I ain't never seen a bald woman before. She didn't talk about nothin' but her problems. I give her a rubdown with that electric cattleprod you wired up for me. She don't have no problems now 'cause she's a ash."

Rick languished a couple of days, after which he seemed relaxed and confident. He even stopped saying "ehhh."

Harla and I rubbed each other's ribs in mutual congratulation.

The next day Rick made his play for Harla.

Of all places, it was at our house. I had gone downtown to sell some securities, while Harla remained behind to work in her garden. As it was warm, she wore her shorts. Rick appeared suddenly, threw his arms around her, and suggested she leave me.

Harla was crying when I returned. Out of memory for his former friendship she had retained his breastbone and one of his knees.

"If only we coulda made you some enemies," she sobbed. "None o' this woulda happened."

"He wasn't worthy, sweetheart." Thus I mollified her. "We shall choose another, a girl this time."

Not long after we found Emma.

Emma was fifteen years old and beautiful beyond description.

Harla happened to be passing by the high school one day in time to witness an altercation. Some female classmates had Emma's face compressed against the chain-link fence, while several older ladies, obviously faculty, looked on with obvious approbation.

"What's your name, honey?" Harla called through the fence.

"Emma," came the strained reply.

"They hurtin' you bad?"

"Real bad."

Harla climbed the fence. Swinging her electric cattle prod, she hurled herself on Emma's attackers, sizzling the skin right off their bones, laughing as she charred the faculty bystanders who rashly rushed in to interfere.

Harla brought Emma home after school.

"Mr. Tim, this here's Emma; she's a orphan with lots o' enemies."

"She singed a bunch of them," chirped the grateful little girl, and began to giggle.

It turned out that Emma was a half orphan who lived with a mother who was ugly and beat her a lot. Also, unlike sweet-tongued Emma, Emma's mother was a garbage mouth.

I flat out asked Emma one day if she wouldn't feel happier if her mother died screaming with pain.

She said she would think on it. The very same evening she informed Harla and me that she had done the job herself, using, of all things, her Girl Scout knife!

Of course Harla and I adopted Emma, relinquishing all other pursuits to concentrate on Emma's education.

Emma progressed rapidly. She quickly massacred her enemies, then started killing sweet people, because, she said, they are nicer to deal with.

Still, Harla seems dissatisfied. I can sense a gathering uneasiness each time Emma comes home to prattle of her little vengeances and murders.

Last night I awoke to find Harla weeping.

"Mr. Tim," she said, "I just got to kill you a enemy. I can't sleep no more otherwise."

I stroked her hair.

"I'm lovable," I reminded her. "I can't make enemies."

"Why, sometimes I think you're your own worst enemy—" She shuddered as she said it. A strange light lit her beautiful green eyes.

"Your own worst enemy," she repeated.

After breakfast this morning Emma killed the postman, whom she loved. "I just like killing nice people," she giggled apologetically. She put her arms around Harla and me. "You two are the nicest people I have ever known." Her eyes took on the same strange light Harla's had. I was too choked up to speak. Harla only looked at me, and said, "Your own worst enemy."

HARLA

I have to stop writing now. Harla wants me to crawl under the house to investigate a crevice which she says has opened there. I'll do it quickly so I won't be late and disappoint Emma, who has been hard at work preparing a wonderful dinner which she says Harla and I will never forget.

COWPANTS

As kids, we played Bashball and Dogdance, Vaudrigo and King-Happy, Pontoon Bridge and Cowpants. These were indoor sports, performed in isolated groups, usually one girl pitted against one of us boys, though I have heard of two or more girls "ganging up" on one boy.

The girls I knew were creative and uninhibited, especially Nancy Yellen, who initiated the games one day after an experience with a baby-sitter named Estrelita. Older than the rest of us—say twelve or thirteen—Nancy introduced us smaller boys to the perilous pleasures of Lick-thigh; it was what she wore, though, as well as what she wielded, that provided the excitement of the thing. I've never forgotten Nancy.

Similarly, Brenda Epcott reigned the specialist in Over-the-Bathtub—but these were rudimentary; it was the other games that developed in time—Bashball, Dogdance, Vaudrigo, King-Happy, Pontoon Bridge, and, eventually Cowpants—that give my life its coloring, so to speak.

The games went on long after Nancy's baby-sitter left town following an animated lesson in Under-My-Bedsheet. In time, the other boys dropped out to take up football, and I had the girls all to myself. Life was wonderful for me—Herbie. I had math at school, good programs over the radio, the matinee on Saturday. But the games were what I lived for.

The games ended in our adolescent years. The girls who titillated my childhood either moved away or affected to outgrow the old games, dismissing them as "juvenile." Life dwindled to dullness. These were the days of corsages and ponytails and sock hops. (I went to one sock hop because of the name; I thought it would be, well, like Dogdance. I never went to another.) I supposed there would never be another girl who relished the good old games.

I was nineteen when I met Roseanne. It was at the library, of all places. I was amusing myself one afternoon by looking into Krafft-Ebing. Roseanne sat in the same section, copying passages from Sacher-Masoch. She was a large creature, with ample everything. I could tell she meant no good by the tight, short dress she wore, and by the defiant way she peered at me, her eyes predatory with mascara. She spoke as if from some forbidden part of her body.

"Hold my books," she ordered. From the way she said it one could have substituted any number of interesting alternative nouns.

Of course she had to be obeyed; that was the way of the old games, especially Vaudrigo. To refuse was to graduate to the more challenging complexities of King-Happy and, eventually, if the inspiration proved constant, to soar to the raptures of Pontoon Bridge. But we were in the library.

I sank my teeth into the cover of her book. My heart raced. Could she know the games, her a stranger who had not grown up in our close and clannish neighborhood? Eagerly, I put my lips to her ear, licked the lobe briefly, and whispered, "Cowpants?"

Her reply was more succinct than the words I use to convey it. Basically, she said it was forbidden to name such secrets aloud, and that she was very angry and intended to give me something that would indelibly impress upon me the necessary amount of smarting consequent to such precipitant speech. We walked over to her house and played Cowpants till my trousers barely fit over the swelling. It was wonderful.

I saw Roseanne a lot after that; each time the welts began to heal, the vision of her standing erect with arched brow and amused smile haunted me unmercifully, till I crept around once more to lick her doorknob, impatient for those wonderful games. She never would tell me where she learned them. I wondered if she, too, along with Nancy Yellen, had been baby-sat by Estrelita. Roseanne. I would still be with her, perhaps even have married her, had she not died.

It happened this way.

As a birthday present I gave her a volume of Tolstoi, at that time my favorite author. At first she demurred over the main story, "The Death of Ivan Ilych," saying she probably wouldn't read it. The next time I saw her, she talked of little else, saying she was on her second reading and contemplating a third. "It suggests dark and dreamy possibilities," she whispered.

A few days later, on a rainy afternoon, I found her in bed with a volume of Keats. She barely gave me a frown, even after

I polished her high-heeled boots. She just lay there reading over and over a line from the "Ode to a Nightingale," not the good part about the "magic casements," but that eerie stuff about being "half in love with easeful death." She made me recite it unremittingly. I derived little satisfaction from the experience, even though she had me bending over a chair at the time.

"Care for a hand of Dogdance?" I asked innocently.

"I crave a more stimulating diversion," she mused, "darker and sweeter." She paused to inspect her net stockings. "Emily Dickinson," she suddenly commanded. "There, on the shelf; bring it to me. Poem number two-eighty." It was the one beginning, "I felt a funeral in my brain." From this we passed to "I heard a fly buzz when I died." After this came Gray's "Elegy."

"Mistress," I cried, "would you not prefer a love story, or perhaps a song of mirth?" She flicked me with the business end of what she was playing with in her hands.

"'Thanatopsis,'" she rapped. "Hurry."

Weeks passed. The games forgotten, I crouched beside her for many a session, reading her favorite death poems while she moaned joyfully about "ecstasies of intolerable pain." Forgotten were the flail, the towel, the shovel, while the crowbar slowly rusted by the bathroom sink. I wasn't present when she took the poison. The newspapers called her the happiest-looking corpse on record. She was happy, all right, but I had no one to play with.

Life dragged wearily by. I got a job stuffing newspapers for the local *Times* dealer, uninteresting work that paid little. Television had come in now, radio demoted to a purveyor of dance music. The movies, too, declined. I took up chess.

It was on the beach, by one of those warped wooden tables with permanently mounted chessboards, that I first saw

Gabrielle. All I saw at first was a thighful of bulging white flesh escaping from a metallic blue swimsuit. I glanced up from my Ruy Lopez opening to behold a broad bland face framed in long frizzy blond hair. Gabrielle was one of those German *Bierfrau* types fresh from the farmlands. Her amused, aloof expression left no doubt that she preferred other matters to chess.

I outraged my opponent by immediately conceding the game in order to pursue her. She turned her back on me and swaggered toward the ocean. I followed close behind. When she was mere yards from the wet sand she turned suddenly.

"I spread this big towel on the ground," she said—her accent smacking of the Wehrmacht—"and will lie on my stomach. You will take this plastic bottle of tanning cream and spread the soft cream on my legs."

Few beginnings were so promising. I found much surface over which to apply the cream and made a thorough and good job of it. When I had finished she readjusted her position, so that she now reclined upon her back.

"It is well for you that you spread the lotion evenly on the backs of my bare thighs; otherwise, I would have been angry. Now, if you are sufficiently humble, you may apply more lotion to the front of my shapely thighs."

It was almost more than my excited juices could bear—after all, we were on a public beach. But I did it, more efficiently, I think, than I had done the other side. By now my fluids had assumed the state that in heating water is known as "crabfroth," e.g., the point just before the boil, when the water begins to resemble a miniature maelstrom. I could stand it no longer. Bending my lips very close to her ear, I whispered the word:

"Cowpants?"

Her brow wrinkled with contempt; then it relaxed. She seemed for a moment to chew the word, gurgitating it, bringing it up. Her brow began to work again, her cold blue eyes to narrow. Then, in a moment, her manner changed; a slow, cold smile animated her lips.

"Ah," she said. "*Die Ku-u-u-h-hose.*" I began to wonder then if Estrelita had invented the games after all. Well, they were all there—*der Hundetanz, der Knallball, die Königsfröhlichkeit, Vaudrigo* (untranslatable into any language), and *die Pontonbrücke.* Oh, times were merry in Gabrielle's parlor. We had the music of Kurt Weil, the sketches of George Grosz, and, best of all, those wonderful games. Gabrielle asked me once how I discovered them, and I told her from Nancy's baby-sitter Estrelita. She laughed and said she had met Estrelita in Germany, and learned from her also. I told Gabrielle not to tease.

This idyll persisted for most of a year, until Gabrielle began to introduce new games. Some were odd. There was, for example, Apehead and the Ballerina, a curious amusement. Sometimes I got to play Apehead. After a while she took to substituting her experimental innovations for the games I loved. Eventually she abandoned the old games altogether, protesting they were "insufficient," and sought out more demanding diversions.

I made halfhearted attempts at first because I loved her—getting through Knee-Kick and Rugburn without much physical damage—but when it came to Branding Iron my refusal was complete.

"Then Skinsplit," she argued; "we play Skinsplit instead." So strongly burned my love for her that I lost two days of work. The very day after my recovery she had me over her dining-room table in a roaring match of Slip-My-Disc. I missed three more days of work.

The progression continued unabated, each successive game improving in mayhem. Still, she would smack her lips after each bout, contract her brow and ingest, chew and then regurgitate what had become her favorite word. "Insufficient!"

The last night I saw her, Gabrielle wore the same outfit I first saw her in at the beach: a banquet of flesh emerging from a metallic blue swimsuit. Both of us stood in her bathtub. Her big blond face blushed beams and smiles as she separated me from the tweed suit I had on.

"Herbie, *kleines Bubchen*," she purred. "I know at last what is . . . sufficient." She left momentarily for the bedroom in order to hang my garments on the coat hanger we formerly used for more romantic purposes. Familiar with her inventions, I did not think it strange when she reappeared a few minutes later wearing a fireman's suit and one of those opera helmets with horns stuck on either side. She concealed something behind her back.

"Happy surprise." She laughed. "See!" and brought forth a gasoline can. "Is sufficient!"

I did not wait for her to light the match, and barely caught her anguished cry as I raced for the bedroom, grabbed for my clothes, and went sailing into the street.

"It was good enough for Wotan!" she wailed petulantly.

So Gabrielle was gone along with her so-called games. She never played the real ones, anyway, except at first—I mean the ones I doted on. Too bad. I think she loved me a lot.

There I was, without a game, without a girl. The nineteen sixties had come upon us; if the girls had improved with their miniskirts, they had retrogressed in their stockings, for they didn't wear any but disfigured their once grand gams with panty hose.

I worked now in the shipping and receiving department of an electrical parts supply house. I was in my late twenties and found feminine consolation only in the garment sections of the mail-order catalogs. There had been one or two attempts at establishing associations with pretty girls, but whenever I broached the subject of the delectable games, the girls proclaimed outrage and disgust, particularly on the first date.

Then, for the first time, I fell totally in love without a thought of garter or lash.

Her name was Angelica, and she was slim and blond and willowy and wore white that first night I saw her in the park. It was during a band concert, and the moon's white rays lit her delicately like a muted spotlight as she sat in her folding chair, listening to Verdi. By good fortune the chair next to her was vacant, and it was only a matter of moments before I engaged her in playful badinage.

Oh, she was wide-eyed and moon-sweet as, in my nervousness, I very nearly spoiled things by asking if she were dominant or submissive. She giggled uncontrollably when, apropos of nothing, I dilated on the virtues of a hard leather strap; then I took hold of myself, and it was all innocent and playful as we chatted and giggled and rustled our programs there in the moonlight, while the band played soft strains from *Traviata*. We stopped for ice cream after the concert, and I walked her home—though we were too shy to kiss good night.

The next few nights with Angelica, an invitation for Pontoon Bridge from the Women's Army Corps could not have deflected me from my seraphic thoughts. I would not have traded them a moment, not even for a champagne enema.

Angelica was the first girl ever to call me by my real name.

"Herbert," she would say, "come sit by me and whisper the secret stirrings of your heart." And we would coo together through perfumed nights as the stars sang overhead.

It was likewise Angelica who expressed dissatisfaction with my career in shipping and receiving and suggested I go to college to study statistical analysis. Thus fate does shape our fortunes. Sometimes I indulged in the feverish speculation that Angelica could be apprised of the games and in time could take an interest in them. If only I could have both Angelica and the games. But I could picture her childlike brow wrinkle as she sought to understand, then the doelike eyes opened wide in horrified disbelief, finally the curled lip of contempt. No, it was Angelica or the rapturous games. I chose Angelica.

It was during an early-afternoon visit to the community playground, as we watched the children playing soccer, that Angelica delicately proposed that we take up sports.

I suggested croquet. Well, we played a few rounds of that, but far from expressing pleasure she only shook her head and smiled sweetly and requested something more challenging. We tried badminton a few days later, and then tennis and finally basketball. But after each session she would only smile sweetly and shake her head and propose still more rigorous sports. In the weeks that followed, in Browning's words, "all smiles stopped together." In desperation I turned to tackle football: she was cold; to kick boxing: she was contemptuous.

The one innocent romance of my life, I told my sympathetic pillow, as I wept alone through arid nights, is a girl to whom the world is a decathlon.

Well, Angelica left me; that was all. She had somehow learned of my lifelong infatuation, I told myself, and tried to wean me from it with wholesome sports. And I had let her down. I turned more determinedly to my studies of statistical analysis and wept for the innocence that was nearly mine.

I took my degree the day before the letter came.

> Herbert,
>
> I am marrying one who can gratify the delicious imperative that has obsessed my life. From your remarks at our first meeting I throbbed with the expectation that it consumed you, too. I was misinformed. When I proposed we take up sports, you spitefully and contemptuously suggested croquet!
>
> Herbert, you knew all the time what I wanted. Oh, if you had condescended to play Cowpants only once a week, I would have been yours forever!
>
> She who was yours, but is now another's,
>
> Angelica

The next years I spent between the leaves of scholarly books or in compiling lecture notes. I was a professor now of statistical analysis, and published articles in learned journals, with now and then a textbook that few cared to read. Oh, the girls still ran in my thoughts, the girls and the games. The likeliest partners were my students, but I learned a lesson early on. Girls involved in statistical analysis seldom take an interest in Dogdance.

I am well into middle age; the once fertile scalp that sometime sprouted bumper crops is shiny now and fallow. My eyebrows are become a profusion of grotesque wires. My stomach bulges convex. I am lost without my reading glasses. Yet I am happy without let or measure, for I at last have found her.

COWPANTS

It happened six years ago on campus. The students had got up some sort of festival in honor of *Cinco de Mayo*. To avoid the off-key trumpets and crack of castanets, I found myself dodging among some seldom-used maintenance buildings, trying to hold on to my cap and gown while I sought escape from what I considered an intrusion on academic hospitality.

I came upon her suddenly, provocatively poised by the drinking fountain, proud as a conquistador, a beauty by any standards. She had her dress pulled high to adjust her stocking. And as I nearly swooned at the wonder of it, our eyes took hold, and her dress remained high. Of course, with no one else about, I was instantly on my knees, chewing at her garter strap. After a lifelong search, this is how I met my wife, my bondage of bliss and unalloyed rapture.

And she, what was it she said on that brightest of May mornings so long ago? Merely this:

"I am Estrelita—want to play Cowpants?"

THE FISH IN SALMON LAKE

Harold Bahr, the great, great detective, have many exciting cases—like time he prove killer dress up like octopus. But everybody know that one. I tell you now of different crime, that happen few years ago when I and Harold rooming together in small flat in city. I working then in fish cannery to pay for rent and food. Harold Bahr go out every day to look for cases. He not known then.

One night after dinner Harold Bahr and Punky Kim—very handsome Korean man who is telling story—talk together in sitting room. Harold Bahr wearing orange bathrobe and sitting in morris chair, white skinny legs propped up on stool. Floor lamp shining off bald bullet head. I seated on sofa facing him.

"Punky," Harold Bahr say in high, rusty voice, "days have burst like clay pots since I last found a crime to solve."

"You silly man," I tell him. "Crimes happen every day. You look in paper."

"Yes, Punky," he say sadly. "But they aren't *my* crimes; they are the paper's crimes, contaminated by police and publicity. No, I want my own crimes—to share with nobody!" Here he clash fist into open palm.

"Not get excited," I tell him. "You get excited you do crazy things. Here, I take up magazine and read soothingly to you." I pick up periodical I buy few hours before, called *Magazine of New Poetry*.

"The problem is," he continue, "just what constitutes a crime? Why, one may be happening right now in this room, a crime of which I am unaware!" He look wildly at furniture and ceiling, so to cool his brain I open magazine and read poem to him.

> "Dead anchor, scaled with flaking rust,
> Insults the tar-roughed planking
> With a stain of orange
> And crushes with appalling weight.
>
> "Wood railing, fever-blistered, worn,
> But finely fenced with salted nets,
> Conforms the soul into a space
> Of fish parts, bones, and broken shells.
>
> "Harsh seagull scream of rope and winch
> As metal grates on metal: Lo!
> A boat strains at the cruel knot
> With torment of a tethered thing.

"A Voice aloft now cries with rapture,
Not the boat but now the gull's cry;
Occult skylark in the sunlight,
The sparkle blinds with diamonds of light.

"Fear not now to strike with might.
Crack the anchor.
Burst the rail.
Sever the rope with upward thrust.

"And plunge into the emerald light.
Swim far and free into the arching waves.
Fear not the sharks that bear thee to thy doom;
They can but bite the flesh and crack the bone.

"After a while, thou wilt be free."

"Hey," I say. "What you think? That one called 'Pier.' You like it?"

"Crimes are a virus obscene, invisible save to microscopy, but killing, killing. They are the unseen rays that produce cancer from sunlight, invisible to those lacking the prism to break them apart. I am both microscope and prism. I am a detective. Read me that poem again."

I read. When I finish he lick lips and purr to self. I not then familiar with his moods and afraid he fancy himself cat. But, no. He merely happy.

"There," he say, "is my crime."

I get very angry 'cause I think he have crazy spell and waste his mind.

"No, Punky," Harold Bahr say. "I mean it. Here we have a

crime right over our rug. That poem reeks with implied crimi-
nality."

I feel face pucker. "Why you get crazy so often?" I yell. I
throw periodical down on tufted carpet.

"Quickly," he say, "tell me who the poet is." I pick periodical
up again and leaf through.

"Name," I say, "is Marc Lamprey."

"A fish name," Harold remark.

"Magazine say he reside at Salmon Lake in Namton."

"More fish," Harold say. He scratch eyebrow. "Namton.
Where is Namton?" I dash to gazetteer.

"Namton in mountains, maybe three hundred mile from
here. Salmon Lake summer resort."

"When was that magazine published?"

"It just come out."

"And that poem—'Pier'—had it a previous publication?"

"No, it say here that all poems first time published."

"Ah," he say. "Ah, ah, ah. It may be an old poem. Or it may
still be fresh." Here he bob back and forth in chair, and say, "ah"
many more time.

"Why you do that?" I ask. "Why you do like this?" I bob in
sofa, and say, "Ah, ah, ah," to shame him.

But he not shamed. He continue to move in chair, and say,
"Ah, ah, ah," till I pinch arm to make him stop.

Suddenly blue eyes grow very clear; he look me straight in
face.

"An uncontaminated crime," he say softly, "and all of it mine.
Better perhaps than that."

"What," I demand, "more better than 'uncontaminated'
crime?"

"An uncommitted one," he say.

• • •

Namton is rocky-woodsy land high up on mountain. Great big mountain it is, full of dripping pine and, as Harold Bahr say, choked with foliage. It next day now, and we drive long distance in Toyota. Punky Kim always drive. One time only, when Harold and I going somewhere, he ask to sit behind wheel. I say okay. He drive well enough till he see potbellied man on motorcycle. Then Harold stand way up in seat, and scream, "Jebusite!" and chase motorcycle man all over highway, all the time pretending to be avenging angel of death. That time I stop car and hide engine key till motorcycle man drive away. Now I do all driving.

Very pretty is way to Namton. Very pretty mountain. Nice winding road. Harold Bahr ask to drive. I tell him no, and he not talk to me all the way up. He just sit low in seat and close eyes. Sometimes he mutter, "Namton-Bampton, sudda-budda-bee." I figure he in training to talk to poet, so I say nothing and listen to glass harmonica music on radio. I think his cracked brain is taking us on goose's run, that nobody going to commit any crime. Still, we stay at lodge maybe two, three days, have good vacation.

At last we arrive at great big lodge. Plenty parking spaces in front, but only two cars parked. No people outside.

I go knock on door, while Harold Bahr sit on car bumper and tie shoe.

Pretty blond girl open door. She wear shorts and have legs. Harold Bahr finish tying shoe, and he, too, go up to door.

"I am Harold Bahr," he say. "This is Mr. Kim. We'd like a couple of rooms."

Pretty girl say she is Alice Thyne. She take us inside and we pay money and sign register. Girl very happy we are here.

"I'm very happy you are here," she say. "We don't get much custom, since the lake dried up."

"You lost your lake?" Harold ask.

"And the ducks and the hunters, and most of our revenue. I'll show you your rooms. We take our meals in common over there in the dining room. Dinner is at seven."

Legs take Harold Bahr and Punky Kim upstairs to long hallway. Hallway not empty like downstairs, no. Creepy old lady sitting on padded chair near top of stairs. Big, creepy old lady with big walking cane that end in three little sticks like camera tripod. She look up from book she is reading.

"Good afternoon, Mrs. Bash," Leggy Alice say.

"Has Mr. Lamprey left his room?" say Mrs. Bash in old lady voice.

"I wouldn't know," reply Alice in tone that remind me of frozen tuna. Then Harold Bahr and Punky Kim go to connecting rooms. Door between is open, and we talk as we unpack.

"Punky," say Harold after he flop on bed and take up "Pier" poem. "I think we are fortunately in time to prevent a murder—or it may be a suicide; the implications in the lines of repression and freedom and death . . ." But I still think he bring us up to abuse wounded goose, so I mumble something about shock therapy and go off in search of place to take bath.

I carry bath brush and soap out into hall. Old creepy lady still there. When she see Punky Kim she stand up. She very big creepy old lady.

"Have you seen Mr. Lamprey?" she ask.

I tell her I not know him.

"*She* knows him well enough." Here old lady nod in general direction of downstairs.

"Fine," I say. "Where is bathroom?"

"And he, he knows just what she wants him to know." She speak to self now, so I smile understandingly and leave to find bathroom for self.

It at end of hall. Fine, bright bathroom that have old-fashioned iron tub with feet. I have long splash. When I come out, old lady gone.

Back in room Harold Bahr still on bed with poem.

"The work implies some violent action and possible recrimination," he say. "Sometimes the energy is dispelled in the creation of a work of art, but the impulse remains, gathering more energy like a battery on slow charge. Listen:

"Dead anchor scaled with flaking rust
Insults the tar-roughed planking
With a *stain* of orange
And *crushes* with *appalling* weight.

"Four images of insult and oppression in just the first stanza."
I interrupt to tell him what creepy old lady say. Harold nod twice, rub bullet head, and read from poem.

"Wood railing, fever-blistered, worn,
But finely fenced with salted nets,
Conforms the soul into a space
Of fish parts, bones, and broken shells.

"Constraint. Constraint and decay and something withheld from its proper element. Oh, let's go down to dinner!"
Nice big dinner. Few eaters but much food. We all sit together at mahogany table with linen cloth. Alice girl serve us,

then sit down and eat, too. She change to white slacks, so not have legs anymore. Creepy big Mrs. Bash with tripod cane is there, talking to large middle-aged man who part black curly hair in middle and wear thin moustache. Other lady there too—fleshy-fortyish, with orange hair—who try to look sexy—and succeed.

Mrs. Bash stop talking to thin moustache man and turn to Harold Bahr.

"Have you seen Mr. Lamprey?" she ask. Before Harold can open mouth, orange-headed lady say Lamprey still in room.

"Still in his room," Mrs. Bash echo. "All he does is sit in that room."

Now I see Harold Bahr is talking to curly-headed moustache man.

"Have you no other guests, Mr. Heifitz?" Harold is saying.

Big man take in, then let out bellyful of air.

"Not often," he say. "Used to. Before the lake dried up. Used to be a lot of duck hunters."

"Why keep on then?"

Mr. Heifitz make funny, ugly face.

"We have our resident guests," he reply.

"I am anxious to meet Mr. Lamprey," Harold say to table people. "I read a poem he wrote."

"He is always writing," say creepy old lady. "Writing secrets."

Dinner talk trail off like sunset, and people disperse. Harold Bahr take out red bandanna and polish head, then go back to study poem in room. I very sad that Harold so crazy he cannot enjoy happy vacation. But moonshining night always cure sadness. So I walk on path under pine trees. Suddenly figure detach itself from shadows and come up to Punky Kim like hermit crab looking for new shell.

"And what do *you* do, Mr. Kim?" voice say. It belong to orange-headed fleshy sexy woman. She talk way down in throat.

I very embarrassed because I not catch her name at dinner.

"I very embarrassed because I not catch your name at dinner," I tell her.

"It's Barbara," throat say. "Barbara Wen." Voice now seem to come from feet.

"I work in fish cannery," I tell her. "How long you people live here?" I ask politely for to make conversation.

"Live here? Alice and Uncle Fitz forever. The place was built by Alice's father. He in turn left it to his brother-in-law Fitz."

"Why he not leave it to Alice?"

"I understand he intended to. Then they quarreled, and he changed his will. They made up, and Alice thought she'd be in again, but then he was killed."

"How he die?"

"He was murdered. Two years ago. Shot with his own gun in a hotel in Crescent City. They never found who did it. Robbery. He had borrowed a sum to try to pipe water to the lake; it is dry, you know. The fool insisted on cash."

Talk getting morbid, so I change subject.

"Why this Marc Lamprey stay all the time in room?" I ask.

"Maybe to think up new ways to make people suffer," she say. Then she make little smile, and ask if I will walk with her in moonlight, but I no longer sad and tell her no. Besides, I very curious to see if Harold Bahr still being crazy over poem. It about time I think for him to be enjoying bright and happy vacation.

Back in room Harold has unknitted afghan bedspread and wound string over furniture. I curse him till he interrupt to make me tell him what I learn. When I talk of orange-headed Barbara Wen, he nod bald bullet head two time, and say:

> "Harsh seagull scream of rope and winch
> As metal grates on metal: Lo!
> A boat strains at the cruel knot
> With torment of a tethered thing.

"More and more repression. Thyne, Wen, Bash, Heifitz, Lamprey himself—which is the 'rope,' the 'winch,' the 'cruel knot,' the 'boat' straining to be free? By the way, have you noticed that 'Heifitz' is a homonym for '*Heifisch*,' the German word for shark? Another fish."

But I am looking at unknitted afghan wound all over furniture, and saying to him some disrespectful words.

"These are the 'salted nets' of the second stanza." He sniff. "I am dramatizing the poem."

I tell him he ready for psychodrama. But he still insist violent act implied in poem; only violent act, he say, not yet come to surface, as poet so far express self only in symbols. I not make much of this, and go to sleep with enchanting thoughts of wandering in moonlight with orange-headed Wen.

Nice big morning breakfast. Day cold and cloudy. Mr. Heifitz say we in for big storm. Alice very friendly to Harold Bahr and Punky Kim, though not friendly enough to wear shorts again, but have on black slacks. Marc Lamprey not at table. Alice say he come down very early to eat and probably now in room. Other guests get up till only Alice remain with us at table. Harold Bahr help self to more potato pancakes and turn to blond Alice.

"I am anxious to meet Mr. Lamprey," rusty voice say. "Have you read his poem 'Pier'?"

"He gave it to me," Alice reply. "He acted like it was a special document. I thought it pretty good and sent it to that magazine. I'm glad they published it."

"Have you known Mr. Lamprey long?"

"He and Mrs. Bash came here several months ago. He can't get along without her, though sometimes he acts like he can't stand her."

"A surrogate mother?"

"A surrogate something. She used to be his cleaning lady. You figure it out. I can't. Two pests. A he pest and a she pest."

"If they're such a pair of undesirables, why not ask them to leave?"

"Uncle Fitz wouldn't hear of it. They began as paying guests; then Uncle Fitz found out that Marc is a handyman and gives him and that old woman free rent and board in exchange for keeping the place up, though as a handyman he's a complete washout."

"You seem not much to like Mr. Lamprey."

"For a while I did. He used to do things—take walks—talk about poetry—sometimes we played cards. Do you know how he spends his time these days? Sitting in his room reading his newspapers."

"Newspapers?"

"Stacks of them. He subscribes to a dozen or so from a dozen different cities. He says they give him inspiration. Something must. He writes good poetry."

"You resent Mr. Lamprey's staying in his room?"

"I prefer it. When he's out of his room he's a pest."

"What kind of pest is he?" Harold ask.

"The very worst kind."

Harold's eyes get narrow.

"This Lamprey," Harold say. "Could he murder somebody?"

"That squirrel? Well, he might start with himself."

Harold's eyes become nasty little squints.

"I think you could be a murderer, Miss Thyne."

"What?"

"A murderess, cold-blooded and lecherous."

"If Uncle Fitz didn't need the money——"

"A murderess with the head of a convict!"

She say something unkind and stamp out of room. I furious.

"Why you bite her with bad words?" I demand to know. "Why unhealthy brain squirt so much venom?"

"A new metaphor!" Harsh voice rise as he point with finger high in air. "This place is a retort of inimical corrosives simmering but not yet volatile. And I, I am a catalyst!"

I not know what catalyst is and think maybe it his religion, so I look reverent as we pass out of room.

"Well, nothing yet from her; let us beard the lamprey in its lair." We trot upstairs to Lamprey room, and Harold knock on door.

There is no answer, so Harold knock again. And again. Then I knock. Then we both knock.

From deep in room squeaky little voice announce: "I'm not coming out today."

"Well, then we'll be going away now," Harold say convincingly, and make footstep sound getting softer and softer.

"We'll wait right here," Harold whisper. "He's bound to come out sooner or later." He take up poem once more. I sit on stair and try to invent crossword puzzle.

"He can't stay in there forever, eh?" Harold whisper. "He's bound to get hungry." I nod and grin.

Four hours later we finally go downstair, pick up sandwiches in kitchen.

"I guess he means it," Harold say. "We'll probably catch him at dinner. What do you say to a walk?"

We start to go outdoors to see woodcraft sights but are withheld by grim old person sitting alone by front door.

"A moment, Mr. Kim, Mr. Bahr," she call out in old-lady voice. "Have you seen Marc Lamprey?"

"He's an elusive fellow," say Harold Bahr. "Have you ever seen a real lamprey, Mrs. Bash? It's a sort of fanged eel with a sucker mouth which burrows into the flesh of other fish to feed on their blood."

"He doesn't feed on my blood, Mr. Bahr. I look after him."

"Eh, and who looks after you, Mrs. Bash?"

"He is a son to me—sometimes a wayward son."

"He is in his room. Why don't you go up?"

"And watch him brood over that woman?"

"Alice, yes, I gathered that."

"He will come round, Mr. Bahr."

"I understand you used to be his cleaning lady," Harold say nastily.

"One rises from humble beginnings. Good day."

We nod courteously and pass out of building.

We follow trail that sign tell us lead to lake. Lake look like desert. Dead pine trees all around baked, cracked lake bed. Overhead big gray clouds piling up on each other.

"Baked, cracked lake bed," Harold murmur, "sudda-budda-bee."

But poetry cut short by sight of Uncle Heifitz standing on wooden dock. Funny to see dock coming from dry land, ending in dry land, and only two, three feet above cracked lake bottom. Uncle Heifitz standing next to big artist's easel. On easel is unfinished canvas of big blue lake. In water is thin man not yet finished being painted.

"Hey-dey!" call out Harold Bahr to Uncle Heifitz. "Painting I see."

"Used to be a lake," Uncle Fitz boom back.

"Freshwater," say Harold, walking onto dock. I follow. "No gulls, eh?"

"Hardly," say Uncle Fitz.

"'Occult skylarks' we call them." Harold wink one eye.

"Indeed," big man answer.

"No 'fish parts, bones, and broken shells,' I expect."

Uncle Fitz give Harold funny look.

"Incidentally," Harold say, "your canvas is bleeding."

"It's the sunset; I try to put it into all my pictures." He look up at clouds. "We'll be in for it in a few hours."

"What's all that wood out yonder?" Harold point to boxy things sticking out of dry lake bed.

"Used to be duck blinds."

"Ah, different from 'tar-roughed planking.'" He laugh.

"I guess." Uncle Fitz laugh.

Punky Kim laugh, too.

"Does Mr. Lamprey ever come here?"

"Not often. Used to. Mostly these days he stays in his room writing that stuff, or else reading his newspapers. He never throws one away. His room must be full of them by now."

"You don't go into his room?"

"Nobody goes in his room. It is fitted with a Yale lock. So far as I know he's got the only key. He's even put bars on the windows, though his room is on the second floor."

"I see. That figure you're sketching—it looks like a drowned body. It wouldn't be Mr. Lamprey?"

"Just a fancy of mine, Mr. Bahr, a pictorial fancy."

"And the lake you are painting; it is full of water, not dry as it is now."

"I'm remembering how it used to look."

"Well, don't fall in and drown," Harold say with stinging wit. We all laugh many times over this; then we leave uncle and return to lodge. All the time air growing colder while dark clouds filling up empty spaces in sky.

Back at lodge, Harold and Punky put heads through open kitchen door, and Harold say to Alice he very sorry he call her murderer with head of convict. Girl vengeful and vindictive; she slam door in faces.

"Still no crime." Harold sigh. "We must increase the pressure."

He politely knock on kitchen door.

Alice open it.

"You're a degenerate!" he shout, and make disrespectful gesture with part of anatomy. I quickly march him upstairs. Once in room he turn all pictures to wall; then he take up poem and recite:

> "A Voice aloft now cries with rapture
> Not the boat but now the gull's cry;
> Occult skylark in the sunlight.
> The sparkle blinds with diamonds of light.

"This is the mystical part," he say. "It is to inspire the defiance of oppression. Listen:

> "Fear not now to strike with might.
> Crack the anchor.

Burst the rail.
Sever the rope with upward thrust.

"And this is the act of violence that has sent us packing three hundred miles. Oh, I simply must talk with Marc Lamprey! Maybe he will be at dinner."

I miserable his brain still so crazy for violent crime. But all he say is that Alice focus of it all, and go on polishing head.

Dinner silent. Everyone resentful. Marc Lamprey still not come down. Uncle Fitz say he in room. Alice very sullen, not look at Harold Bahr. Punky Kim try to spread merriment by telling several funny jokes, but no one laugh.

After dinner Harold talk with creepy Mrs. Bash, while Punky look for Barbara Wen to walk with in moonlight; only now is no moonlight, only clouds. I not find Wen, but as I pass Uncle Fitz's room, I hear voice that sound very much orange-headed, so I shrug shoulders and go back to room and read "Pier" poem, but still not find hint of violent crime.

That night is big black storm. Yellow flashes tear all across sky till whole world crash with noise. I peek into Harold's room to see if he up, too; but no, he snore very loudly.

I sleep few hours, then get up to enjoy storm. Rain stop about six-thirty; it too early to get up, so I go back to sleep.

When I awake clouds outside blacker than ever, and I think we in for more storm. I go into Harold's room. He raveling yarn back into afghan. I ask if he enjoy storm. He very angry he sleep through it, and say storm best time for violent crime, and that maybe Marc already kill or wound someone.

He relieved to see Alice, Uncle, and Mrs. Bash at breakfast table; Barbara Wen and Marc Lamprey not there, though. Alice glare hard at us, then tell Uncle Fitz storm has uprooted telephone line.

Front door bang open very suddenly. Barbara Wen come puffing in like marathon racer.

"Mrs. Bash," she say with little breath, "have you got the key to Marc's room? I met him out back; he asked me to bring him something."

Old lady eyes look squinty and mean.

"To my knowledge there is only one key, which he keeps on his person. Why did he not give it to you?"

Wen start to speak, then dash upstairs. Bash glare. Heifitz glare. Alice look at Harold, and she glare. I start to glare, too, but Harold take arm and say we go for walk.

Everything wet and drippy outside; ground shiny with little pools of water.

Light very queer and eerie.

"Notice the queer and eerie light," Harold say. "It is the light between storms."

It hard to see clearly. I start to walk to spot in forest where I talk with Barbara Wen about moonlight walk, but Harold grab arm and steer toward lake bed.

"Barbara Wen acted mighty suspiciously," Harold say. "What do you make of the case so far?"

I tell him he is case. Sure, everyone act suspicious; everyone always act suspicious when you have crime on mind. Sometime even I act suspicious, though I am innocent good man.

"Don't you see the Wen was clearly lying?" Harold say.

I tell him maybe old lady lie or make mistake about number of keys.

"No," Harold insist. "Uncle Fitz corroborated her when he

told us that Lamprey has the only key to that room. Remember? But look—we have a lake!"

He right. We pass out of forest and see lake bed covered with big sheet of water. Light still very eerie. Very, very hard to see. Suddenly Harold grab arm.

"What is that on the dock?" he ask. "It looks like a gibbet."

I not know what gibbet is, so file that one away like 'catalyst.' Besides, object on dock look to me like hangman stand. But then we laugh because we both wrong. It only Uncle Heifitz's easel.

"What's that black bundle in the mud at the foot of the dock?" Harold ask. We walk to dock and go to end.

Black bundle is human body facedown in mud, half in half out shallow puddle water.

"May as well save our shoes," Harold say. He take up easel, bend down, use foot of easel to turn body over. It very hard to turn over because face buried much deeper in mud than rest of body. But at last he turn it on its back.

"Ahhh!" Harold say, and recite:

> "And plunge into the emerald light.
> Swim far and free into the arching waves.
> Fear not the sharks that bear thee to thy doom;
> They can but bite the flesh and crack the bone.
>
> "After a while thou wilt be free."

Ugly white corpse covered with black mud. Harold kneel down and splash face with puddle water till mud off face. Slim, skinny corpse with mouth open remind me of Harold's description of eel fish with sucker mouth.

"Let's get him out of the mud," Harold say. We kneel down and lift skinny corpse onto dock.

Harold put hand inside corpse's coat pocket and bring out transparent plastic bag. Inside bag is what look like dagger; but, no, Harold remove it from bag and unroll it, and I see it is piece of paper, all rolled up.

"Oh, listen to this!" Harold cry out. He read writing on paper.

> *"I met at a museum a man named Andy Thyne, who showed me only kindness and courtesy. We got together a few times at his hotel room and drank and talked of art and poetry. I killed him for his money, as I now kill myself for justice.*
>
> *Marc Lamprey*

"This is insulting!" Harold say with disgust. I afraid for a minute he going to tear paper up. But he only shake head and put paper carefully in pocket.

"We'll have to verify the handwriting and the identity of the body," he say. He return to corpse.

"He hasn't been long in the water, Punky. Look at the smooth skin; water wrinkles, you know." Suddenly he begin to whistle and then stop to recite poem all over again. I very happy that Harold at last have his tragic and grisly death. Now maybe he can have swell time enjoying vacation.

"So," I say knowingly, "this Lamprey bad murderer, who kill Alice's father, then brood long, long time till he finally drown self like poet Longfellow."

"If you drown yourself," Harold say, "you don't do it in three inches of muddy water, two feet from a dock!"

"But maybe lake deeper when he drown."

"When you drown," Harold insist, "you float down; this fellow was impacted in the mud. No, depend upon it, this murderer was murdered. Witness also that lunatic confession."

"But it is suicide note!" I say. I start to get very angry because I think brain on its hind legs again.

"Let us see what else is on him," he say. Harold turn out every pocket of slimy dead corpse but find only key; he put this in pocket alongside confession, and we start back to lodge.

"So Barbara Wen met her Marc along the way, and he sent her to his room!" Harold roar as we pick our way around water puddles.

In big main room we see Uncle Fitz is talking to Mrs. Bash. Alice not there. Wen not there.

"Give me a few minutes, then tell them, Punky," Harold whisper. "I'm off to the locked room. Meet me there when you have a chance."

I give him few minutes, then stroll into room and put on friendly face to soften shocking news.

"Hey," I say. "Marc Lamprey's dead corpse in dry lake. You got wheelbarrow?"

Mrs. Bash grab old-lady heart; Uncle Fitz nearly fall out of chair. Fitz and Punky go to toolshed to fetch wheelbarrow, and then hurry over to lake.

Corpse not prettier for being left alone. Uncle Fitz start to go through dead person's pockets.

"The key!" he snap. "Where's his key?"

I coy and tell him I once hear of key being lost in water and advise him to jump in lake. It only funny joke, but he plunge in and rake mud all over.

"Have you got the key?" he demand. "I'm minded to search you."

He very big, tough man. I make oriental sounds and twirl hands so he think I know karate.

"No!" he say. "Bahr. It's Bahr!" and run back way we come, leaving Punky to deliver corpse by self.

When I and corpse arrive at lodge, Alice, Bash—sad and crying. Wen look scared. Uncle Fitz clashing big fist into palm. I assume karate stance again, but he wave me off.

"That's not the way they do it," he say in tired voice. Then he get angry again.

"That bastard has locked himself in Marc's room!" he shout.

I angry 'cause he call Harold Bahr bastard, and call Uncle Fitz bastard in return; but he only shake head and look tired. Body still outside in wheelbarrow. I nip upstairs to Marc Lamprey's room and call to Harold to open door.

Door open slowly, and I step into messy room with bed, writing desk, and ferocious stack of newspapers.

"What we do with dead man?" I ask.

Harold smiling. His smile very terrible.

"It's all in this little tin box," he say, ignoring question. "Our Lamprey trusted to his locked door and barred window."

He show me tin box, take from it what look like legal document, along with what is clearly newspaper clipping with photograph.

"And a little notebook, too." Smile more terrible now. "Look. Symbols."

I study page he indicate. Find funny drawings of violin and something that protrude from face like boil—followed by small sums: eight dollar, twenty dollar, forty-three dollar.

Harold give me note we find on body.

"Just compare the handwriting on this with the writing on these manuscript poems," he say.

I study long, long time, while Harold root around room.

Finally: "They all look same," I say.

"Yes," he agree. "It's clear that Marc Lamprey wrote that confession—that precious, pretentious, sententious, over-written, feeble, and febrile—" Here he start to get very angry.

"All except for stationery," I say quickly. "Stationery different."

Harold's eyes clear. "Yes," he say. "I haven't been able to find any writing paper exactly like it."

He pocket papers and notebook, and we go downstairs. Uncle Fitz help Harold and Punky carry wet corpse up to Lamprey room and dump it on bed. Barbara Wen come, too, along with Bash and formerly leggy Alice.

"I take it this is Marc Lamprey," Harold say.

Others agree.

"Has anybody called the police?"

"The phone lines are still down," Fitz say.

"I'll drive to town," Barbara Wen say.

"That is ill advised!" Harold roar. Suddenly he hold up finger.

"I am a detective," he announce, "and shall represent the police *in absentia*. We must all remain here at the lodge. We'll go downstairs now and I'll relock the door."

"I think I'll stay up here," Barbara Wen say.

"Me too," say Uncle Fitz.

"It will do you no good." Harold shake head. "I've already pulled all the plums. We'll go down now, and I'll lock the door."

Uncle Fitz ball fists. "This is my hotel!" he shout.

Harold's lip curl. "Is it, Mr. Heifitz?"

Harold lock door, and we all go downstairs and gather in dining room. Harold make speech.

"Marc Lamprey was dead and drowned in a few inches of water," Harold say. "Yet his skin was not much wrinkled. Therefore, he could not have been in the water very long. According to Mr. Kim, the rain stopped this morning at about half past six. The assumption is—that whatever his motive for going to the lake—he would hardly have done so while the rain was still falling. Mr. Kim and I found the body at around half past seven. Therefore, I suggest the murder was committed between the hour of, say, six-thirty and a quarter past seven. Oh, don't gasp, Mrs. Bash. I said 'murder.' You don't drown yourself in three inches of water."

I very impressed. It big confrontation scene like in old movie—the kind you never supposed to put into story nowadays, because it is cliché.

"Where were you at murder time, Mr. Heifitz?" Harold ask.

Uncle Fitz say nothing.

Harold shake bald head. "The police will ask the same question." Uncle Fitz still is wordless.

"And you, Mrs. Bash?"

"I was in my room, though I did go out on the porch for a few minutes to get some air."

"Better. And you, Miss Alice?"

"I was in the kitchen working on breakfast. I didn't go out at all."

"Did anybody see you not go out?"

Alice turn back on him.

"Now you, Miss Wen. You are apparently the last one to see Mr. Lamprey alive."

"Yes. As I told you, I met him in the woods. He asked me to get him something from his room."

Harold's eyes shrink to tiny dots. "You met him on the dock and killed him. We both know why."

Wen get very upset.

"No!" she blurt out. "I found Marc dead. I saw my chance to get something from his room, something he threatened to send to my parents. I didn't kill him!"

"Where were you before you went out?"

Wen turn puce; Uncle Fitz look like sheep who swallowed canary.

"Is that right, Mr. Heifitz?" Uncle Fitz silent.

"Oh, Barbara Wen, Barbara Wen"—Harold put hands to bullet head—"all a-flutter for the secrets of the locked room. Did you really not kill its occupant? Or you, Mr. Heifitz; you, too, were awfully keen to get into that room—did you kill him? Incidentally, Alice, might you not take vengeance on the man who murdered your father?"

Bombshell burst. Harold read confession. Alice cry some and sink into chair. When things quiet down, Harold point finger at old lady.

"And finally there is Mrs. Bash, who daily saw her ersatz son lose interest in her, in favor of a poetic vision. Jealousy is a potent motive for murder. And one of you, you know, is a murderer."

Harold take out red bandanna and burnish head. Then he replace bandanna and sit on back of chair.

"Let us hoist up all our linen," he say. "Our Lamprey was not only the murderer of Alice's father; he was a blackmailer as well, if only on a small scale. Oh, now, Miss Wen, don't look that way; lots of girls have been arrested before." Here Uncle Fitz look squinty at her.

"It would kill my parents," she say.

"Mr. Heifitz, your culpability was greater. Incidentally, when did Marc confront you with the will leaving this place to Alice?"

"What?" Alice scream.

Uncle Fitz look like spent whoopie-cushion.

"Not long after he arrived," Fitz say softly. "In a moment of weakness I agreed to give him and that woman free lodging in exchange for his silence."

"Uncle Fitz!" Alice shoot out of chair.

"Yes, Alice. I cheated you out of your inheritance. And ever since I've felt like an excremental heel!"

"But, Uncle Fitz"—Alice beside him now—"I never cared for this place—I stayed on only as a favor to you—you can have everything!"

"You don't detest me?"

"The only one I ever detested was Marc Lamprey—oh, and Mr. Bahr, of course."

Tender scene fill Punky Kim's eyes with mucus, so I wipe them off with shirtsleeve. I still not know who murderer is— Heifitz or Wen or Bash or pretty Alice with blond legs.

"Let's take it from the beginning," Harold say. "Marc Lamprey is living in Crescent City. Too weak to work, indolent by temperament, he possesses a poet's sensibility, if not a poet's talent. One day in a museum he strikes up an acquaintanceship with a hotel owner who is on a business trip to borrow money. The two find they have much in common and meet a few times to talk. They also drink. The hotel owner tells Marc about Salmon Lake and invites him for a visit. Apparently, in a fit of drunken confidence, he even tells Marc about his daughter and the hiding place of the will restoring her inheritance.

"Now they are in the hotel owner's room. The man shows Marc the money he borrowed—all in cash—as well as the gun he carries to protect it. Marc sees his opportunity, kills the man with his own gun, steals the money, and slips away.

"Back in his own quarters Marc is smitten by remorse, hagridden with fear. He lies low for a time, but is terrified to remain in Crescent City. But where will he go?

"Where else? One name echoes within Marc's wormy little brain: Salmon Lake. Where else but Salmon Lake, where he had been invited by the man he murdered? His disordered poetic fancy probably sees it as fitting.

"But not alone. Never alone. Marc is a mamma's boy raised to be dependent. He will take with him his cleaning woman, Mrs. Bash, a person willing to mother him.

"So he and Mrs. Bash establish themselves as paying guests at Salmon Lake. But the payment is made with Marc's own money because he is afraid to touch any of the stolen cash for fear it may be traced to him. Incidentally, I found it. It is upstairs in Marc's room inside a little tin box.

"To get back to Marc, he is desperately fearful for his safety. He must keep abreast of the progress of the murder investigation, so he subscribes to the *Crescent City News*. But he feels this might look suspicious, so as a smoke screen he orders a dozen other small-town papers.

"After a while Marc's money is nearly exhausted; but he has a plan. Had Alice's father not told him about the will and its hiding place? Marc retrieves it, tempts Mr. Heifitz, and Mr. Heifitz falls.

"But good things fly in tandem. No sooner has Marc established himself as a 'handyman,' with free room and board for himself and his companion—than another windfall fills his basket.

"In a *Kansas City Globe*, one of his 'smoke screen' newspapers, he finds an incriminating item about a—dancer." Here he nod to Barbara.

"Once again his demands are modest—everyone's demands are modest in this case—and she agrees to pay up. It looks like Marc has arrived. He has a place to live, food to eat, money in his pocket, and a quiet and apparently safe existence.

"Then, suddenly, everything falls to pieces. True to his poetic nature, he falls for Alice, the daughter of the man he murdered, the person he has helped to cheat out of her inheritance. It doesn't occur to his bloated ego that the girl might not have him.

"In the throes of his infatuation, everything dishonorable in him cries out for expiation. He tries to suppress it. But it ferments in him, finally taking the form of some indifferent verses which accidentally get published. Mr. Kim and I are not the only ones to read that poem. One closer at hand ponders those lines, and wonders.

"Marc's behavior becomes increasingly peculiar. He takes to his room and broods, till it becomes obvious—at least to one—that Marc's secrets are no longer safe. For he is on the verge of confessing everything he knows, regardless of consequences.

"'Fear not the sharks that bear thee to thy doom,' his little poem runs,

"'They can but bite the flesh and crack the bone.'

"The sharks are the police, the courts, the cost of his crimes.

"'After a while,' the poem concludes, 'thou wilt be free.'

"The 'freedom' I take to mean his clear conscience after he has confessed and made himself worthy of Alice.

"Well, it is obvious to someone that it is only a matter of

time before Marc explodes with that confession, just as it was obvious to me when I first heard the poem that the writer was about to explode into something—I didn't know what, though I fancied at the time that it was either murder or suicide. Here was my problem. The explosion was inevitable, but it might be weeks or even months away. I came here to stir things up.

"I had no sooner arrived when it became apparent—by conversations Mr. Kim had with Mrs. Bash, and I had with Alice—that Alice was the center of the whole problem. And I reasoned that if I could put pressure on her, she might in some way influence Marc to release all that fermenting energy while I was on hand to absorb or deflect it. Well, I applied the pressure, and one of you killed him."

It is Punky Kim who get excited now.

"Which one kill him?" I demand to know. "Is it Barbara Wen who is demented murderer? Is it Uncle Fitz? Or is it two together?"

Wen and Heifitz both look despitefully at me. Harold pat them both on shoulder.

"Of course, Mr. Heifitz did not kill him. Of course Barbara Wen did not kill him."

"How you know this?"

"Because he was blackmailing them."

"Blackmail!" I scream. "You not know that blackmail victim have perfect motive for killing blackmailer? Who you think kill Marc Lamprey?"

"I know who killed him. It was Mrs. Bash."

"Why?"

"Because she was blackmailing him."

"What?"

"Listen. Marc killed Mr. Thyne, had a seizure of remorse,

and wrote out that suicide note. Well, he changed his mind about killing himself but kept the note nonetheless. Some writers save everything.

"At this point Mrs. Bash enters. She is his cleaning lady and is probably not above a bit of petty pilfering or at least snooping. My guess is that she found the note, confronted him with it, and offered her silence in exchange for his protection. Well, they went to Salmon Lake. But he was too timid to use any of the money for which he had committed murder. So instead, Marc paid his blackmailer with what he could get by blackmailing others—Barbara Wen and Mr. Heifitz.

"I suppose it worked for a few months, till suddenly catastrophe struck. Marc fell in love, had a poetic seizure and a change of heart. He wrote that poem, then took to his room to brood upon his crimes. Mrs. Bash read the poem and brooded, too.

"Mark was about to explode. Would the explosion implicate her? Proclaim her a blackmailer as well as accessory after the fact to a murder? If so, she must act. Yet she dared not act hastily. Marc was, after all, her golden goose. Perhaps this latest craze would pass, defused for lack of a detonator.

"Alice was the detonator. I made sure of that. Alice, did you treat Mr. Lamprey differently after I insulted you?"

"You made me so mad that I was merciless to his moonfaced whining."

"That did the trick. He was crazy now to confess what he was once desperate to conceal. And Mrs. Bash at last made up her mind. She made an assignation with him to meet her at the dock.

"Here. Just let me borrow this, Mrs. Bash. This cane (notice the brass handle slips off—like this) is hollow inside. The scroll of the confession (observe) fits perfectly.

"Having lured him to the dock, she planted the document on him, tripped him into the mud, and caught him by the back of the neck with the tripodal end of her cane and held him down. Isn't that so, Mrs. Bash?"

"I did not trip him, Mr. Bahr. I threw him into the mud."

"Hmm. Just so. How did you get him to the dock?"

"He told me he was going to confess. I suggested I turn over to him the old confession to show the police. I said it was in a secret place at the end of the dock."

"I suppose you removed it from your cane when he was not looking?" She nod head.

"He was not dutiful, not dutiful at all."

"Mr. Heifitz and company, I ask you to amuse Mrs. Bash while Mr. Kim and I drive for the police."

Alice see us to car. Then she do terrible thing.

"I was wrong about you, Mr. Bahr," she say. She kiss him hard on his disgusting, nasty cheek.

"Why," I ask, as car turn down winding road, "why you so positive sure it Mrs. Bash who kill Lamprey? Lamprey murder Alice's father; Lamprey cheat Alice out of property. Alice have more better motive for killing Lamprey. Why you think it Bash?"

"Consider," Harold say as he polish head. "Why would anyone, even an orker like Lamprey, trot about such a disagreeable old woman, if he were not compelled to?"

"Just so," I muse. "But on face of it, Alice still have better motive."

"Oh, I never suspected her, Punky."

I feel eyes getting mean.

"Why you not suspect her?"

"Why, she's blond, Punky. Blond girls never kill anybody."

"What?"
"And besides—"
"Yes?"
"Did you notice her legs?

    "She's a willow sapling, a billowy cat;
    Twigs and whiskers, fancy that!
    A birch for you, a Manx for me,
    And sudda-budda-budda bee!"

We drive into sunset.

THE VERMS

Don't think too much," George said. "It slows down your killing. Talk instead. Talk all the time you do it."

Steve looked after the departing cruiser, now a tiny speck in the white sky.

"Do I have to kill them all?" he asked. "Even the infants?"

George scratched the stubble on his tanned cheek.

"I saw a man attacked by infant verms. There wasn't much left of him. You're a sharpshooter. They chose you for your ability to kill."

"I never even shot a rabbit," Steve said moodily. He continued to scan the sky. The cruiser was gone now; they were alone in the desert. "All I ever fired at was targets. The only reason they sent me out here was that I was good shooting at targets." He looked about him. Bunches of dry grasses spotted the soft, gray dust as far as the horizon. A dark cluster of stones loomed nearby.

Now it was George who looked into the sky. "The nights come fast here," he said. "We'd better get started." They inspected the power packs on their Lancer Specials; each had enough firepower for a thousand rounds.

"Head for the rocks," George said. They began to tread the soft gray soil.

"How long you been here, George?" Steve asked, as they walked along.

"Nearly three years now—since we started this project. Three years to clean up this one sector—and we still haven't done it. I guess you know it's not all desert like you see here; farther on there are streams and meadows and other good places to raise our children when we finally finish the job. Did you know that of the hundred two-man teams we send out each week, several never make it back?"

"Why's that, George? The verms aren't armed, are they?"

"Armed? What did they teach you at training school? No. They're not armed; we are. That's how we can kill them."

"Then what happens?"

"People get careless."

"Back at Fort Hayes they didn't show any pictures or tell us anything about the verms. They said we'd learn better from you fellas that were here before."

"I don't think your commanding officer wanted you to know too much about them."

"Can we rest a spell?"

"Sure. The atmosphere here is thinner than ours. It's harder to breathe. We'll stop for a few minutes."

They unslung their carry-alls and sat in the soft, dry dust.

Steve looked at the rocks ahead. "It's hard to believe that just a little while ago we were sitting in the cruiser with a lot of other fellas."

"Cheer up. They'll be back in three days to pick us up. Then it's three days of R&R, and then three more days in the desert. Life goes on in a succession of threes. It's not a bad life."

"We learned at the academy that the verms came to this planet a long time ago and took over."

"Yes, they exterminated what was evidently a peaceful and benign race. Still feel uncomfortable about killing them?"

"The major back on Earth said it wasn't like killing; he said it was more like swatting insects. That right?"

"You can judge for yourself. Let's go."

They shouldered their packs and moved on toward the rocks.

"It's safest to hunt them in daylight," George said. "The verms are strongest at night, and the nights are awfully dark here. We'll get as many as we can, then bed down."

"Like I said," Steve said, gasping in the thin air, "all I know is target shooting; I never killed anything—especially anything as never did me harm. These verms—they supposed to be big?"

"Ordinarily they crawl on their bellies and don't reach your knees. When they get riled they stand up on their bottom legs; they're taller than we are then. Stop, we're close enough."

"I don't see anything; you sure they're here?"

"I know they are. Look."

"What is that coming out of all those holes? Gawd! There must be fifty of them."

"Put down the Lancer. Wait until they're good and close. Steady. Now face the target, but stand at an angle—like this— with your shoulder against mine. This way we're protected. When I tell you, shoot everything that moves."

"They're getting close."

"Not yet. Wait until we have more targets. Steady. Steady. Now."

Their Lancers made a tinkling sound as they spewed out an almost constant stream of light. Dozens of dark bodies leaped high in the glare to crumple like burned locusts in the soft desert dust.

"It's not so bad," Steve shouted. "It's not bad at all. I go for this. I can do it all night."

"You may have to," George yelled back. "Don't turn your head. Keep doing what you're doing."

"What? Why?"

"More of them are pouring out of a big crack off to my right. I never saw so many at one time."

"Good, let them come. Know what they look like to me? Bugs! Big, ugly, black bugs!"

"Can you smell them, Steve?"

"I sure as hell can. Gah!"

"They tell you at the academy that they smell?"

"No, and they didn't mention any bugs, either. I didn't know what they'd look like."

"Maybe you wouldn't have come if they showed you a few pictures."

They continued to fire.

"Tell you one thing; I sure as hell don't mind exterminating a mess of bugs. But why don't they use poison, instead of fellas with Lancers?"

"And maybe poison the whole planet? Not likely."

"George, when are they going to stop?"

"They don't stop. They haven't got the sense. Keep firing."

"There's too many of them."

"Keep firing. Keep talking."

"What happens if one of them catches you?"

"They hold you face-to-face with them with their big claws, while they rake you over with all their little legs. Then they stick a long hollow tube down your throat and suck out your juices. Keep firing."

"Damn! I missed one."

"Fire steadily. Get them all. And keep talking."

"Why do we bother with this one sector when we got a whole damn planet to settle on? Are these bugs everywhere?"

"Possibly. Maybe there are worse things in other places."

"There couldn't be anything worse; they give me the willies. Gad, their carcasses are piled up like a wall. Still they keep coming."

"I told you. They're stupid. Ah, but you have to watch out for them. They play tricks sometimes. There's supposed to be a major nest somewhere around here; looks like we found it. Buck up, I'm probably wrong. They seem to be petering out."

"They're not coming as thick or as fast—it's getting hard to see. Can they see in the dark?"

"They can do everything in the dark. They're much smarter at night. I don't know why; no one can figure them out."

"I can't see any more of them."

"I can't either."

"Reckon we got them all?"

"Look around you and shoot anything that looks like a verm. Don't shoot me. I'm going to toss some coglights."

George slung his Lancer onto his back and reached into his carry-all.

"Here," he said. "It'll be bright at first. Don't look directly at the lights." He twisted the tops off four cylinders and flung each cylinder a dozen yards in a different direction. The desert shone as with daylight.

"This is more like it." Steve laughed. "Yes sir, now a body can see to Kingdom Come."

Beyond the daylight square prowled the desert, a solid wall of hostile blackness. Within the square lay several crumpled bodies. The light gleamed dully off the polished shells.

"I move we set up the tent and call it an evening," George said. "Tomorrow we'll mop up whatever remains and move on. Did they tell you about the tents?"

"They said nothing could come through one."

"Not even a Lancer beam. Let's get it pegged down."

They stretched the bright orange fabric tautly over its hollow metal frame, then hammered eight spikes two feet into the ground to anchor the flooring, made of the same material.

The two men climbed inside. George switched on the lamp and sealed the entrance. Their world shrank to a six-foot cube.

"The coglights used to keep them away," George said, "but they're bolder now. They may come around in a bit and scratch at the tent. They can't get in. They can't knock it over. They can't tunnel up. You'll know they're here because they'll push against the sides. You won't hear them because the tent is soundproof. The reason it is soundproof—I don't think they told you this—"

"They didn't tell me anything."

"The reason it is soundproof is so we won't hear them talk."

"They *talk*? You're pulling my leg!"

"Have it your own way." George smiled. "Say, you hungry?" He distributed an assortment of food packets. Like all their equipment it weighed practically nothing.

"Not another bite till breakfast," George said. "You know that at this season the nights are ten hours long?"

Steve nodded between mouthfuls.

"And that the days are only six hours?"

Steve nodded again.

"To help us sleep away the long hours we use a Somnex Timer; it's a clock that emits a little resonance that lulls you to sleep. All you do is close your eyes and listen."

"We have them on Earth."

"Really? I didn't know."

"I use one because I wake up a lot and can't get back to sleep again."

"If you wake up here, remember what I told you. The verms may push against the tent, but they can't get in. Don't panic and start shooting. You use a Lancer, and the fabric will deflect the beam so it'll bounce around the walls and fry us. Whatever happens—don't use the Lancer. If you get scared, wake me."

"I'm not scared of them, George. I killed bunches. You saw me."

"So did they. The verms have it in for you now, and they're not above playing tricks."

"They're just a bunch of dumb bugs."

"Dumb? Yes, by day. But at night they think. That's when they're most dangerous. They play tricks. You wouldn't believe some of the gruesome tricks they've played. I'll tell you about it tomorrow while we're hunting."

George yawned. "I'm setting the Timer so it will tell us when it's time to get up; the tent won't admit any daylight. I— where's your Lancer, Steve?"

"What?"

"Where's your Lancer?"

"My—oh, hell!"

"Where is it?"

"Damn! I set it down while we were putting up the tent."

"You unplugged it from the pack?"

"I guess I did."

"Didn't they teach you anything? You're never supposed to unplug it when you're outside. Your supposed to sling it over your shoulder so it will be ready at all times. I don't even unplug mine when I sleep."

"I'll go and get it."

"With what? Phooey. You've messed up enough. Here, I'll go and get it—if the verms haven't carried it away. With one Lancer between us we'd be in fine shape."

George knelt by the tent flap, his Lancer poised to shoot.

"Now unseal the door—just a little; let's see if we have any visitors." He peered out into the square of light surrounding the tent.

"See anything?"

"No, we're lucky. Now listen. When I say the word, unzip the flap and let me out; then close it fast—except for one little chink—and wait for my call. When you hear it, open up in a hurry and stand aside."

"You don't have to do this, George. I left it there."

"All right, here I go."

George stepped outside. Steve drew the zipper.

"Damned stupid rookie dumbness," Steve murmured. "Why in hell don't I have any brains? I have to make this up to George." He paced nervously back and forth.

George was taking a long time. Steve peered through the few inches of open flap.

"George, where are you? You all right?"

There was no answer.

"George?"

"Be quiet. I found it. It was farther away than we thought. I'll—oh, hell. Hell."

There was a bright flash and a crackling.

"George."

"Open the flap."

Steve had just enough time to pull the zipper and step back as George staggered in with the Lancer. Blood flowed from his neck. He laid Steve's Lancer down.

"Disinfectant and bandages quick. Antitoxin pills."

"Wait." Steve fumbled inside his carry-all. "Here, here. What happened?" He began to clean and dress the wound.

"One of them bit me; it was hiding behind the tent—a big one. I killed it." He swallowed two capsules.

"Does it hurt bad?"

"It burns like a Lancer beam. Ow! Yes, it really hurts bad."

"What do we do now?"

"Nothing. The cruiser will be back day after tomorrow. I guess I can hold on till then. Help me into my sleeping bag."

"Does it feel any better?"

"I'm sleepy. I'm very sleepy."

"George, I'm really sorry this happened. George, can you forgive me?"

George was asleep with his mouth open. His breathing was heavy.

"That's right, George. You sleep now. You'll feel better tomorrow. I'm really sorry this happened."

Steve made sure of the tent flap before he switched off the light. Everything became solid black and silent, except for George's breathing.

He climbed into his own bag. The lining felt thin but soft and comfortable. The coglights would burn the ten hours until dawn. He tried to picture the bright square surrounding the tent. Beyond that waited the desert, savage and sightless. He thought of home and listened to the hum of the Timer.

He sat up. Was it morning? He looked at the Timer's glowing dial. He had been asleep a little over two hours. Eight to go. He shifted his position. Too bad the tent was soundproof; he would have welcomed a friendly night sound. He remembered George's joke about the verms talking. The only sound he heard was the rasping of George's breath. He leaned back against the tent wall.

The wall bulged inward. He scrambled out of his sleeping bag, stood up, and felt with his palms. The entire side stretched tight into an inward curve. He felt around to the adjoining wall. It protruded, too. "They're massing all around us," he said aloud. He reached for his Lancer.

No. Better wake George.

He snapped on the light.

George looked horrible. His neck—swollen like a cushion—had turned black and shiny. His eyes were opening and closing, opening and closing. His breathing was frenzied.

"You want water? You want anything? Dear God!"

George's eyes focused on Steve.

"Turn off the light," he said in a whisper.

"You look bad. You look really bad."

"I'm getting better. Turn off the light."

Steve shifted his gaze. "George, those things are right up against the tent."

"Turn off the light," came the whisper. The breathing slowed.

"All right, George." Steve switched off the light and crawled back into his sleeping bag.

He was just being stupid. Those verms couldn't break in. Tomorrow, at first light, he would open the flap just a little and point the Lancer outside and shoot any that were still there. Who knows? Maybe George would be all better by then. He listened intently. George's breathing sounded normal—in and out, in and out. The medicine must be taking effect.

He dreamed he was shooting verms, one by one, as each reared up to attack him. The Lancer cut cleanly, leaving each one a crackling black husk. But, oh, the smell. The smell they made when they came at him was disgusting. He began to cough.

He opened his eyes and focused on the glowing dial. Still it was not morning. He had hours to go.

The smell was still there. It was inside the tent.

He dove for the light and rubbed his eyes against the glare.

No, nothing had got in. George was in his sleeping bag, his face turned away.

George's body began to stir inside the sleeping bag. The verm smell grew stronger.

Suddenly George began to kick. Once. Twice. Steve watched wide-eyed as George's body writhed beneath the covers.

"Wake up!" Steve shouted. "Please wake up!" The writhing ceased.

George's head rolled around.

"What is it, Steve?" he whispered.

George's head was black and shiny; he kept darting it around; the head never kept still. The sleeping bag began to move again.

"What is it, Steve?"

"Oh, Gawd, George. You look so—you look so—Oh, Gawd, I can't stand to watch!"

"The light hurts my eyes, Steve. Turn it off. Turn off the light, Steve."

Steve snapped off the light.

"Steve," came the whisper from the other sleeping bag. "What you see happening is the poison working its way out. I'm getting better. I'm nearly well now. Only let me sleep."

"You're really sick."

"It's the poison leaving my body. Sleep, Steve. Listen to the Timer."

"No, I'd better—"

"Let the Timer catch you."

"I think I'd—"

"Let it catch you."

Steve closed his eyes. This time he dreamed of home, where there were no verms, no George—no Lancers, coglights, carry-alls or orders to exterminate—only rich, green fields and warm smiles of people who mattered.

"Steve?" A whispered voice like an expulsion of breath. "Steve?"

He rubbed his eyes. His home slowly faded.

"Wake up, Steve."

"Is it morning, George? I'll get the light."

"I don't like the light, Steve. Steve? This is their planet. We don't belong here."

Steve felt for the light switch.

"What are you doing, Steve?"

Steve turned on the light. Then he dove for his Lancer.

"No," the voice whispered. "Don't shoot George."

"You're not George anymore." He aimed at the triangular head.

"If you shoot, the beam will rebound and kill you, too."

He lowered the weapon.

The body began to emerge from the sleeping bag.

"I'm going out to them, Steve. I must complete my growth."

"All right, George. Just don't touch me; don't brush against me." He undid the tent flap.

George crawled out, his Lancer strapped grotesquely to his misshapen back.

"Good-bye, Steve."

Steve sealed the tent and threw himself on his bedroll. He pleaded for the Timer to take effect.

•   •   •

The alarm chirped gently, melodiously, persistently.

It was time to get up.

For a moment Steve thought of breakfasting with George. Then he clicked on the light and saw the empty sleeping bag and took his head in both his hands. Is this what happened when they bit you? Why the whole thing was such a secret? Why they had to be exterminated? He began to moan. Anything was better—than this.

He sat up abruptly.

Or maybe it was a trick.

That was it. What a fool he'd been, what a stupid, green-livered, brainless jackass.

George hadn't changed at all—it was an illusion, hypnosis, one of their gruesome tricks.

And he let George go to them. George was dead now. He had helped him die.

Or maybe George *had* changed.

Steve readied his Lancer and opened the flap a few inches. Then he unsealed it all the way. Sunlight poured in. Lancer poised, he stepped outside.

There was nothing to shoot. Only the empty, metallic-looking husks that littered the gray dust. These and the burned-out coglights.

"What am I going to do now?" he asked the desert. With George gone, how could he continue the mission? The cruiser would be along tomorrow; maybe he should sit tight till then. He stared at the tent.

"No," he said. "I have to do what I was sent to do. And I have to find George."

He made a scratch meal and checked the contents of his carry-all.

"I have to travel light in this thin atmosphere." One by one, he unloaded each superfluous item and laid it in the tent. "Won't be needing my flashlight, because I'll be working in the bright sun. Won't need the extra power packs, because George is not here to share them with me. I'll take a few coglights to serve as grenades in case I find any holes full of them."

He surveyed the black carcasses; then he checked the gauge on his power pack. It read FULL.

"One way or another I'm going to find George," he told the desert. "And I'm going to kill as many verms as I've got rounds of ammunition. Then I'm coming back to wait for the cruiser."

He made a circuit of the tent and saw nothing but more empty carcasses. He began to move toward the rocks.

Two of the creatures crawled over a flat boulder. The Lancer flame licked at their shells.

Two less to worry about, he thought. Something had happened to him during the night. He felt more sure of himself.

Among the rocks he found shallow empty caves. Here and there deep fissures penetrated the ground. The widest crack had a particularly strong verm smell. He dropped a coglight in and held the Lancer poised. A sharp crackling below told him he must have got whatever was there. He moved off across the desert.

He wandered for hours, searching the rocks and the cracks in the desert floor. Now and then he found a small nest of five or six and left them face up, their legs kicking at the sun. Occasionally he met lone travelers and dispatched them quickly. There was no sign of George.

He drank copiously from his canteen. So far he had killed maybe fifty. Once he saw a nest of baby verms worrying the carcass of one of the larger ones. Odd, it never occurred to him to ask what they ate. He shot them all.

Halfway to the horizon loomed a big hill. From the top of the hill he should be able to see the whole desert floor. Maybe he would find George. He checked his power pack and saw it was nearly full.

Getting to the hill took longer than he'd expected. He had thought it fairly close and low. Now as he stood sweating beneath the towering mass of gray boulders, he cursed the planet and the thin air and the confusion that made far-off things seem nearby.

Carefully he scanned the pile of stone. No verms. He slung his Lancer and began to climb, using both hands to grip the rocks and propel his body upward. He moved steadily toward the summit, glancing all around him as he climbed. Once he looked back to see the outline of the tent standing against the bright sky.

Eventually he found the top—a wide, flat surface—and stood up to survey the ground beneath him.

Beyond the mound lay a great bowl-shaped depression, crawling with verms pouring like black beads from a rift in its center. He rubbed his eyes. This must be the major nest George told him about.

George. Poor George. He unslung his Lancer.

"Damned bugs," Steve muttered. "Damned, tricky, murdering black bugs. I'm going to damage every last one of you."

They made superb targets as he pointed and squeezed, pointed and squeezed, wiping out rows, bunches, battalions of them. It was not Steve who shot; it was the brain of the Lancer, the eye of the Lancer. Steve grinned, intoxicated with the straight, clear beams and the way each scurrying bead dropped still.

"Every last one," he whispered. "Every last one."

The Lancer spat flame till he had to strain his eyes to make out the few beads that still moved. He collapsed onto the hilltop and wiped his forehead.

"I've been up here too long," he said. "It's beginning to get dark."

He shouldered his Lancer and headed down the way he came.

Maybe it wouldn't be too bad. After the shooting he'd done there couldn't be many of them left. He should be able to get back to the tent in time.

Descending was more difficult than climbing had been; he had to use all his concentration to find the best places to put his hands and feet. It was getting harder to see. But he was nearly down. He unstrapped his carry-all and set it beside him while he sat on a boulder to catch his breath.

The verms waited ten feet below, a jungle of twitching antennae and writhing legs. Their smell made him gag.

He raised the Lancer and began to kill them in bunches. His back was shielded by the rock; if he kept his head, he should get them all.

Still they came on. They just kept coming on.

The night came, too. The intermittent Lancer blasts afforded him some vision, but it was time for coglights. He felt behind him for the carry-all.

It was gone. He must have knocked it over while he was shooting. He took a breath. He was a sharpshooter. His back was protected. With enough light he could probably get them all. With enough light—but where was the light to come from?

Something reared up before him, its writhing legs a flurry of movement. The Lancer flame knocked its head off. He could hear it twitching in the soft dust.

The night grew darker after the momentary brightness.

The tent. He had to find the tent. But how could he see to find it? His eyes fell on the Lancer.

He could switch the power pack to maximum. Each shot would throw enough energy to blast through a cruiser; the power drain would be enormous, but the light emitted would be dazzling. He turned the dial to the FULL ON position and fired into the army just below.

The night lit up around him as the insects burst with the explosion of power; pieces of them continued to burn, showing him a path through their midst. He jumped down off the rock, landed in the dust, and nearly stumbled over his carry-all. He snatched it up and ran for all he was worth.

Movement ahead, a wall of shifting shapes against the blacker wall of the night. He discharged another blast. The shocking glare showed him he had a path once more. Again the blast left burning remnants, grim torches to light his way. He ran till the lights were far behind and only a sickening smell told of the presence all around. His lungs were nearly bursting. He had to rest for a second to catch his breath.

If he could snatch a few seconds to get a coglight out of his carry-all— No time. He pivoted, squeezing the trigger, firing all around him till the landscape shone as bright as noon.

His hand plunged into the carry-all and brought forth a coglight. He twisted off the cap and tossed the cylinder a dozen yards ahead. Now he could see. He was momentarily safe. His heart pounded as his lungs fought to take in the thin air. He looked down to read the gauge on his power pack.

The gauge stood on empty.

"There's always *something* left!" he cried out. "Even if the dial says nothing—there's always *something*." He switched down the power level to minimum. "Got to save what's left," he said. He looked up.

Two of the verms were entering the circle of light.

"This may not kill them," he panted, "but it'll slow them up some." He shot both of them, took a breath, and ran again for the tent, another coglight cylinder in his free hand.

The rustling all around him told him he should use it. He twisted the cap and heaved the cylinder like a grenade. The result was a crackling bonfire of bursting shells. He raised the Lancer. Even with the power switched down, he still had the ability to stun them on their backs. He had only one coglight left; he had to cover a lot of distance before he used it.

He did not get far. He practically collided with a beetling shell, used the Lancer, and detonated his last light. He was a long way from the tent. He readjusted the power pack, back to its middle position. Why bother to conserve energy? It was all but gone anyway.

He could see them just beyond the circle of light. They were on their hind legs, a forest of legs and antennae. At least he could kill a few more. Possibly he had power to kill three or four more—maybe even five. Who knew?

He crouched and slowly pivoted, trying to be alert to the attack that might come from any direction.

"Steve." A voice came out of the darkness.

His body jerked erect.

"Steve, it's me—George!"

George.

"We want you to be like us, Steve."

"Go to hell!"

"I can see in the dark, Steve. Don't you want to see in the dark?" The voice came from a big verm standing just outside the circle.

Steve took careful aim and fired. The verm went down.

"That wasn't me, Steve." The voice came from another direction now, where half a dozen clustered. Steve fired three times. Three verms went down. He fired a fourth time. But the power was gone.

"None of them was me, Steve." The voice was behind him.

Steve whipped around. A giant verm entered the circle of light.

"Follow me, Steve. I'll take you to a secret place."

Steve pointed the barrel menacingly.

"The tent is good enough for me." Maybe George didn't know the Lancer was empty.

"I wouldn't hurt you, Steve." The creature's triangular head towered a foot above his. "Trust me. I want to show you something." What choice did he have?

"All right," he said. "But don't try anything crazy, or I'll blow right through you."

"I wouldn't hurt you, Steve. You know me." The big verm crossed through the circle of light and passed into darkness.

"Steve?"

Steve followed a few yards behind. As far as he could tell, the other verms were keeping clear of him.

The verm stalked ahead just on the perimeter of his vision.

"You can come closer, Steve," it said.

"What are you going to show me?"

"We're almost there."

The verm stopped.

"It's at your feet, Steve—the something I wanted to show you."

"Where?"

"Walk a little farther."

"I don't see anything."

"Look down."

Something white lay on the sand.

Steve knelt down.

He turned it over.

"Oh, my God!" he cried. "It's George. It's George's body. He's dead and cold. He didn't change at all!"

Steve stood up and howled at the darkness around him.

"If this is George, then who's been talking to me?"

The voice came back at him.

"I wouldn't hurt you, Steve."

Suddenly there were voices all around.

"I wouldn't hurt you, Steve. I wouldn't hurt you, Steve. I wouldn't hurt you, Steve. I wouldn't hurt you, Steve."

Steve covered his ears and knelt.

"You weren't joking; they do talk. They talk, George, and they play gruesome tricks."

"I wouldn't hurt you, Steve." The voices were much nearer.

George looked peaceful, like he was asleep—except for the long gash on his neck.

"Wouldn't hurt you—hurt you—hurt you—"

And he was still wearing his Lancer!

He never would unplug it.

Steve picked it up and made it spit fire.

"Big dumb bugs!" he shouted. "Damned big, dumb bugs!" He whirled and shot and continued to shoot.

WE THREE AND THE STARS

October. It was early evening and very dark as she walked the three blocks from the hospital to her apartment, her crisp nurse's uniform crackling like the leaves beneath her feet. She passed the park—the empty swings sagging, the tennis courts forsaken. Beyond the courts was the park bench—their park bench—too dark to see now. She walked on, past silent houses with darkened windows. People retired early here. What was to keep them up? It was just a small rural town on the edge of an Air Force base.

No moon tonight, she thought, *but lots of stars.* Bright and cold. Odd, how rarely she looked at the stars. Stars above stars above stars. Too high up and far away. For a moment she wondered if it was October up in the stars. Then she realized she was thinking nonsense and continued on to the front door of her apartment.

She was disappointed not to see Richard's car parked in front. Oh, but it was early yet, much too early. He'd have to go through debriefing now that his assignment was finished. She climbed the stairs and let herself in.

Richard's blue eyes and dark wavy hair greeted her from the picture on the nightstand as soon as she switched on the light. She drew a breath. He should be over before ten, and they would leave immediately—that was their plan. That was why she had her nicest things packed; that was why she had taken a leave of absence from her nursing job at the hospital.

The clock on the end table said eight-ten. She looked out the window for Richard's car but saw only the stars.

They had sat together, by chance, on a park bench, nearly a year ago: he to read his newspaper, she to nibble at a sandwich. They hadn't met; they didn't speak. He read his paper while she finished her lunch and went back to work. They met the next day—not by chance. They spoke a lot this time, about life and loneliness and the things that made them laugh. What time was it?

Eight-seventeen. The time didn't matter. They would leave sometime tonight and marry tomorrow. She leaned out the window to see if his car was there, then turned to the photo by her bedside. Richard was different from all the other Air Force pilots she had met, working as she did so close to the base; their happy-go-lucky posturing annoyed her. Richard was always serious, except about his flying partner Al Gordon. She laughed. Zany Al. To listen to Richard, Al had got into more trouble than seemed possible short of court-martial. She smiled happily. Their project had ended now; at last she would meet Al Gordon.

Her arms reached up momentarily, her mouth expanding

into a yawn. She had risen early to pack, too early, really. She yawned again, then shook her head to drive the sleep away as she contemplated her beautifully packed suitcase lying on top of the bed. Suddenly she found herself yawning uncontrollably. It wouldn't hurt to lie down for ten minutes; that way she would be fresh when Richard arrived. She lay fully clothed upon the bed next to her suitcase and closed her eyes. Waves of sleep washed over her. She fell upward toward the heavens, past silver stars pulsing with light, till she ascended to a black place and found Richard there, along with another man, a stranger who kept trying to take his head off as a kind of joke. She smiled and knew it must be Al Gordon.

She woke abruptly. The clock said a quarter to twelve. She had overslept by hours. Where was Richard? Maybe he had come and she had not heard him. Maybe he was waiting outside in his car. She peered through the window but saw only the stars.

The phone rang.

"Richard?"

No one there. Just a dial tone.

"I'll call him," she said suddenly. Something must have happened. The number at the base. She had never used it. Where was it? In her purse.

Six rings. Eight. Please answer.

"Three-Fourteen," said a crisp voice.

"What?"

"Air Force Three-Fourteen, Corporal Jackson speaking."

"This is Ellen Crane. Please help me. I'm looking for my fiancé, Major Richard Lockyer. He was supposed to finish his mission today. He should have been through by now. Can you check to see if he's still there?"

"I'll see, ma'am. One minute."

He was probably still at work. Maybe the debriefing took longer than he had planned. She hoped he wouldn't be annoyed for calling him like this. She hoped—

"Ma'am?

"Yes."

"I have no information on Major Lockyer."

"Can't you tell me at least if he's left the base?"

She heard voices in the background. A deep voice. A softer voice.

"Maybe you should call tomorrow, ma'am."

"Why? Why should I call tomorrow? What can you tell me tomorrow that you can't tell me tonight?"

"The department that Major Lockyer works for is not answering their phone. I think they're all closed up for the night. You should call tomorrow, ma'am. Good night, ma'am." The phone hung up.

That's how they act when someone dies, she thought. *They never tell you over the phone. They make you wait until morning, when you're less hysterical, when they can send someone to hold your hand.*

You're being silly. Even now he is probably on his way. Even now—

She lifted the phone again. This time to call the police. He could have had an accident. He could have crashed his car speeding to his marriage.

A desk sergeant spoke at the other end.

"My fiancé, Richard Lockyer," she explained. "We're supposed to get married. He isn't here. Can you tell me anything? Was there an accident?"

A pause. What would she say if the sergeant told her Richard was killed? Please, God, don't let Richard be killed. Don't let him be hurt—

"No one of that description has been reported in any accident," the voice came back.

"Then where is he? We were supposed to be married."

"Maybe he changed his mind."

She hung up the phone.

He wouldn't do that. He would never do that.

But why didn't he call?

The doorbell rang.

She flew to the door and flung it open.

Two men in gray suits stood in the doorway.

"Miss Crane?"

"Yes."

"My name is Drake," said one, showing her a badge in a wallet. "This is Reynolds. May we come in?" She stepped back, and they seemed to fill the room.

"Is it about Major Lockyer?" She was nearly in tears.

"Yes, it is."

"Is he dead?"

"Don't *you* know?"

"No, no, I don't."

"May we look around?"

"Yes, are you from the police?"

"No, Miss Crane."

"Where is Richard?" she asked.

"He was on a mission. Something went wrong with the mission. That's all I can tell you."

"Is Richard dead? Is he injured?"

"Something went wrong. That's all we can say."

They looked at everything in the apartment, even under the bed.

"It isn't here," Reynolds said.

"Is Richard all right?"

"No," said Drake. His eyes fastened on the framed photograph on the nightstand. "Sorry to disturb you."

And they walked into the October night.

Her beautifully packed suitcase still lay on the bed. Richard's picture still smiled from the nightstand. Richard's picture—maybe that's all she had now—that and the stars that seemed to come into the room.

The phone rang.

"Ellen?"

It was Richard.

"Ellen? Ellen?"

Richard's voice.

"Thank God," was all she could say, over and over. "Thank God."

"Ellen, something's happened."

"What happened, Richard? Richard?" For a moment he was missing again. "Richard."

"I can't talk now. Listen, Ellen, it's nearly midnight. Meet me at the park in an hour, by our bench. Don't let anyone see you. Don't tell anybody you've heard from me."

"Some men were here."

"Are they gone?"

"Yes."

"Meet me at the park. Don't let anyone follow you."

"What's wrong, Richard?"

"They want Gordon, Ellen. But they won't find him."

"Richard—"

But the phone had stopped speaking.

It didn't matter. Richard was all right. Nothing mattered but that.

• • •

She found the streets empty of all but leaves as she waded through shadows toward the park. The bench—their bench—lay buried in shadows, too. All was so dark that even the stars seemed to have gone away.

Something stepped out of the shadows.

"Ellen."

Richard's arms held her. It was too dark to see his face, but she knew Richard's arms.

"What's happening, Richard?"

"I took Gordon, Ellen. They're after me because I've got Gordon."

"I don't understand."

"I was flying, Ellen—Gordon was with me—but not a plane. It wasn't a plane, Ellen. We were piloting—it doesn't matter now—we were piloting a spacecraft, heading for something that was sending out signals. We were supposed to take pictures of it.

"We started our cameras when the object was nearly in sight; the next thing we knew, our lights were gone. We heard the hatch open. Bodies crept in. They took us somewhere—a dark, narrow place—it reminded me of—I don't know what. They kept repeating the same words over and over. They did something to Gordon.

"Then I was back in the spacecraft at the controls. I didn't know Gordon was in there with me. I knew only that I was over the base, about to land, the thing they told me shouting in my head like an alarm. I climbed out as soon as I landed; they covered Gordon right away and put us into an ambulance—both of us still in our space suits—that's important—and drove us to base hospital. They left Gordon in the ambulance while a couple of them took me inside and got my space suit off and began to examine me. I tried to tell them the thing that was buzzing in my brain, but they paid no attention. I guess I got a little crazy. They ran to get help. They had clothes there waiting for me. I saw a white coat hanging from a hook on the door. I put it over my clothes and left by the window. The ambulance with Gordon was still outside."

"Why did you run away?"

"They were going to pull Gordon out of his space suit."

"Why shouldn't they?"

"They mustn't do that. That's the thing I was told over and over. Gordon has to remain in that space suit."

"Why, Richard?"

"He has to remain in the space suit."

"Why? Why should he stay in the space suit? He's dead, isn't he? How can it matter?"

Richard's voice lowered to a whisper.

"Maybe not so dead, Ellen."

"Then the quicker they pull off the suit, the better he'll be. If he's alive, he has to eat. He has to breathe. Alive or dead— why should he stay in a space suit? It doesn't make sense."

"That's what they said, Ellen. They burned it on my brain."

"Richard. Bring Gordon back. Let the doctors look at him."

"They must not pull off that space suit!"

"Why not?"

"Terrible things will happen if they do."

"What?"

"I don't know . . ." his voice faltered.

An early-morning breeze arose from nowhere. She held him, silently, and felt the air wash over them. Only they existed—herself, Richard, the wind, and, of course, the night.

The breeze stopped after a while.

"Where have you got him?" she asked softly.

"In an abandoned farmhouse a few miles outside of town." He was calm now. "It's fenced off from the public, surrounded by empty fields and sycamore trees. I used to play there as a kid. I drove a fair distance after I hid Gordon's body. I left the ambulance on a side street and caught a ride here. Will you help me, Ellen?"

"What can I do?"

"We've got to get Gordon away from them. There's no time now; it's nearly daylight. It will have to be tonight. In your car. They won't suspect a woman alone. We'll put him in the trunk. You'll drive him somewhere where they can't find him, then phone me to join you. Meet me at the farmhouse as soon as it's dark."

"Richard, call the base. Tell them everything. They'll listen to you."

"What if they don't listen?" His grip fastened on her arm. "We may have to hide out for a couple of days. Bring water and food—and blankets; it gets cold in that farmhouse—also, any money you have. If you get there before me, I've got Gordon inside, covered up. Don't look at him."

"What are you talking about? I'm a nurse. I'm used to . . . sights."

"Not this one, Ellen. No one can look at this one and remain sane."

"Richard!"

"I'll try to be there before you. But if not, remember, whatever you do, don't look at Gordon."

"What you're asking is crazy. We are breaking the law. You took an ambulance; you stole Gordon's body. On top of that, you don't even trust me to do the things I've been trained to do. I don't care how bad Gordon looks. If I'm going to help you, I need to know what I'm getting myself into."

"You're right, Ellen. It's better if I do it alone. I can rent a car, alter my appearance. I'll call you once I've got Gordon safely away."

She laid her arm on his shoulder. "How do I get to this farm-house?"

"You sure?"

"I'm sure."

"Take Sycamore Road to the end. There's a hole in the chain-link fence directly across from the road marker. You can't see the hole till you get behind the trees. Once through the fence walk straight till you come against a wooden post. Then bear right. You'll come upon the farmhouse suddenly out of the trees. Above all, make certain you aren't followed. Got that?" She nodded.

"Ellen"—he took her hand—"I'm begging you to humor me in this other thing. Please promise me you won't look at Gordon. Trust me, Ellen. Please."

She bit her lip. "All right," she said. "I promise."

"It will be light in a few hours. I'll have to hide somewhere."

"Do you want me to drop you at that farmhouse, now?"

"No. I need to be close to a phone. Not your house—it will be watched. I'll try to get them looking in the wrong direction."

She was beginning to see him now in the pale flush of the false dawn. He looked tired and—frail, so frail. He held her close for an instant.

"Richard——" she started to say.

But he was gone.

She had seen it dozens of times in patients that sustained injuries. The wild talk, the paranoia.

"But at least he's alive," she said aloud. Richard was in trouble; that was all that she knew. If he went to jail for breaking the law——well, so would she. She sat for a moment on the park bench——their park bench——and smiled. This day was to be their honeymoon.

• • •

The first thing she did when she got home was to put together a bag of groceries, along with a parcel containing a flashlight, blankets, and her old Girl Scout canteen, all of which she stowed in the trunk of her car, beside her beautifully packed suitcase. She slept some, and spent the day in her apartment, resting to be refreshed against the night. Drake, the government man, stopped by at noon but left after a few minutes. As the day wore on, she was aware of cars and vans moving down her street, parking along the curb and waiting.

Just before sunset, she drove to the hospital and stopped inside at the nurses' station to extend her leave of absence, then headed downtown.

When she had driven the length of the business district, she turned suddenly down a residential street, making certain no one followed her. Cautiously, she guided her car back to the main street, then onto the highway. Except for an occasional car coming the other way, hers was the only car on the road. Finally she reached Sycamore Road.

The October sun scorched the fields red as it settled into the Earth. She left her car alongside the culvert where the street dead-ended and forced her way beneath a forest of branches till she came up against the chain-link fence, invisible behind the clusters of dusty sycamores.

She found the hole only because Richard had told her where it would be, drowned in foliage. Beyond the hole she waded through a wilderness of closely packed trees, bushes, and vines, suddenly coming upon something wooden, nearly smothered in the mounds of dusty vegetation, and knew it must be the farmhouse. Brushing aside the creepers, she gained the porch and pushed her way in through the partially opened wooden door. It was an old, shabby farmhouse, of one big room and several smaller ones, nearly dark for the foliage outside, full of dust, dry as October. And something else, not of the farmland.

In a corner of the main big room something lay covered up by an old blanket. She could just make out what must be the bulge of the helmeted space suit. Dust motes floated in the disturbed air, almost like stars swirling. Maybe it was the flat, dead air that made her feel a giddy sense of motion. She took a breath to steady herself. Richard would join her soon. Maybe by then he would have come to his senses. Maybe even now he was reporting to the base. Maybe.

The sun had gone out of the room, and she switched on her flashlight, scattering shadows, playing the beam around the room, all except for the corner. Everything of value had long ago been removed or rotted away. What remained were the broken things that peel off people's lives. The frayed and tattered ghosts of what might have been window curtains. The skeleton of a bureau. The fragments of a chair. For a moment she darted the beam onto the wrapped thing in the corner. And Gordon.

Why was she here—alone with a corpse? Why was she

breaking the law? For what? To humor a man in shock, a man with delusional fantasies?

But the man was Richard.

She stared at the splintered walls, the floor littered with blown leaves, the dark mass of foliage growing through the glassless window and partially opened door. And she thought of the tattered things that peeled off *her* life—her life before Richard.

She hadn't wanted to become a nurse. She wanted to study art. Medicine was too close a reminder of what happened on that field trip with the Girl Scouts. A nurse can always get a job, her mother told her. You have to take care of yourself because you might never know. She went on to nursing and found she enjoyed it. Nursing became her life. And now Richard was her life, just as her Girl Scouts had been, and her years at college.

The room grew colder. She wrapped herself inside a blanket and made herself comfortable on the floor.

It hadn't been a bad life so far. The only really bad thing that ever happened to her was on that field trip to the science fair; that is where she saw those things—babies that should have been teething and crying, but floated white and wrinkled in jars of alcohol, curls of unraveled skin fluttering dreamily from tiny exposed bones. Because of this she nearly fell apart; she left the Girl Scouts, and her mother kept her out of school for a semester. Years later she became a nurse.

Now she thought of all the happy movies she ever saw, and the funny things that happened to her at nursing school, and how good it would be when she and Richard were married. She yawned and wrapped her blanket more tightly around her. She forgot the jars of alcohol, and she forgot Gordon.

She woke because something was making sounds. Stray

shafts of moonlight found their way down to Earth to steal through the gaps among the dusty foliage and into the farmhouse, so the room was not wholly dark. Moreover, her flashlight, still turned on, lay on the floor a few inches away, fruitlessly scattering its beam against the splintered wall.

Something was making sounds, a kind of heavy breathing, painfully loud in the compressed silence. Her mouth went dry; icy spasms invaded her back. She couldn't breathe; she couldn't move. Yet her body shook; her whole body shook. The sounds grew louder. The flashlight lay a few feet away. Could she crawl over and get it? Did she want to see what breathed?

She made her body move, but it shook so she could not at first hold the flashlight. Chilling waves coursed up and down her trembling body as she made her fingers grip the handle.

Rising to her feet, she deliberately aimed the beam straight at the sound. The blanket over the body was heaving up and down. She looked at her watch and mentally made a note. At 3:10 A.M, her training told her, the body began to breathe. Gordon's covered body stirred with motion. Like rats crawling under the blanket. Ghostly fear gave way to the rational. Maybe that's what it was—rats. As awful as it was, she had to know. Gingerly she crept over, her flashlight gripped in one hand, the other hand extended till, with thumb and forefinger, she lifted a fold of the blanket. The flashlight beam illuminated a glimpse of padded space suit, the shoulder and chest—the fabric alive—rippling back and forth—like wet glistening skin. The head, still in shadow, was turning slowly into the light. But before this happened she fainted onto the floor.

It took her a while to remember where she was when she awoke. And when she did, she didn't want to. It was still dark, and something stood over her. It was better, her mind screamed, to lie here, and never to move, never to move or think or be, because this is a thing that should not happen. But maybe it could. Something made a noise.

"Gordon?" she whispered.

"They nearly had me." Richard's voice. "I couldn't get away till a few minutes ago. They tried to follow me, but I lost them. I'm sure I lost them. Ellen, where is he? Why have you moved him?"

"Moved him?" was all she could say. "Moved him?"

"Gordon. He's gone."

• • •

"We've got to find him. How? How?"

"It's out of our hands now. Call the base. Let them deal with it."

"No. No. I can't. Whatever they did to him up there, they must have done for a reason."

"It must be a horrible reason."

"Whatever it is, we've got to find him. What happened tonight?"

"I fell asleep. I woke up when I heard the breathing. I pulled the blanket back a little. Gordon's space suit was . . . quivering like live skin."

"Did you see his face, Ellen?"

"No. I fainted."

"Thank goodness." He slammed his hand against the wall. "Who are they?" he exploded. "What do they want? Maybe it's some experiment in genetic engineering. Maybe they want to make Gordons out of all of us!"

"You say we need to find him. How will we find him?"

"I don't know. I don't want you even to look at him. I don't want anyone to look at him."

She put her arms around Richard's shoulders.

"Let's wait till morning, darling. We can't do anything till morning."

They sat together on Ellen's blanket, his arm around her waist. The night air blew through the partially opened door.

"I never told you, Ellen, but I used to have dreams about beings that changed people into monsters. When I was eleven, I was horrified nearly into a nervous breakdown by a science fiction picture I saw.

"And there was the principal of the high school I went to—I used to work for him—cut lawns, clean up. One day he invited me inside the house and showed me what was in one of the closets. It was nothing but a bag of golf clubs. But those golf clubs scared me half out of my mind. We moved right away to another neighborhood, another school. But for months I expected the principal to come and take me back to that closet."

His arm grew tighter around her. "All my life I've been afraid of—I don't know what."

"I have been too, darling. I saw something at a science fair that frightened me so much my mother kept me out of school."

"Gordon, too, was terrified as a child; he wouldn't say how or what did it. He became the class clown; otherwise, he would have exploded, he told me. Want to hear something else? I've had a phrase in my head, nearly as long as I can remember: Fear rules the universe."

She moved closer to him. "Richard, that sounds so familiar . . . I've heard that, too, or maybe I dreamed it. It's so odd. You and I and Gordon . . ."

"I'm not even sure why they kept us in the space program. Both of us made a lot of blunders early on, but everyone just seemed to ignore them."

"Richard, there's someone outside."

"What?"

"I hear someone outside. Listen."

Something cracked a dry board on the front porch.

"He's come back. I hadn't thought of that."

The partially opened door began to open wider.

Richard snapped off the flashlight. "It's better if you don't see him. Gordon, Gordon, in here!"

The room erupted with blinding light.

"Richard!"

"Close your eyes, Ellen. Don't look at him. Gordon, in here."

"Who are all these men? Let go. Let go I say!"

· · ·

She sat in a black-padded armchair in a white room, empty of furnishings save for a desk, a larger chair, and meaningless modern art on bleak white walls. Behind the desk, on the larger chair, sat a man with a smooth and quiet voice.

"Feel okay now?" he asked. The nameplate on the desk said COLONEL SHELDON.

"Yes. Much better."

"It's always upsetting to be arrested." He smiled, and studied his watch. "That was nearly three hours ago. You were fed, made comfortable, treated well?"

"Very well."

"Well enough to talk to me?"

She nodded.

He opened a manila folder before him on the desk, consulted the sheaves of paper inside, then returned to her.

"I understand you are a nurse. Did you examine Major Gordon's body?"

"No."

"Did you, ah, study his face?"

"I haven't seen it. Richard—Major Lockyer—told me not to look."

He wrote something down.

"Miss Crane, what has Major Lockyer told you of his work here?"

"He said he pilots spaceships." She knew it sounded wrong even before she saw the raised eyebrows.

"Spaceships. I see." He wrote something more. "It makes sense now. Miss Crane," he said gently. "You know, don't you, that your fiancé is addicted to watching cheap science-fiction movies?"

"No."

"Then you probably are not aware that he suffered a nervous breakdown from watching a science-fiction movie when he was eleven years old."

"Yes. He told me about that."

"Did he tell you that when he was sixteen, he was expelled from school for insisting that the principal was an alien from outer space?"

"No. Yes. He talked a little about it—at the farmhouse."

"That seems to be his pattern, Miss Crane, to retreat into science fiction when life becomes unbearable. Miss Crane, the Air Force doesn't conduct spaceflights. And spaceflights don't originate at Air Force bases. Your fiancé and Major Gordon were testing an experimental plane. There was an explosion, which killed Major Gordon. Major Lockyer adverted to science fiction because he can't accept the fact that his best friend is dead."

"No," she said. "Major Gordon is changed into something horrible. I saw his space suit. It was like skin."

"You saw this?"

"Yes. The skin moved back and forth."

He consulted the sheaves of paper once more. He seemed annoyed with her when he finally answered.

"Miss Crane, that space suit is made of a synthetic that looks like skin. It has a built-in respiratory process. It is supposed to move."

"But the whole body moved after I fainted. The whole body walked out the door!"

"I'm afraid Major Lockyer carried it away while you slept."

"Gordon—"

"Gordon is dead, Miss Crane. The body needs to be buried. We need to find out from Major Lockyer where he hid it. Did he say anything—I mean anything short of science fiction—as to why he took the body?"

"No, only that the space people told him he had to keep Gordon inside the space suit. May I see Major Lockyer now?"

He closed the file on the desk.

"Major Lockyer is restricted to base pending further investigation."

"When can I see him?"

"I'm afraid not for a while." He smiled and took her hand. "I wouldn't worry much. We'll soon have him well again. Good night, Miss Crane. Someone will drive you home."

She let herself be led from the room at the base, conveyed to a jeep, driven to her apartment. All the time she was as silent as the man who drove her home. It was not until she was inside her apartment with the door safely locked that she felt she could breathe freely. Now as she stood by her bedside, the useless suitcase again on the bed, the picture of Richard, unwinking from the nightstand, she pondered the question she was reluctant to ask.

Why, if the Air Force knew Richard was such a mental cripple, did they accept him in the first place?

• • •

It is winter now. October's leaves lie clothed in snow outside the hospital walls. The wind blows cold, to sift the snow like laundered sheets on a patient's bed. The wind sings as it blows, into a lullaby of air and snow. Work, Ellen, fold your sheets as the wind bestows the snow.

Be mindful of your patients, Ellen. Work hard and wonder less where Richard is. Work, Ellen. Fold down the sheets like drifts of snow.

Snow piles on your park bench now. They sweep it clean as often as it falls, yet more will come. Sit on your bench while you can and write the letters which are never answered. Read your paper in the lull between the snow; search the stiff pages for reports of something too terrible to be believed stalking the shadows at night. There is nothing in the news. Go back to the hospital. Mind your patients, Ellen. Unfold your sheets and cure your sick, then hurry back to your park bench to scan the pages once more.

Finally, it comes. On a leaden, weary, windswept day, the rising wind gathers the finely fallen snow into goblin mounds as you sit on your bench unfolding the chalky pages of a frozen newspaper. What is it the pages whisper to you? Merely an account of a military maneuver in the depths of night near an abandoned warehouse. Something covered by a blanket is carried out and hurriedly taken away in a guarded vehicle. That is all. Only a drill. It is enough. You know now.

Sleep, Ellen. Sleep, Town. Sleep, World. All is well. They have Gordon now.

• • •

The snow gave way to rain that Tuesday morning when the government men arrived at her door.

"Remember us, Miss Crane—Reynolds and Drake? Major Lockyer wants to see you. Can you come with us for an extended trip?"

"I'm nearly late for work. I can't just leave."

"We've cleared it with the hospital. Please come with us, Miss Crane. We'll wait while you pack a bag."

"Major Lockyer is waiting for you."

She threw some clothes into her suitcase.

They put her in a closed car and drove her to the base, past the buildings, to an airfield. All the while the rain fell till her plane rose above the clouds, only later to reenter the rain when the plane landed outside Washington. Another closed car drove her to a well-known building.

They put her in a room like the room she sat in when she spoke with Colonel Sheldon, except the walls held no modern art. A man named Colonel Edwards sat facing her.

"I understand that you've never been a parent, Miss Crane." She nodded.

"Nonetheless, wouldn't you admit that a good parent protects his children from painful and upsetting knowledge—like death and disease?"

"I suppose so."

"I ask you, what good does it do a five-year-old to know its mother might fall apart with cancer? Don't you agree?"

It was a different room and a different face, yet, oddly

enough, the voice wasn't so very different. The two of them—
Ellen and the new face—sat staring at each other across a sim-
ulated wooden desk. Just the two of them, each in a padded
chair. No windows, so she could not see the rain.

"The government, you know, tries to be a good parent. How
does it benefit anybody to worry about—well, visitors from
other planets, for example? Why frighten and confuse people?"

"There is such a thing as truth," she hazarded.

"People don't want truth; they want security. Ask anyone
what he thinks of flying saucers. You'll get an almost hysterical
skepticism."

"They told me Major Lockyer made the whole thing up."

"That was to protect you, Miss Crane. Things are different
now. What I am about to say is classified. If you reveal any part
of what I am about to tell you, you may be arrested. Do you
understand?"

She nodded.

"When Major Lockyer returned from his mission, he and
Major Gordon were put aboard an ambulance and taken to base
hospital. Major Lockyer was brought in while Gordon's covered body was left in the ambulance."

He paused.

"It was left there because the ones who put Gordon's body
into the ambulance were reluctant to handle it again. Does that
sound probable?"

"I don't know what's probable," she said.

"By the time a suitable team was assembled to deal with the
body it had already been taken by Major Lockyer."

Again the pause.

"It took us a while to find it. A passerby observed something
crawling through a vent under an abandoned warehouse. He

called the police. They called us. We sent out a team to secure the body and flew it to a certain facility, where it was examined."

"You took it out of the space suit?" she interrupted.

"No. It was evident that the space suit is now part of him. We didn't take it out." He busied himself for a moment with a glass paperweight on his desk.

"Gordon affected everyone right away——like a high-pitched sound or a bad smell. It was worse for the ones guarding the laboratory where the body was housed. One night a guard deserted."

"Is Gordon alive or dead?" she asked.

"The man inside the space suit is dead. The space suit itself may be alive——in some sense."

He adverted a moment to his glass paperweight. "We've got the body stretched out on a table in a sealed room. It just lies there——till someone comes in. Then it half rises up to stare at him.

"That's precisely the way things are——were, until yesterday, when someone thought of bringing Major Lockyer into the room. That's where you come in, Miss Crane."

"Me? How?"

"Gordon sat up and spoke your name."

• • •

A uniformed soldier courteously escorted her to an apartment in the same building as the office she had just left. It too was clean, brightly lit, windowless.

Richard sat on a sofa.

When they could talk again she sat beside him.

"They believe me now." His arms were around her. "They

always did, but not officially. I'm free. But they want something. I don't know what. There's supposed to be a meeting; they say they need to talk with both of us."

"What did they do to you in the hospital? Are you all right?"

"Yes, I'm all right. They didn't do anything except ask questions. I'm fine now that you're with me, except that phrase we talked about keeps running through my head. 'Fear rules the universe.' Over and over. I can't get rid of it. Another thing. The principal—in high school . . . I'm beginning to remember little pieces of the things the principal told me. But I can't get any of it to make sense. You know, Ellen, all I really want is you and a place away from the stars."

"We'll have it all, darling. We'll have everything."

"That phrase; I just can't get that phrase out of my head."

"Don't think about it now. When is the meeting supposed to start?"

"At three." He consulted his watch. "We've a couple of hours. What would you like to do?"

Until the time of the meeting she sat with Richard on the sofa, holding his hand.

● ● ●

A gathering of impressive men—in uniform and civilian suits—sat around an oval conference table in a well-lighted room. Among the ones in civilian clothes she recognized a certain famous man. Another man she recognized, also a civilian, bald, red-faced and robust, laughing and whispering to a knot of men standing by him. She, too, sat at the table, Richard next to her, nodding as introductions were made all around.

The Robust Man spoke first.

"Miss Crane," he said, laughing, bending his bald head forward, "we're going to let our hair down with you." Nobody else laughed.

One who introduced himself as General Wilson took over. His eyes focused on Ellen and Richard.

"I'll tell you about the space people," he said. "They call themselves the Grider. They're people." He narrowed his eyes. "I suppose they could be people. We started picking up their signals from outside our atmosphere just after the war. We tried signaling them back, but they didn't respond, so we kept our ears open and pretended they didn't exist. This was our policy for years—we listened, we sent back signals, we pretended they didn't exist.

"Everything changed about three years ago. They sent us a message one day that rocked us on our heels and put our entire military on alert. The Grider, it seems, have the ability to project images from deep space. What they showed us convinced the President and the Joint Chiefs, convinced the top military and the Secretary of State.

"Apparently, some power in the galaxy is attacking and destroying every life-form in its path. The Grider are in its path. So is Earth. The Grider say they alone cannot stop the menace. They need our help. They'd already taken some steps to defeat this destructive power. Two young men were applying for our astronaut program, they said: Lockyer and Gordon."

"Me!" Richard started from his chair.

"Yes, both were to be accepted. Both were to be trained for a secret space mission. It was the only way to stop the invasion coming at us. They didn't say any more. They only showed us more pictures, very convincing pictures. The Grider never say more than they feel they have to. I suppose it is part of their psychology. Considering the magnitude of the crisis, we felt they asked for very little—two of our astronauts to help them save the galaxy from destruction." He nodded to Colonel Edwards.

"Everyone was curious as to why the Grider chose you two, Major Lockyer," Colonel Edwards resumed. "They were examined, minutely, Miss Crane. Neither had any knowledge of beings from another world. In the interest of security, we told them they were part of a secret team to investigate objects in space; we created a special unit—military, you see—not civilian—attached to the Air Force, not to NASA. During this time we had no further communication from the Grider.

"Until last October, when they sent another message, giving a navigational position and specifying a certain time. 'We are waiting for Gordon,' it said. 'We are waiting for Lockyer.'"

General Wilson spoke. "Colonel Edwards told you about Gordon saying your name when Major Lockyer went to view the body. What you don't know is this. The same day, the Grider sent us a message telling us what they want."

"They want you, Miss Crane," said the Robust Man.

"Me."

"They want you and Major Lockyer to go into space together."

"Why? Why do they want me?"

The bald Robust Man answered curtly. "They say you are necessary, Miss Crane. You, Major Lockyer. Oh, yes, and Gordon."

Ellen studied the faces at the table. They were all looking at her.

"If you're worried about your life, Miss Crane, we think that these beings, the Grider, wouldn't go to so much trouble just to kill someone," said the Robust Man.

"What if they change me into something like Gordon?" she asked.

"Really, Miss Crane, we hardly think so," The Robust Man laughed. "I really think we should trust them."

"What I'm here for, Miss Crane," said the Famous Man, "is to authorize your journey into space."

"Of course you don't have to go," said General Wilson.

"Though the fate of our world may depend on what you do up there," said the Robust Man.

"It's your decision," said the Famous Man.

"The fate of our world," Ellen repeated. She stared at the faces around the room, her eyes coming at last to rest on Richard, sitting next to her. "I'll go," she said.

· · ·

The best part was that space wasn't black and gloomy as she'd supposed. It was gorgeous with stars. Wearing white space suits, they occupied adjoining seats in the cockpit, Richard piloting, all of heaven revealed through the wraparound windows. After the initial thrust all was perfectly, motionlessly still. Takeoff had made her only slightly giddy for a moment. The hasty training they had given her must have helped. Now, being free of Earth's atmosphere, she surrendered herself to the glory of unending stars.

She wanted to shout at so much beauty, at least to shout to Richard, but he was talking on the radio to the men at the base. She settled back to drink it all in. She had never thought of heaven as a real place of light and quiet.

The only disquieting note was their fellow passenger, stowed in the baggage chamber adjacent to the cockpit. She reached over to make sure that the hatch was firmly shut.

Richard droned on over the radio, with someone from the base interrupting every few minutes to ask questions or give instructions. She returned to the window and the stars.

How she had stared at the stars that October night when it all began—as she hurried home to meet Richard for their wedding and honeymoon. Now here they were, drifting through fields of stars.

She settled back farther in her seat. She had nothing to do while she waited for Richard to get off the radio, nothing to do but savor the stars.

Something hid the stars.

The cockpit shook.

"You, at the base," Richard shouted. "Something's happening. Why don't you answer? Hello!"

The cockpit went dark, utterly, completely black.

Richard screamed in the darkness.

"What's wrong?" she cried.

"I'm remembering things—terrible things."

"What, Richard, what?"

"That movie I saw as a kid—it wasn't a movie. That's when they got me.

"And the high school principal—he was one of them. The thing in his closet he made me remember as a bag of golf clubs—it was shriveled and black and half a machine. It had once been a man. Oh, my God, it was so dry and shriveled. And it wasn't in a closet. It wasn't a closet at all. Oh, my God!"

"Lockyer," the voice came over the radio. "What's happening? What's happening?"

All collapsed in screams and darkness.

• • •

"Fear rules the universe, children," Mrs. Webster, the Girl Scout leader, insisted. "Pay attention. You must observe *everything* at the science fair." She sounded so cross. Or was it Dr. Bradley, from Sunday school? No, now that she thought of it, the voice was more like the teacher's from the third grade. What was her name?

"Outer planets." They all spoke at once—The Girl Scout leader, Dr. Bradley, Teacher, their outlines glowing like neon lights right in front of her. "Far without time." This time she recognized Dr. Bradley's spectacles. It was Dr. Bradley speaking.

The science fair unwrapped all around her, exhibit after exhibit, perched on curious metal counters—lights, bottles, apparatuses that made no sense. And she. Was she lying or sitting? It was hard to see. Sometimes she thought she was standing. Now which one spoke?

"They come."

She was sure now. The voices came from bright glass cylinders on one of the tables. She missed the first words, because she had to bend very low to hear, but it was Mrs. Webster's voice, coming from something that wore a blue-and-white-checked gingham dress. That is how she knew it was Mrs. Webster. The others—Teacher and Dr. Bradley—were speaking, too, but they only made sounds she could not understand. The three of them—Teacher, Dr. Bradley and Mrs. Webster—seemed to have wrapped white gauze around their faces, while the room filled with the reflection of water.

"They make us explode," Dr. Bradley explained. She was sure it was Dr. Bradley speaking this time, though she could not see Dr. Bradley's dark spectacles or Mrs. Webster's checked dress because of the gauze bandages around them.

"We explode, but we do not die. We cannot die."

"They make us explode," said Dr. Bradley, nodding his spectacles.

"Who are you?"

"We are the Grider."

She was looking up at them. Each inhabited a towering glass cylinder filled with fluid. The gauze around their bodies began to unravel, floating dreamily as swaying tongues of white skin. She smelled alcohol. Mrs. Webster, Dr. Bradley, Teacher—they were the horrid dead babies preserved in alcohol.

Instantly she knew. She had been here before, as a child—talking with these things. There had never been a science fair. Her mind had made it into a science fair—as Richard's had made his horror into a set of golf clubs. She covered her eyes.

"Something coming." The voices cut through her fear.

"What? What is coming?" She removed her hands from her face and stood on tiptoe to see them. The gauze unwound.

"We chose you as a child." Teacher was a tall peeling thing in a rising cylinder. She had to crane her neck to see its face—Dr. Bradley's face. "We chose you as a child. For this moment."

"Me? What for? What for?"

"For something coming. Something out there. We chose you."

The thing in the cylinder talked from Mrs. Webster's checked dress.

"We have modified your vehicle."

"We have an instrument to focus your thoughts."

"I don't understand."

"We have prepared you to meet them."

"Who are they? Why should I meet them?" The liquid in the

bottles turned so bright she had to shield her eyes. "What should I do?" she cried.

"Stop them." The voice was a high-pitched whine.

"How far away are they?"

"You will meet them where there is neither time nor distance."

"It will take no time at all; you are going beyond time."

"You will be simply there." The light was going.

"Who said that?" Ellen shivered. The lights burned out. Most of the science fair was collapsed now into wrong angles. In the dark surrounding the table with the bright cylinders, she sensed shadowy forms moving rapidly about.

She tried to pierce the collapsing darkness. "Richard," she demanded. "Where is Richard?"

"He is alive aboard your vehicle. You will not see him because you must be alone." The lights came up for a second more. "Fear rules the universe," someone said. She saw them now as horrid dead babies in little glass bottles—swirls of peeling skin exposing tiny bones.

The science fair dissolved. She was in the spaceship in her seat next to Richard's. The lights were off, but the faint starlight through the windows outlined the figure seated at the controls. She turned to the seat beside her.

"They got me away into their ship," she said. "But I'm back now." She took his hand. "They're gone." She squeezed the hand held out to her. "They said I wouldn't see you because I had to be alone. What did they mean by that, Richard? Did you get all that? Richard, why don't you answer?" The angle of the helmet prevented her seeing the face. But she knew, even before the lights came on, that Gordon sat at the controls.

• • •

He is safe in the ship with me, her inner voice told her, *tucked away in a corridor or crawl space. He is safe because he is part of this mission, and they said he would be safe and on board.* She glanced around the tiny cockpit chamber but saw only darkness. *Richard is here with me, somewhere.*

She gazed straight ahead to lose herself through the window. Streams of light shot toward her and past her as the spaceship plummeted on. *Richard is safe, and I am safe; and whatever this thing is that pilots the ship, it is safe, too.*

From her position in the adjoining seat she could see only the profile, slightly glistening in the subdued light, squatting like a limp crab over the controls. The vast dark head lay mercifully in shadow. Outside, the lights streaked by.

"Why us?" she asked the lights. "Richard and Gordon—and me? Why did those horrors choose us? Why couldn't they do whatever had to be done?"

You heard them, Ellen: they explode.

Yes, she thought, *they explode, even inside their glass cylinders, and I suppose we don't explode.* "Maybe we don't," she said aloud. All she knew for certain was that she was rushing out to meet something the horrors feared. Whatever it was must be worse still.

She felt them long before they came into view, the way one feels a disease. First the depression that precedes a malaise. Then the sick headache turning to nausea. At last the wrenching illness that all but threw her stomach out of her mouth.

"I thought the worst thing was that you died!" She screamed. A wash of memories overflowed her from the science fair.

"But you don't die," she remembered. "You don't die at all. They keep you alive—forever. They hurt you and hurt you—forever."

Now she saw them. Through the window. Streamlined bodies dashing at her. Not spaceships, as in all the science-fiction movies—but things with fish eyes and fish faces, trailing streamers of whipcord appendages, flinging a kind of palpable atmosphere as they streamed past her.

Fear that doesn't end. Forever. Shrieking fear that goes on and on. And sadness and being alone. And terrible things happening to people you love, and you can't do anything about it. All the things that drive people screaming mad.

Dying is not the worst thing, her insides screamed. Nor is it the pain—the body can faint with pain. It is that other thing—being helpless in fear. They keep coming. It would take an army—an air force—to defeat them. No, nothing could defeat them. They were all around her, dragging her through panic fears to which she couldn't even put a name.

I'm exploding like the Grider, she thought, *but inside where no one can see it. They're killing me with fear.*

Whose fear? said something like Richard's voice. Whose fear is it, Ellen?

Fear? Her fear, of course. Whose else could it be?

No, Ellen. It couldn't all be your fear.

It couldn't be all her fear.

Then whose fear am I feeling? She gazed out at the things swarming around her—and her eyes met something beyond them, pursuing them like a shadow. Only the seat belt kept her from collapsing out of the seat.

It is their *fear I am feeling. Their* fear. *They* are afraid. *They are not advancing. They are fleeing. They are fleeing something they* fear.

That is why they will destroy whatever is in their path. In their haste to get away they will destroy us because there is no weapon to stop them.

Fear is a weapon. Richard's voice. Fear rules the universe. Get more fear.

More fear?

Much more fear. What gives you fear?

Something looking in the window. Being buried alive. No.

She turned to the thing at the controls. Deliberately she put her face into its, their plastic bubbles almost touching—like a kiss—and stared long into the bulging eyes.

The scream inside her nearly tore her head off. "No!" she screamed. "No! No!" She screamed till she thought she would die, then screamed again, her screams shooting round the cabin till the whole ship was one scream of fear.

"Fear rules the universe," she sobbed. "And God knows I have fear."

Put all your fear into a thought, said Richard's voice. The Grider have an instrument aboard to concentrate your thought. I am that instrument.

Something touched her shoulder; Gordon's face was thrust into hers. She reeled as thoughts ripped from her mind, her heart, her spine. Her body shook with terror. Excruciating shocks burst from her screaming mind.

Outside the procession stopped. Thousands of lidless eyes trained on her. Thousands of eyes locked with microscopic precision on her. They hit her back with a despair that nearly sent her gasping her lungs out.

Through the glass one creature emerged distinctly, a hair-covered length hurling quill after quill of fear into her heart, her lungs, her stomach. That thing outside, is it large like a building, she wondered, or tiny like a gnat? Inside the spaceship Gordon's helmet looked bigger than the universe. *How big is the universe?* she asked. *What is size, anyway? Does it really matter?* She knew only that she had never hurt so much, and that she could not faint or die. Maybe, just maybe, they would let her die now, though she did wonder if the quilled thing that swarmed past her was small and close or large and far.

She sought the answer in Gordon's eyes. The shocks exploding from her tore her across like gauze. She wrenched her head around to focus on the creatures just outside.

They swirled around the spaceship, turning, fleeing back upon the advancing shadow. Like squid swarming in millions. Like squid bursting into parts. Expanding. Exploding. Popping. Destroying themselves in a panic of suicide, caught between her throbbing thoughts and the shadow driving them on. Suddenly she was through them.

Beyond was the shadow, a writhing wave of fingers—or worms. More soulless monsters, she said. Already they were working on her, piercing her chest with shadows of fear, invading her brain.

"Worms, what do *you* fear?" She laughed. "Ha. You fear me!" This time she had no need for Gordon. She burned the worms to red confetti as the spaceship streaked on.

Nobody had ever told her of the cosmic graces of little people. Somehow she remembered a line her high school teacher had said. "I am a little world made cunningly," she quoted. It made sense now, for the whole world was within her.

The spaceship tore through a panorama she could never have imagined. Vast red clouds rose about her, unfolding into shapes like crenellated walls. All her life she had been told the universe was empty space. The ones who told her were wrong. The spreading red walls momentarily expanded to a complex, multiturreted castle; then, for an instant, they shifted to take on the contours of her own apartment, before they transformed again. She would remember this the next time she sat in her tiny apartment with the windows open to the stars. The universe is crammed with good things, she decided. She was at home in the universe.

She laughed. The Grider—for all their scientific gadgetry—what did they know of the universe? Nobody could know all about the universe. They can't even begin to comprehend people like Richard or Gordon or me. We are too deep for them. They lack—what was that word her teacher had used?—ethics. And the highest ethics are the theological virtues that Dr. Bradley had talked about, whatever they were. It was something to think about. A new thought struck her. Maybe all the things they said about God are true.

Suddenly she thought of Earth, their park bench, and her one-room apartment.

"Let's go home, Gordon," she said aloud. "I am weary of the stars. Richard, wherever you are in the ship, I want to go home. I want to have supper at home!"

• • •

Through the window the stars came up suddenly, as a great wall of red cloud shifted out of vision. The spaceship must be turning. She abandoned herself to gazing beyond the window as the spacecraft quit the remnants of the red cloud to shoot through a dazzle of meteors that glittered like sequins on a sky-blue gown. She was going home. She knew it. She was going home.

Home? What of Gordon?

She looked to see Gordon draped limply over the controls, like a flabby stingray, ropes of skin protruding from his underside to manipulate switches.

"You can't ever go home, Gordon. You are changed into something that doesn't belong in the world." A thought struck her. "Maybe I am too changed to ever go home."

Outside, the meteors shimmered with silver flashes.

"I got drunk on the universe, Gordon, and I've killed— living creatures. I killed them with my thoughts. I've been so far away, if I ever get home, can I go back to just being me?

"Fear does rule the universe, Gordon, because life goes on forever. That's what I learned at the science fair. Life doesn't stop. That's why the Grider feared the ones that chased them across the galaxy, and those creatures feared the shadows that pursued them. Life goes on forever, and you can't stop it, even if you're in agony.

"I'm changed like you, Gordon, but inside. Maybe I'm too changed to go home. But I am going home, whatever I am changed to. That planet ahead of me. That can only be Earth."

It was only a small speck near the shining splendor that must be the sun. Nearer was a fleet of floating things.

She smiled. The Grider, hovering by hundreds in their absurd cylindrical spacecraft with odd, long appendages protruding, looking for all the world like something spawned in contaminated pools. Maybe they had a planet or maybe they dwelled permanently in those spaceships of theirs; she didn't much care either way.

She saw nothing now but the dead bodies of all the other little girls who had been abducted to the science fair.

Her mind was opened. She remembered all she had learned as a small girl, the first time they took her. All they had made her forget. Till now.

Fear rules the universe. That is the law of the Grider. They could not withstand the things that made them explode with fear, so they went searching for something that could. All those terrible stories about alien abductions. It was the Grider experimenting to learn how much fear we can take. She looked at Gordon and wondered how long it took them to discover our horror of the living corpse.

She was nearly upon them, the jointed appendages from their cylindrical spacecraft extending and distending like the mandibles of some crustacean.

New thoughts crowded into her mind. Richard's. Richard was in her mind and remembering, too, everything the principal had told him. Richard's memories merged with hers.

You, Grider, her thoughts raced, *you kidnapped and tortured us till your experiments showed you that Earth people can tolerate fear on a level that makes you explode. So you chose Gordon as a fear factory, and Richard as the instrument to focus the fear. And you chose me because I was the one little child who did not die with fright with what you did to her. You prepared us, Grider, to do the thing you could not do, and we succeeded and killed all your enemies, which you convinced our government are ours, too.*

I have one more task to perform. She was very close to the flotilla now. "I wish you could hear me, Grider," she said aloud. "It is not nice to inflict gruesome experiments on innocent people. It is not nice to terrify children with appalling figures in dark closets."

Gordon had risen from the controls and stood erect, nodding, swinging his arms up and down.

"You terrorized Richard," she said to the Grider. "And made this thing of Gordon. You know so much, do you?

"You can't begin to understand Gordon or Richard or me.

We have kindness and humor. That's why we are people. And you are shallow monsters that can only invent things.

"Enjoy yourselves, Grider." She hugged Gordon, putting her face close to the one inside the helmet.

The fleet tried to scatter before it exploded. She felt the panic reflect back upon her. But all that was left were burning remnants of their jointed spaceships.

She turned away from the window because Gordon's body began to shake, swayed back and forth, the mouth to make sounds. Gordon was laughing. The worst sight in the world was to see Gordon laughing. The body made violent jerks, slamming against the bulkhead, doubling, twitching till it began to fall apart. She watched in terrible fascination as Gordon's body exploded with laughter. A moment more and it was over. Only the bubble helmet, empty, lay a few feet away. Gordon had disintegrated.

The Grider were wrong, Ellen said to the expanding Earth and to the dazzling sun radiating through the window. Fear rules only part of the universe. She contemplated the empty helmet on the floor. Laughter rules another part. And something else. She leapt to throw her arms around Richard, who now sat smiling beside her in the pilot's seat. Something far more wonderful rules the universe.

Ashes Fall on Timberlake

I

I laid my pen down early that hot, moonless night. All day I had been at work piling up manuscript; now to relax I slipped from the cabin and hiked to a little clearing where I could recline among boulders and try to guess the secrets of the stars. Everything felt almost supernaturally still; not a pine needle stirred. The night was a vacuum, empty of air, sound, and motion.

Around me rose the pines of Timberlake Mountain, where I came to write my book. It was June when I moved into my isolated cabin; and all was so pleasant, so placid and productive, that I stayed on into September, then into October.

Now it was October on Timberlake Mountain that I stood among pines, far from the rural activity of the Village, where Joe the fix-it man hung out at the dry goods store waiting for things to break, and Walt in his restaurant imparted homespun wisdom from behind the zinc counter. Timberlake

233

Village, the vacation place that never quite succeeded as a resort.

But I was miles from there. I was deep in the forest and exhilarated because I had written most of my book and cared only for the sheer wonder of existence. I peered about the clearing in the hot, still night, till I found a likely boulder for a chair and settled in to stare up at the sky.

Above me shone a cosmic ocean, its silver lights a host of tinsel islets. You view but fragments, my excited fancy whispered, as when you stand upon the shore to gaze across the waters. Though all seems bottomless ocean, you stare at shallows, seeing nothing of the great seas beyond. Surely in the skies, too, you see but coastal waters.

My mind was so charmed with this notion that I fancied our planet an island in a cosmic sea. I lowered my gaze to take in the forest about me. The very clearing in which I sat was an island, too, washed by an ocean of dark pine. Then I looked skyward again and nearly fell from my boulder, for marvelous things were happening in the sky.

Incandescent fireballs exploded into streaks and bubbles of colored light—bursts of the purest silvers and greens—dazzling electrical showers. Fireball after fireball hurled across the sky to erupt into a Vesuvius of dazzling silver sparks. I watched openmouthed as the display increased in magnitude until the blaze of light was almost too much for my unprotected eyes.

It was no mere meteor shower; it was an exaltation of comets, a vast celestial pyrotechnic that had the skies almost singing with light. I had no notion of the passage of time; I knew only that I was in some way a part of this splendor, and I told myself that whatever was happening in the sky was what man was made for.

And as, overhead, star burst upon star, gradually, very gradually, I became aware of *sound* all around me, as of the softest of soft rains, and felt the eyelash flutter of ashes gently descending; and I saw that the sky rained ash that fell in delicate soft flakes. This I saw by the green-and-silver light as the glowing balls burst to fragments overhead. And I heard other sounds, a pop-pop-popping as from far away.

The ashes piled in drifts around my feet, but harder to see now, for the spectacle was dying. The lights waned rapidly till all was washed a sickly green.

Then it was I heard a dull thud, so near me that I started, as something heavy fell among the tufted ashes at my feet. And in the waning, sickly light I looked down to behold a demon hand with an enormous ring flashing purple fire. The last of the stars must have burned out, for all was darkness except the purple fire.

Then I knew what the lights meant, and I knew, too, the significance of the ashes. And I realized I must take that demon hand as proof that I had witnessed a terrible battle in the skies. As one possessed, I seized that hand and ran with it in the silence of that haunted night, through the forest of clinging pines, back to the safety of my lonely cabin.

II

I arrived gasping for breath and set the hand on the table. I bolted the door and pulled down the window shade. Only then did I light the oil-burning lamp. Only then did I gaze upon the hand.

It was dark green, twice the size of a man's hand. Wide it was and flat, studded with bony knobs, with six spatulate fingers ending in black claws. The hand had been neatly severed at the wrist, which was dry and shiny, as though cauterized by smoking iron.

But the ring it wore enthralled me. Silver, it was, with a perpendicular disc sparkling with purple flashes. It was impossible to look anywhere but at those purple flashes. The color seemed to get inside my head and gather in a pool at the bottom of my brain.

Suddenly my brain exploded with tremendous thoughts, reeled on the threshold of vistas splendid and terrible. I plunged through corridors of light ringed to infinity, more light than I could bear. I tore my gaze away and staggered back. And when I looked up in wonder to see the ring's reflected sparkle on the walls and floor and ceiling, it seemed I stood inside an immense refracting jewel. Spellbound, I lowered my eyes.

Purple fire poured from the ring, spilling onto the floor. I put out my hand to catch the fire. The pain pierced like a soldering iron. I cried out. Seizing a thick towel nearby, I threw it over hand and ring and all. Instantly all motion stopped. The only remaining light came from my oil lamp. By this light I saw my own hand was purple.

Now that I could no longer revel in the ring's colored circles, a quiet horror stole over me. I felt drained and peculiarly vulnerable. The room I stood in, the cabin, the night itself—all seemed tense, as though expecting something. Always I heard noises from the forest, cracks and sighs and pattering. The world seemed hushed as though terrified to silence.

I blew the lamp out and stole to the window. In the darkness came the unsettling notion that the hand might choose that moment to crawl out from under the towel. But I would not heed such thoughts. I took a deep breath and carefully lifted a corner of the window shade.

Shapes with round heads moved through the forest, blackly silhouetted against the trees. They moved slowly, deliberately.

My first thought was to run for the car. But could I start the engine in time? Maybe I could hide in the forest. Or had I better stay where I was? Perhaps they would bypass the cabin.

Someone knocked on the door.

It was a queer knock, a double knock, a sound one might make who had been told we knock on our doors.

Knock-knock.

Knock-knock.

Knock-knock.

I had a feeling, almost a certitude, it wanted only the ring. I had merely to open the door, perhaps just a crack, and pass the ring through. But I could not. For whatever was on the other side of the door might have a hand to match the one on the table.

Knock-knock.

The night was still once more.

I sat in darkness in a big armchair set in a deep recess next to the mantelpiece—out of sight of the window—and stayed there, not daring to move. Some time after, long, long after, I heard a bird chattering and drew comfort from the sound. Quiet thoughts possessed me as I listened to the night bird, and I fell to pondering. A few hours before, my world had a ceiling. Now it lay unroofed to whatever might leap from the skies. Who was I to face such things? A writer. One schooled in the impracticalities of dream. I must turn the hand over to someone better fitted to deal with it.

The thought was reassuring. I felt no longer alone and powerless. The night bird still sang outside, its voice now joined by others. They sang throughout the night as I crouched in my armchair, till the window shade lightened, and I knew morning was near. I must have dozed, for I woke to full daylight.

What woke me was someone knocking on the door.

It was a persistent rapping, unlike the uncertain double knock that came in the night. But the world had shed its terrors with its darkness. Without further thought I flung the door open.

Joe the fix-it man slouched in the doorway, framed in morning sunlight. "Hullo, Garvin. I've come to take it away," he said simply.

"Take what?" I asked foolishly.

He walked past me over to the table and thrust the bundle into his coat pocket.

"It's a good thing you didn't give it to them," he said.

I grabbed his arm.

What's going on, Joe?" He glanced at my purple hand.

"Buy yourself a pair of gloves." He walked out, closing the door behind him.

III

Joe knew all about it. Whatever it meant, he understood it. Joe was a practical man who could deal with it. It was Joe's problem now.

I felt much better as I wandered outdoors. Joe would know what to do. The pines met me with a heady fragrance. I walked for an hour or so trying to think things out. In the morning sunlight the whole appalling incident seemed much less real. *Could there really have been a severed hand?* I asked myself. *A ring of purple fire? Beings stalking through the woods?* I made my way back to the clearing where I had witnessed the wonders in the sky. I found the boulder where I had sat, but not the heaps of ashes.

The morning grew very hot. I tramped through the forest till I stumbled on a nest of ferns buried beneath the pines. I settled comfortably among the ferns as a cool place to rest and think things over. *There couldn't really have been a devilish hand,* I said. There must have been something in those meteoric lights that hypnotized the brain. I felt very drowsy. How did I know I even saw the lights? I was out of it anyway. I yawned. Joe had the hand; Joe had the ring; I didn't. Real or not, it was Joe's problem now. The only thing I had was the purple stain on my hand. I found myself yawning uncontrollably. Later on I could drive to the village and ask Joe about it all. It was Joe's problem now.

It was late afternoon when the voices woke me. I was too comfortable to move. I hoped they would go away, but they paused a few feet from where I lay covered by the ferns.

"That Rooshian lady in the spa'ship," the first voice was saying, "she starts yellin' that the spa'ship is yawin' back and forth and that she can't keep no equalibr'um."

"What she done then?" asked the other voice.

"She puts her eye to the porthole, an' her face gits kind o' crazy when she sees what's comin' t' git her. She don't stop screamin' till her face breaks apart. Then the whole spa'ship sort o' dissolves. Crotan!"

"He don't like 'em out there," said the other voice. "They ain't supposed t' know what's goin' on."

"Yep. Jus' like Roanoke hunnerts o' years ago. They seen some stuff they shouldn't. He took the whole colony away."

"What about the Unified Field Experiments? You bet that made 'em all crazy!" Both voices grew excited.

"Made 'em invisible."

"Whole durn ship disappeared and showed up a second later at another dock miles away."

"The folks aboard——"

"One walked clean through the side o' the ship."

"Walked inta horra!"

"Stendec!"

"Shhh!"

"Stendec's got 'em."

"No, they's Crotan's."

"I tell ya, they's Stendec's. Crotan don't have nothin' under the sea."

"How about all them skeletons in airplanes down there that seen white water?"

"Them's Stendec's. Crotan don't have nothin' under the sea."

A pause. A shuffling of feet. The men moved on.

"Who's got the ra-a-ang?" the first voice drawled.

"Garvin. Garvin's got it."

My name! They were saying my name!

"Crotan wants it back."

"I reckon Stendec'll come t' git it."

"No, Crotan'll git it first."

The voices died as the figures moved away. I got up and parted the bushes. I saw them clearly. Laboring men from the next valley—East Slope types, as they are known around here. Two workmen carrying their lunch pails, talking together on their way home.

They were still looking for the ring. They didn't know I'd given it to Joe. I had to drive to the village and find Joe. He would tell them I no longer had the ring. When I went for my car, I found the cabin door open.

I stopped at the car long enough to arm myself with the tire iron. Then I went inside the cabin.

All seemed as I had left it. Except that the top dresser drawer, which I always keep closed, was halfway open. Except that a pile of linen that I left at the foot of the bed was now at the center. Except that my briefcase, my valise, my corner cabinet—everything that could conceivably hide a ring—had been searched, probed, put back only in its approximate place. I'm sure they got the car, too. Unless I hid it in the woods, they must figure the only other place for the ring was on my person. I had to get to Joe. I started the car and drove to the village.

I talked to the owner of the dry goods store where Joe hung out; he told me Joe had not come round that day but was expected in the morning. I could wait till morning, but not in my isolated cabin. I started toward the hotel when I realized I had eaten nothing all day. The village's best restaurant was an old-fashioned barbecue pit with picnic tables and sawdust on the floor. It was always pretty lively, and I was minded not to be alone.

Walt, the proprietor, stood by the cash register. He nodded when I came into the crowded restaurant.

"You're doing good business," I said.

"Lots of folks came to town early," Walt said. "Been hanging around all day. East Slopers. Now what do they want?"

"I wouldn't complain," I said, "as long as they pay their checks."

"Something's not right," Walt said. "They never come to the village in such numbers. Look at them. They don't say hardly a word. They just eat slow and stare at people. I right out asked one, why are all you folks here? Know what he said? He said they're here for the hunting."

"So?"

"Man, there is no hunting here. There's nothing to hunt. Don't you know that? They just look around and stare, like they're searching for something. And they're silent. They're real silent."

"That fellow isn't silent," I said, indicating a smiling, red-faced man with spectacles, who seemed to be holding court at one of the picnic benches.

"Him? That's old Scotty. No East Sloper him! He's an engineer or something. Been coming here for years. Talks like a phonograph, don't he? Look at him, with that grin on that red face of his, just a-jabberin' away. Oh, the Johnsons are leaving. I reckon Scotty talked their appetites to death. Do you want to sit next to old Battermouth? It's the only empty space unless you want to wait a bit."

I told him the seat would do. I preferred the noise and the crowd to finding myself seated next to one of the taciturn East Slopers. I took my place on the bench and looked around for the waitress.

"Beans are real good today." Scotty laughed.

"They're always good," I replied.

"You bet. Real good." He glanced at the other diners as if for confirmation. Then he smiled at me.

He looked to be in his sixties: a tall, red-faced man with black spectacles and closely cropped, bristly white hair. He wore a short-sleeved dress shirt and a black tie. He smiled a great deal.

"I'm Scotty," he said.

"Jim Garvin," I replied.

The waitress brought a place setting and took my order.

"Say, Scotty," one of the diners said, "d'ja see the meteor shower last night?"

"Sure did. Why it was better than the Fourth of Ju-ly." He turned to me. "You see it?"

"I saw some of it," I said.

"What do you think made everything so bright?" Scotty asked candidly. "Could it be gases, do you think?"

I said I didn't know.

"Sometimes pieces of those meteors fall to the ground. I knew a fella once found a chunk of iron ore as big as your fist."

"Happens alla time," said someone.

"Man," said Scotty, "would I like to get me a souvenir of a meteor shower." He laughed with his eyes. His red face and closely cropped white hair seemed to laugh with him. "Anybody hear of any rocks falling?" None of us had.

My dinner came. I ate as Scotty talked indiscriminately to all of us at table—general talk, of travel and weather and his home in St. Louis.

The people at the end of the table got up to go. A woman with a little girl took their place. The waitress cleared the table and brought menus and place settings. Scotty beamed at the little girl.

"How do, Missy?" He smiled.

The little girl tugged at her mother's arm.

"Go, Mummy."

Her mother said something.

"Go, Mummy." She was crying. She was looking directly at Scotty and crying bitterly. "Go, Mummy. Go now!" The woman got up.

"I'm sorry. I'm real sorry," she said, as the child pulled her from the room.

"Takes a face like mine to scare little children." Scotty laughed. Some laughed with him.

I finished my meal. Scotty ordered more food. I put some bills on the table.

"Say, Mister." Scotty winked. "Where'd you get that purple hand? You been pickin' grapes?" He laughed. Joe warned me to hide that purple stain. Now Scotty had blurted it out. I wondered if any of the East Slopers had taken notice. I laughed, too, as I left the restaurant.

It was very dark outside. The street was quiet except for a couple of loungers leaning against a wall. Neither seemed curious about me, yet I walked a block out of my way, darted through a short alley, and slipped into the side entrance of the hotel.

In the dimly lighted lobby I could make out a weasel-faced man behind the desk. Two other men sat on a sofa, their faces hidden in shadow.

"I'd like a room for the night," I said to the clerk.

"Certainly, Mr. Garvin."

He had called me by my name.

And I had never met him.

"I'll have to check first. We are crowded tonight—lots of folks are in for the hunt. Excuse me a moment." He disappeared into an inner office.

Names get known quickly in a mountain village. Maybe Walt or Joe or someone else had pointed me out to him. Still, it bothered me that he knew my name. I looked around the lobby. The two men still sat in shadow. One lit a cigarette. I saw their faces momentarily. The clerk returned.

"You're in luck, Mr. Garvin. We have one room left." He told me the price and handed me the register.

"I nearly forgot," I said. "Have you a pay phone?"

"A pay phone? Yes, right around the corner there. Do you want the room, Mr. Garvin?"

"Yes, I do," I said.

I tried to look casual as I walked over to the phone booth and closed the folding door behind me. I hoped my hand did not shake as I dialed the number of the airport. I looked at my watch; it was then a quarter to nine. I could be down the mountain and catch the 12:35 flight to Decatur. I reserved a seat. Calmly, very calmly, I returned to the front desk.

"Do you want to sign the register now, Mr. Garvin?" The desk clerk asked. The two other men had risen from the sofa and stood now beside the main desk. I signed the register and made for the front door.

"Where are you going, Mr. Garvin?"

"My luggage," I said.

"My men will get it for you. Give them your car key."

"No. It's a book I'm writing. That's all my luggage. Just a book." I stepped past them.

"That call I made was to the movie theater," I said, pausing at the open door. "I have to hurry. The picture's already started." I was out the door a second later.

I retraced my steps to the alley and over to the street where I had left my car, then drove the half block to the theater and parked in the alley close by the side entrance. I walked around to the front, bought a ticket, and went inside. I hoped no one saw me leave through the side door. I slipped into my car and started the engine.

That desk clerk—could I have got past him if he knew about my plane ticket? What about the two men on the sofa? What would they have done if they suspected I overheard their conversation in the woods?

I was clear of town now, heading for my cabin to put together a few things, collect my manuscript, then leave for good. Timberlake was a hotbed of them, whoever they were. I looked at my watch. I had two hours or so before the movie let out. When they missed me at the hotel they would come looking. I pulled up in front of my cabin, then got out of the car, walked the few steps, and opened the cabin door. I fumbled for a match to light the oil lamp. The door shut behind me.

Everything was wrong. Shining particles glutted the air. My ears felt a surging as of air singing through a breathing tube. The very walls seemed to strain as if containing an immense pressure. I felt around for the oil lamp. The room suddenly blazed with green light.

Scotty sat in the big chair. He was saying something. I remember watching the reflection of the bright particles on his shiny, black-rimmed glasses. The room stretched on and on. I felt euphoric.

He was telling me about a Unified Field, but I was more interested in watching the solid walls pulsate through the dense air. All the while Scotty smiled and joked with me.

Once he said, "You have something that belongs to us."

"Not anymore." I laughed.

"Will you give it up, or shall I take out my ray gun? Ha! Ha!"

"I gave it to Joe." I laughed, as though my doing so was the funniest thing in the world.

His red face leaned way over.

"You don't look as if you gave it to Joe. Where is Joe?"

"He is gone."

Scotty winked at me. "Of course," he said. "You gave the ring to Joe, so you don't have it anymore."

"Not anymore," I agreed.

The room vibrated with a loud buzzing. I looked up to find Scotty standing by a door I didn't know was there.

"Say." He smiled. "Somebody wants to see you." He took my arm and walked me to the door. "Go right in." I paid little attention to him or to the angry buzzing coming from beyond the door. I was laughing uncontrollably because I could talk with such a being as Scotty was.

"Who are you?" I almost shouted. "I mean, what are you really? You aren't human, are you?" The euphoria nearly exploded inside me as I waited for his answer.

The buzzing stopped. "I don't look like them," he said, pointing at the door he was trying to get me to walk through. "I look like one of you. Go on in now." But I wanted to ask him more questions.

Then Scotty wasn't there anymore. The room sang in my ears with its escaping pressures. The buzzing started up again and died in a devilish whisper. My purple hand felt like it was on fire. Scotty reappeared. In the pulsing confusion of that pressurized room, with his glasses flashing and his bristly hair almost glowing white, Scotty bent low and whispered.

"Go in now, go in and see Crotan!"

IV

I was up and out the door, reeling with a concussion of sound and an agonizing pain in my ears; then I was driving down the mountain, the word "Crotan" crashing through my mind like a scream inside a cave.

I had booked a reservation on the 12:30 flight to Decatur. What time was it now? I glanced at my watch, but my watch had stopped. How long had I been inside the cabin with Scotty? Had I time to get down the mountain and reach the airport before my flight left? What time was it now?

I tried the car radio but found only static. I pushed button after button, but only the same eerie static.

Then a voice came over the radio, a horrid voice between a croak and a whisper, a voice that said the same thing, over and over:

"Go back and see Crotan!"

I switched off the radio and floored the gas pedal. I drove recklessly, maniacally. I wanted only to reach the bottom, find the airport, and get on a plane—any plane to anywhere.

A tunnel was coming up that marked the halfway point down the mountain, beyond that a long straightaway, then more twists and hairpin curves, all the way to the bottom, to the main highway, then on to the airport.

When I saw the tunnel I braked sharply.

Men stood outside, behind lighted barricades.

I knew then I could not get down, not on that road. What then? Suddenly I remembered the old toll road, abandoned now. I had hiked part of it some weeks back; up from the highway it ran past a long-deserted lumber camp. Was it dri-vable down from the highway? I had passed the junction a few miles back. A chain blocked the entrance from the highway, but I suspected I could get around it by going a few yards cross-country.

I drove back up the highway to the junction, then eased the car over a dirt mound and down onto what remained of the toll road. Most of the asphalt paving was gone. I threaded my way down, zigzagging to avoid potholes and fallen boulders. The surface grew so bad I barely crawled over what remained of the road.

Abruptly it thinned to a mere asphalt strip that terminated in an infestation of growth. I could go no farther. I had either to return to the highway or abandon the car.

I craned my head out the window as I backed uphill in search of an area wide enough to turn around. The sputtering tires kicked up a cloud of dust. Still, I made progress. I backed onto an island of pavement and was about to start my turn. I faced forward and peered through the windshield.

Something tall and lean and with a perfectly round head was loping toward me. No time to turn around. I backed recklessly up the hill. The tires threw up a wall of dust as the car fled backwards. Though the headlights seemed to blind it, the thing came after, its long, thin arms flapping as it dove for the hood. That's when I ground the gears and gunned the engine. The car shot forward. With a dull thud the creature hit the pavement and lay still.

In a frenzy I shifted to reverse again and turned the car around. I could drive forward now. Just before I rounded a curve I braked a moment to look back. The creature lay like a broken insect, slightly shining in the starlight. Was it Crotan's, I wondered? Or—what was that other name I overheard in the forest?

I returned to the highway junction. I had two choices. I could try to crash through the blockade in the tunnel. Or I could return to Timberlake. The tunnel meant sure death. And Timberlake? By now they would be waiting for me. The highway would be watched. There might be more blockades.

What if I stayed on the toll road? What if I drove up the toll road? The paving seemed sound when I hiked the road a few weeks back. If I could get through to the Village, I could find the sheriff and ask his protection.

The sheriff? What was wrong with me? I had not thought of getting help from anyone except Joe. Did these beings wield such hypnotic power?

No chain blocked the toll road up from the highway. The surface seemed intact. I had another thought. If I could not get through to the Village, I could hide perhaps in the old logging camp till morning—and then take my chances in the tunnel along with the morning traffic. I drove on.

The trees grew denser as I gained altitude. After a while the road left the cliff side to wind beneath a pine forest. The headlights began to pick out dilapidated shacks, an indication I had reached the abandoned lumber camp. I hit the brakes suddenly to avoid hitting something.

A fallen tree blocked the road. I got out. The tree looked manageable. I hefted one end to drag it off the road.

"Hold it right there, Mister!" a voice cried out.

I found myself staring into the barrels of a shotgun.

V

"I got nothin' against you, Mister; but don't move. I got to shoot you if you move."

It was a young voice, a nervous voice. I could just make out a skinny youth with a blond haystack of hair.

"I don't know you," I said. "What do you want?"

"Jest move, Mister—right over to that shed. You jest move, Mister." The voice fairly shook.

"You're an East Sloper, aren't you?" I asked as we walked along.

"Never you mind what I am. Jest you move."

We kept on till we stood in front of a ramshackle wooden hut.

"Why are you doing this to me?" I asked. "I'm human like you."

He turned on me with hatred.

"Don't talk that way!" he cried. "Jes' don't you talk that way! I ain't got nothing 'gainst you." He was almost pitiful. "Don't y' see? I got orders." His voice dropped.

"Who gives the orders?" I shouted. He could have shot me. I would not have cared. "Who? Who?"

"Monsters, that's who!" he shouted back. Then he caught himself and peered fearfully into the woods. "No." His voice dropped. "I didn't mean that. They's good. They's real good."

"Who is Stendec?" I demanded.

"Don't say that name?"

"Who is he?"

"The—the other side."

"Then you're with Crotan!"

"You got no right to name 'em like that. It don't pay to name 'em."

"What was that thing guarding the bottom of the toll road? It had a round head. I killed it."

He nearly dropped the shotgun.

"Gads!" he whispered. "You killed one? You killed one o' their devils?" He spoke in awe. Then, "Wouldn't wanna be you, Mister. No, sir, wouldn't wanna be you."

"Who are they?" I was whispering now.

"My boss," he said meditatively. "My boss don't look like none of them. He looks like you 'n' me."

"But on the inside; what is he on the inside?"

"Don't, Mister. He *looks* like you 'n' me."

"Who are you?"

"Name's Tommy—just a poor fella—'n' they pay; they pay good, if you can stand 'em. My daddy worked for 'em, till he got *taken*. Say, I'm tellin' you too much."

"What are they? Where are they from? What do they want?"

"Listen!" He made a motion as to stop my mouth. From somewhere in the darkness came a snapping of branches as of some big thing moving toward us.

"A bear," I said. "It's a bear."

"T'aint no bear." He was almost chanting. "They heer'd, they heer'd me tell you they was monsters' now they's comin' to git me. They took Pa, you know. They took Pa. Now they's comin' for me!"

"Don't be silly," I said. "It's a bear. It won't hurt you. It will go away." It was closer, a crackling of undergrowth, something rushing out of the densely packed darkness.

The boy stood staring at the forest, straining his eyes to see.

"Oh, Gawd," Tommy cried. "Oh, Gawd!" He broke from the clearing and ran yelping through the trees. I made for the car, swung round the fallen tree, floored the gas pedal till the lumber camp was far behind.

VI

The toll road proved passable all the way to the Village. I resolved to tell the sheriff everything. He would not believe such a fantastic story, but at least he might offer protection.

Why was I so sure he would not believe me? These beings can hypnotize; maybe they put it in our heads that we will not be believed. The sheriff might help, maybe not. In any case, there was Joe. He at least would tell them I no longer had the ring.

What time was it getting to be? I turned on the radio.

And got the news. The announcer was speaking of a disaster. An airplane had crashed just minutes after takeoff. Flight 17 to Decatur.

For a second I lost control of the car, then wildly steered to avoid leaving the road. Flight 17 was my flight—the plane on which I had a reserved seat. They were taking no chances in case I made it down the mountain.

The early-morning light was just breaking when I reached the silent, empty streets of Timberlake. I drove halfway across town to the sheriff's station.

Joe was leaning against the wall of the brick station house.

I parked and walked over to him.

"You need to tell them I no longer have the ring," I said.

"What ring?"

"The ring you took from my cabin!"

"I never took no ring."

"Joe! Don't you understand? You need to tell them I don't have it."

"Won't do any good." He yawned. "You took it. You've got to give it back."

"Give me the ring then."

"I killed the sheriff," Joe said simply.

"What?" I stared in disbelief. "Why?"

"Had my reasons. His body's hung up in the office if you care to see it." I shrank from him.

"You horror," I said. "You crawling, murderous horror. Whatever you are—whatever you all are—you do not belong here."

He yawned again.

"Your kind don't see things right. Usually you see only what we want you to see. Look." He put his arm through the solid brick wall, then withdrew it. The wall was unmarked.

"Illusion!" I cried.

"No." His voice was bored. "The wall is the illusion. Your

kind sees only bits and pieces of things; we put it all together. Don't you get it?"

"No."

"Mister, when you think you're sittin' safe in that cabin of yours, you're thinkin' blind. There's things in there with you—things so terrible your stomach would stretch right out of your mouth if you saw 'em."

He reached into a coat pocket and brought out my wrapped towel.

"Let's give 'em another try at it." He handed me the bundle. "I'll tell 'em you're comin'. Know the old lumber camp?"

"I just came from there."

"You come from there? Man, they're playin' with you. Just you go on back now and give 'em the ring."

"When will you send them the message that I'm coming?"

"What?"

"When will you send the message?"

He looked closely at me.

"I've already told 'em," he said.

"I don't understand."

"Your kind never does. Tell you one thing, though. Me and that fella you call Scotty may be on different sides, but at least we can mix with your kind. Those others—those ones at the lumber camp—it don't pay to look at 'em." He started to go.

"Wait!" I said. "You are with Stendec, aren't you?"

His eyebrows lifted.

"Is Stendec," I asked, "the right side?"

He looked at me quizzically. "The *right side?*" he repeated. He turned to walk away.

"Then tell me this," I cried. He turned around. "Joe, are you and Scotty from—another planet?"

"Some things," he said, "are real, and some things only kind of real."

"I don't know what you mean. But, tell me, is this village real?"

His eyes were strange.

"I do not see a village," he said, and disappeared into the wall.

VII

I drove back down the toll road to the lumber camp. I drove automatically, without feeling. All was still. Besides Joe, I had seen no one on the streets. Yet it was morning. It was as though the world was in suspension. The only sound I heard was the noise the car made traveling over the bumpy road.

Eventually I came to the clearing where I had met Tommy, the East Sloper. I stopped the car and got out, the bundle in my hand. From somewhere in the bush came the sound of trickling water.

"Here, over here," said a voice.

"Where are you?" I cried.

"Here. Here."

It came from deep in the woods. I trekked through the gloom toward the voice.

"Which way do I go?"

There was no reply.

"Where are you?" I called.

Then I went on a little farther and saw a sight.

Bound to a tree was Tommy, his eyes staring, his mouth gaped open in a silent shriek. That was all of his flesh. The rest was skeleton.

Scotty stepped from behind the tree. He wore his short-sleeved dress shirt and black tie. His eyes twinkled behind his black-rimmed glasses.

"Hi!" He grinned. He took out a red bandanna and began to polish his spectacles.

"Right over there," he called cheerily, "into what looks like a nice little cave." He took the bundle from me, plucked off the towel, and presented me the hand. It looked horrible in the sunlight. "Don't be shy." He grinned. "Just walk right in and say 'Hello'!" His red face seemed to burn beside the dead white one on the tree.

I walked on. What kept me going was a new thought. Don't be so quick to condemn what you don't understand, said something deep inside me. I have Crotan's ring. Crotan wants it back. What harm has Crotan done me? How do I know the men in the hotel or even the creature in the woods would have harmed me? It was Joe working for Stendec who killed the sheriff. Maybe the forces of Stendec shot down the plane. Maybe they killed Tommy. It is Stendec who is evil; Crotan is Stendec's enemy; Crotan must be good, maybe even benevolent. I will find out, for Crotan wants his ring.

I walked over to what looked like a cave in the hillside, though it wasn't there the last time I hiked the area. The surface seemed made of metal. "Just walk right in," Scotty had said, "and say 'Hello'!"

I stepped into darkness. Once again the blood sang in my ears with the weight of intense pressure, as I felt my way along a wall textured with protruding knobs of hard leather. My ears were popping with the pressure. I had the odd, impossible notion that I had been there before.

From somewhere ahead I heard that unmistakable buzzing.

Suddenly I saw myself talking to Scotty inside my cabin. But the pressure—that buzzing—that extra room! Where had that conversation taken place?

In total darkness I carried the hand toward whatever was making the sound, feeling my way along the leathery fixtures on the wall. Abruptly I felt emptiness and knew I stood upon the threshold of an inner chamber. Something large moved in the darkness a few feet away. The buzzing stopped.

The ring gave off a violet light, bright enough to show the silhouette of two arms—one terminating in a hand reaching for the one I held, the other ending in a stump.

And the light lit up the leather fixtures on the walls, and I saw what we meant to the beings haunting Timberlake. They decorated their walls with human parts. So might a fisherman adorn his hut with spoils of the sea.

I dropped the hand and hurled myself outside. I ran a ways, then walked quietly to the car. What was the use? I drove down the mountain slowly. No one hindered me.

What is it all about? Is it a war? Can it be a game?